COMING FOR HIM

Benedek heard it again. It was a creaking, thumping sound. At first, he thought it was coming from inside the house, but the second time he heard it, it clearly came from overhead.

Someone was on the roof.

He heard a different sound, this time something that was not connected to the house. It was a flapping sound, but it only lasted briefly. It was immediately followed by more movements on the roof.

"Oh, my God," Benedek whispered. A cold explosion of fear in his chest spread throughout his body and made him tremble, made his heartbeat increase. He hurried into his bedroom and got the twelve-gauge pump-action shotgun that leaned against the wall beside his bed. It was loaded and ready. He took the gun back up the hall to the living room.

He had decided many years ago that he would fight to the very end, that if possible, he would take one or more of them with him when he went. Benedek had no intention of going out easily.

The front window that looked out on the lawn exploded inward, and a pale figure flew through....

Other *Leisure* books by Ray Garton:

LIVE GIRLS
THE LOVELIEST DEAD

NIGHT LIFE

RAY GARTON

LEISURE BOOKS   NEW YORK CITY

Dedicated to Dawn, with love.

A LEISURE BOOK®

April 2007

Published by

Dorchester Publishing Co., Inc.
200 Madison Avenue
New York, NY 10016

ISBN-10: 0-8439-5675-5
ISBN-13: 978-0-8439-5675-7

Printed in the United States of America.

Visit us on the web at www.dorchesterpub.com.

ACKNOWLEDGMENTS

I'd like to thank some people who provided support and aided me in the writing of this novel—Scott Sandin and Derek Sandin; T. M. Wright and Roxane White; Dr. Sheela Stocks; my friends at Shocklines and the Message Board of the Damned; my publisher and friend, Bill Schafer; and my wife, Dawn, who generously, every day, removes all distractions so I can write.

NIGHT LIFE

When the man and woman arrived at their destination, she laughed with surprise at the red blanket already spread out on the ground at their feet. A champagne bottle with two deep-red lillies hand-painted on the side stood in an empty silver ice bucket. Two crystal champagne glasses awaited them. Standing in a simple white vase, a dozen blood-red roses trembled in the warm breeze.

She turned to him and they pressed their naked bodies together. She gently placed her palms against his chest. Although she continued to smile, welling tears sparkled in her eyes. Her voice was soft as she said, "Aw, look at this. This is so sweet. You're more of a romantic now than when we first met."

"I refuse to take the blame for that," he said. "It's your fault."

Bodies pressed together as one, they were a pale

flame under the glow of the full moon. She put a hand to the side of his goateed face as she kissed him. They finally separated and knelt, then sat close together on the blanket, facing each other. He took the champagne bottle from the ice bucket in his right hand. He kept his left hand—a twisted, gray, withered claw— out of sight in his lap or behind his back. It was usually concealed in a custom-made glove of black calfskin leather, but not tonight.

With the bottle held between his knees, he removed the cork with his right hand. It did not pop out with the typical celebratory report, nor did foam hiss from the bottle's mouth. The sound was soft, a moist *fup*.

"Wine?" he said as one eyebrow rose playfully high on his forehead.

She feigned a heavy Hungarian accent. "I never drrrink—"

They finished the quote together. "—vine."

They smiled, as if about to laugh. Instead, their eyes briefly broke contact as the moment darkened. It was only a little joke, but it still held too much pain for both of them, conjured memories they had spent years putting behind them.

He carefully tipped the bottle over her glass. The dark liquid that poured out was thick and slow as it slapped the bottom of the glass and slid up one inner side, then dipped back down and left behind a clinging, drooling film. After pouring some for himself, he lifted his glass.

"To us," he said in a breath.

"To us."

They delicately touched their glasses together. Heavy

with the thick liquid, the glasses made a flat *clack* on contact.

Small creatures stirred in the brush around them. Crickets chirped some distance away. Cars and trucks and buses and trains gave slow and rhythmic breath to the city far below.

Glasses drained, he poured again. When they finished their second drink, each bore a dark, glistening, pencil-thin mustache. Eyes closed, they took a moment to appreciate their drinks, then threw the glasses into the night. Crystal shattered far below them seconds later.

Lying back on the blanket, they embraced, kissed. Legs intertwined, toes wiggled as their feet played together. The warm, gusty breeze carried her soft laughter away as he tickled her ribs, kissed her mouth, cheek, neck, moved down to cover an erect nipple with his mouth. Her laughter became a feather-soft sigh.

She made a soft, high-pitched sound behind tightly pressed lips as he entered her. She lifted her legs high, knees bent, feet curled downward. He rose above her, hands flat on the blanket, elbows locked. He smiled down at her with a low, feral sound deep in his chest.

Propping herself up on her elbows, she sharply arched her back, dropped her head backward, mouth open. Her long, strawberry-blond hair pooled on the blanket. Needlelike fangs slowly curved downward from beneath her upper lip as she opened her mouth, until they reached their full length. Moist with saliva, they glimmered in the moonlight.

His became visible as he growled with each exhalation. He clenched the blanket in his fist as he thrust harder. She dropped down on her back, raised her right hand and clutched at the pale skin of his muscular back while her left arm swung in a spastic arc and toppled the roses. The vase rolled off the blanket and clinked over the pebbled ground.

Their piercing cries of release sent small animals scurrying in terror around them. Startled birds flew from their nighttime perches in all directions.

Lying at the base of the forty-five-foot tall Y in the HOLLYWOOD sign atop Mt. Lee in Griffith Park, they remained motionless for several seconds as a deep stillness settled around them.

They had married sixteen years ago in a small chapel in Carmel, then had gone south and settled in Los Angeles. Their marriage had been the first good thing to happen to them after the nightmare their lives had become in New York City.

They lay on their backs together, staring up at the stars. She snuggled into the crook of his arm, passed her hand up over his flat stomach and rested it on his chest. They took turns gulping from the champagne bottle, whispered I-love-yous, and laughed secretly at things only they found funny.

When the bottle was empty, they stood and kissed again, then he threw it off the mountain. It shattered below, long before it reached the diamonds that shimmered on a vast expanse of black velvet spread out far below them. The lights twinkled through the haze of pollutants that hovered over Los Angeles.

"Happy anniversary, Davey," she whispered.

He squeezed her tightly and said, "Happy anniversary, Casey."

They were gone in a fraction of a heartbeat, abandoning the red blanket bunched and tangled around the empty ice bucket. There was no one around to hear the fading sound of rapidly flapping wings of flesh on the breeze.

CHAPTER ONE

Karen Moffett arrived at the Beverly Hills Hotel on Monday afternoon, just minutes before her appointment. She went to the elevator, her footsteps silent on the plush, smoky-colored carpet. She pressed the button and waited.

A man came to the elevator and stood beside her. He was tall, in his early forties, with a chiseled face and a five o'clock shadow shortly before two in the afternoon. His black hair was streaked with silver. Although trim and fit, he looked tired. He carried a black briefcase in his left hand and wore a dark gray suit that looked expensive, but slept in. He smiled and nodded at her.

Karen returned the gesture, then the elevator opened and they both stepped inside.

"Floor?" the man said.

"Three."

The man smiled again as he pushed the button. "Me, too."

Karen turned her gaze up to the floor lights above the door as the car rose to the third floor. It opened up and they both got out and turned right. Karen worried for a moment that the man was following her—she hoped not. She stopped outside room 308.

So did he.

"Are you following me?" Karen said.

He cocked his head to the left curiously. "Are you here to see Martin Burgess?"

"Yes, I am."

"Well, so am I."

"Oh. Well. Okay, then. I didn't realize there would be anyone else here for the two o'clock appointment."

"Neither did I." He stepped forward and knocked on the door.

"Come in," someone called on the other side.

The man opened the door and let Karen go in first.

Martin Burgess was forty-seven, a man of medium height, his dark hair thinning on top, a paunch pressed against the black T-shirt he wore that read, I'M WEARING BLACK TILL THEY COME UP WITH SOMETHING DARKER! His T-shirt collection was well-known—he received so many from the millions of readers of his horror novels, he probably didn't need to buy any more. Karen had read up on Burgess as soon as she accepted the invitation to meet him at the hotel only a couple days ago. He'd become a rich man by writing best-selling horror novels, most of which were made into bad movies. But the quality of the movies had no effect on the amount of money he'd made from them. He lived in a sprawling mansion near Mt. Shasta in northern California, and had a house in Topanga Canyon, and another in

Florida. Every Halloween, he threw a big party at his mountain home for underprivileged children, particularly kids who were terminally ill. He'd divorced Sheila, his wife of almost twenty years, to be with a much younger woman, Denise, whom he'd married ten months ago.

Karen had read a couple of his novels. They were easy reading and the stories were quite good, as was the development of characters. She'd encountered moments when the books actually had given her chills. Burgess's writing was effective, but he wasn't going to win any major book awards anytime soon. It was apparent in interviews with Burgess that he did not labor under any such delusions. He'd once said that his books were the literary equivalent of an order of spicy nachos.

"Please come in and sit down," Burgess said with a smile.

The man closed the door, and they crossed the suite, and Karen sat on a couch with two chairs facing it over a coffee table. On the table was a fat black binder. The man sat down in one of the chairs.

"So, I take it you two have met?" Burgess said as he planted himself in the other chair. Burgess wore khaki pants and black loafers, a pair of wire-framed glasses. His black T-shirt was untucked.

"No, we haven't," Karen said.

Burgess said, "Karen Moffett, meet Gavin Keoph." He turned to Keoph. "I hope your trip down from San Francisco was a pleasant one, Mr. Keoph."

Keoph shrugged. "I don't travel well. Never have." He leaned forward, reached out a hand to Karen, and they shook. "Nice to meet you, Miss Moffett," he said with a smile.

"Karen is fine."

Burgess said, "Can I get you anything to drink? I'm only here for this meeting, but the room has a bar, or I can have room service bring something up, if you prefer."

They both declined.

"I'm very interested to know why you sent for me, Mr. Burgess," Keoph said.

Burgess got up and went to the small refrigerator behind the bar and took out a beer, popped it open on his way back to the chair. "I called you here because you're both very good at what you do. I've done extensive research, and I've found you to be among the most respected people in your fields. Your agencies— Moffett and Brand, and yours, Mr. Keoph, Burning Lizard Security and Investigations—have great reputations. And to get to the point, I have work for you. But this won't be a typical job."

Burgess put his left ankle up on his right knee and sipped his beer.

"I want you both to work for me," he went on, "full-time. I want to be your only client for the duration of the investigation, so you'll need to clear your schedules for awhile. I know this is asking a lot, but I plan to pay a lot, because this will be unconventional work for both of you, to say the least."

"What kind of work is it?" Karen said.

Burgess put his left foot on the floor, moved his chair closer to the coffee table, and put down his beer. "I'd like to show you both something. I've been researching this . . . event, this . . . *phenomenon* for about eighteen years. I've scoured newspapers from major cities all over the world for every reference to this story." He laughed. "I've even paid off newsroom clerks to get my hands on the original negatives of the only couple of photographs that have been taken. Before anyone was even calling it 'the Internet,' I bought a computer and got connected to it in hope of finding any scrap of information I could, of meeting any person who might know anything about it. I've made phone calls to six continents looking for the truth. I've traveled coast to coast following what little evidence I've uncovered. But I've taken it as far as I can on my own. From here on out, I need you two. For all the work I've done, I've gathered surprisingly little information, but that's the nature of these . . . things. The highlights of my work are contained in this scrapbook. I've condensed it to this body of newspaper clippings and photographs and notes from my interviews with witnesses."

Burgess reached out and opened the scrapbook to the beginning, a news clipping under the plastic. He turned the book so they could both see it.

The author of the article, published by the *New York Post*, was someone by the name of Woodrow Hill. The headline read VAMPIRES IN NEW YORK? EYE-WITNESS SAYS YES!

Burgess sat back in his chair and said, "It seems a little peep-show in Times Square—this was back before they cleaned it up and turned it into a family theme park—was owned and operated by vampires, a little place called Live Girls. The article claims the vampires bit the horny male patrons on the penis while performing . . . sexual favors through a hole in the wall. They would take just enough blood to satisfy themselves, not enough for the victim to lose consciousness or anything. The victim might've felt bad for awhile, but that was all. The writer of the article claimed that, because of Live Girls, a friend of his had been transformed into a vampire by one of the peep-show girls, and someone near and dear to him had been killed."

A cat came out from behind the couch, hopped up onto the table, and stretched out beside the open binder. It was a sleek gray cat with long hair and a luxurious tail. It had some Persian in its blood—it didn't have the classic Persian face, but fur grew out of the bottoms of the big puffy paws. Karen recognized it because she had a couple Persians at home.

"This is Angie," Burgess said as he stroked the cat. "That's short for Angelica, to which she also answers. I take her everywhere with me. My wife thinks I'm crazy. But, then, I've found that when you marry a woman who isn't even half your age, she will almost *always* think you're crazy." He smiled, then laughed a little. He seemed disappointed that they didn't find his remark funny. He picked up Angie and put her on the floor, and she wandered off.

Burgess leaned forward in his seat, elbows on his thighs. He said, "The *Post* story begins with a brief editor's note, which claims that Woodrow Hill is a pseudonym for a prominent reporter who prefers to remain anonymous. I was very intrigued by this. The day after the article was published, I called a friend of mine at the *Post* and asked him who it was. This guy told me he wouldn't make any promises, but he'd try to find out. A few months later, he called me back and said the writer of the article was one Walter Benedek. He was a reporter for the *New York Times*. It's all in the scrapbook. I tried contacting him, but he returned none of my calls or letters. He eventually retired and disappeared."

Karen frowned. "Wait a second," she said. "If he worked for the *Times*, why did he write something for the *Post*?"

"Because he probably knew good and well that the *Times* would never publish such a piece," Burgess said. "In the article, he also named a New York night club called the Midnight Club, which he claimed was run by vampires who preyed on the clientele. Within twenty-four hours of the explosion at Live Girls, the Midnight Club folded up and cleared out, hardly leaving a trace. This information came from the *Global Inquisitor*, but I had it checked out. I hired a New York detective to look into the Midnight Club. It had never appeared in any phone book and had never advertised. It was almost as if it had never existed. Anyway, Benedek seemed to know the *Times* would never print his story. The *Post* is a tabloid, they had no trouble publishing a piece about vampires in Times Square.

He stood and walked over to a small table against the wall. He opened the briefcase on the table and took out two thick manila folders.

"I've had all the pertinent information in the scrap book copied and compiled in a file for each of you. Each file contains a check for your first payment."

Burgess handed them each a folder, then sat down again. He took a drink of his beer, and put it back down on the table.

"I still don't understand what you want us to do, Mr. Burgess," Karen said.

"I've managed to track down Walter Benedek. I hired that New York detective I'd used to look into the Midnight Club. It took awhile. Mr. Benedek had done a good job of covering up his tracks. He didn't *want* to be found. But my guy managed to find him . . . sort of. He lives in upstate New York, up in the Finger Lakes District. Unfortunately, all he could find was a post office box, which he staked out for awhile. Mr. Benedek never showed up. He's in a town called Honeoye, but that's as specific as my information gets. Miss Moffett, I'd like you to track him down. Before you do anything else, I would like you to pay a visit to Mr. Benedek and get him to tell you all he knows about these vampires."

"What do you want me to do?" Keoph said.

"I'd like you to wait until Miss Moffett learns all she can. In the meantime, Mr. Keoph, you might want to bone up on vampire mythology. It might come in handy. Then I want you both to work together toward one common goal. I want you to find the vampires for me." His eyebrows rose and he grinned at them.

Karen slowly turned her head to Keoph, who turned to her. They looked at each other for a moment, then turned back to Burgess. He seemed a perfectly reasonable man, pleasant and unassuming.

"Are you serious, Mr. Burgess?" Karen said.

"Serious as a heart attack." He continued to grin.

"You know," Keoph said, "I have other clients who are depending on me."

Burgess nodded. "You also have an excellent staff of investigators to take on those clients. I'm paying you a ridiculous amount of money to do this. If you choose not to, of course, there's nothing I can do about it. But before you make that decision, I suggest you open your folder and take a look at the first check."

Karen and Keoph opened their folders. The check was paper-clipped to the first page of the file. Karen's eyebrows rose. It was, indeed, a ridiculous amount of money for a first payment. She and Keoph exchanged another look.

She closed the file and said, "Let me get this straight, Mr. Burgess. You think these vampires really exist?"

"That's what I want you to find out," Burgess said. He smiled again. "Of course, my mind is pretty much made up. My investigation turned up enough evidence for *me* to think I was onto something. Yes, I'm inclined to believe they really exist. But like I said, even over eighteen years, I've been able to gather surprisingly little information. These things don't *want* to be found. So, I guess, while I'm already convinced they're out there, I'm curious to see if you can *find* them. I've provided you with all the information I have. The tabloid papers all followed up on that *Post* article with lurid stories of vampires in the New York sex trade, particularly the *Global Inquisitor*. The *Inquisitor* has done a story on these vampires two or three times a year ever since, milking it for all it's worth."

"You believe the *Inquisitor*?" Keoph said.

"Ah, welcome to my world, Mr. Keoph," Burgess said with a chuckle. "Many people think that tabloids print only lies. But you'd be surprised. During the O.J. Simpson media explosion back in the nineties, the most accurate reporting came from, of all places, the *National Enquirer*. Yes, it's true, tabloids publish a lot of utter bullshit. I mean, we all know the story about Batboy meeting the Pope is bullshit, right? But sometimes, they're the only place to find the truth, because unlike the legitimate press, the tabloids will go to whatever lengths necessary to get it. And they're a ruthless bunch. All the articles are in the file. You may find some helpful information in them, you may not. But don't dismiss them just because they're from tabloids."

"Why aren't we both going to see Walter Benedek?" Karen said.

"I'm sending you because I suspect that Mr. Benedek will be more forthcoming with a woman than a man."

"Have you talked to him?" Karen said.

"No, I haven't, but I've talked to someone who knows him, a man named Ethan Collier. They knew each other professionally and personally for many years, but Collier hasn't heard from him in a long time. It's all in the file. Anyway, Ethan Collier tells me Mr. Benedek is an incurable flirt, and that women love him."

Karen said, "Am I supposed to interview him, or flirt with him?"

"A little of both couldn't hurt," Burgess said. "Look, I'm not asking you to have a relationship with the guy, just don't be afraid to be charming if you think—"

"Mr. Burgess, with all due respect, I've been doing this for fourteen years," Karen said.

"You're right, I'm sorry. Forget I said that. I don't mean to tell you how to do your job. Forgive me. I just think he'll be more receptive to a woman than a man. By all accounts, the man's a perfect gentleman, so it's not like I'm sending you into a situation where you'll be—"

"I understand, Mr. Burgess," Karen said.

"When would you like us to start?" Keoph said.

"Immediately," Burgess said. "I realize you'll need some time to farm your clients out to other investigators at your agencies, but I'd like you to get started as soon as that's done. I recommend doing that today."

Karen paged through the file, thinking. It sounded like a wild goose chase to her, but Burgess was paying a lot. Vampires. It was probably going to end up being some group of goth misfits who wore a lot of black clothes and phony fangs and wrote bad poetry. But she was intrigued by the fact that a reporter for the *Times* would write a pseudonymous piece for the *Post*—why would he do such a thing? Obviously, he truly believed he had encountered vampires. Mental illness? Possible, but how likely? Karen's curiosity was stirred by Walter Benedek.

"All right," she said. "I'll do it."

Keoph thought about it a moment longer, then nodded. "Yeah."

Burgess grinned again and clapped his hands once, then rubbed them together vigorously. "Wonderful, wonderful. You'll want to go over all the information in the files. Miss Moffett, I've taken the liberty of booking a flight to Rochester, New York for you. It leaves at six forty-five in the morning."

Karen said, "Sounds like you were pretty confident we'd take this job."

"Like I said, Miss Moffett," Burgess said, "I'm paying you a ridiculous amount of money to do this, and I know how loudly money speaks to us all. I had every confidence you would come on board, if not just for the money, then certainly out of curiosity. I would imagine people in your line of work to be very curious in general, am I right? Just a little?"

Karen smiled. "Yes, you are. Just a little."

Angie hopped into Burgess's lap, and he stroked her back as she settled down across his thighs.

"My cell phone number is in the file," Burgess said. "I'll be staying at my Topanga Canyon house for another week or ten days, so I'll be in town if you need me for anything. If you have any questions or important information to share with me, feel free to call me at anytime, day or night. Don't worry about waking me. I'm a night owl, anyway. I do most of my writing at night. If you wake me, it'll be in the morning, when I sleep." He turned to Keoph. "You've been awfully quiet, Mr. Keoph. What do you have to say about all this?"

One heavy brow rose over Keoph's right eye. "The truth?"

Burgess smiled. "Always, Mr. Keoph, always."

"The truth is," Keoph said, "I think you're a taco short of a combo plate."

Burgess released a single abrupt, "*Ha!* That's exactly what I expected. I'm sure you both think I'm insane. But I'm not. I'm just curious, very curious. I've made my living by making up stories about vampires and ghosts and demons and werewolves for the last twenty-two years—things that are so ingrained in our culture that, even if only for the length of a book, people are able to believe in them. Then there are those who *do* believe in them, with great sincerity."

"Like you?" Keoph said.

"Those old legends and superstitions have to come from *someplace*. I find it difficult to believe they're all completely false. They started somewhere, somehow. I believe there may be more behind them than we think. I want to find out. And now I can afford to do it. Based on your reputations, I've hired you to do it for me. I want to start with these vampires."

"You want to *start* with the vampires?" Keoph said.

"Yes. This isn't the only scrapbook I have, and this

isn't the only story I've been following. But I think this is a good starting point."

"I usually work alone," Keoph said. "Why two of us?"

Burgess said, "To save time. You can do twice the work. I'm not saying you have to work together every minute. Spread out, follow separate leads, just . . . do whatever it is you do," he said with a big boyish smile.

Karen turned to Keoph and said, "If it's okay with you, we can use my Century City office as a base of operations."

He nodded. "Sounds good." He put his briefcase on the coffee table, opened it, and put the file in, then closed it again.

"Well, then, that's that," Burgess said. He put the cat back on the floor and stood. "I'm sure you want to get to those files, and you have preparations to make now that you've signed on."

Karen stood as Burgess headed for the door. As Keoph stood, she said, "Do you have a car yet?"

Keoph said, "No, I took a cab straight here from the airport."

"Where's your luggage?"

"I didn't bring anything but this briefcase. I hadn't planned to spend the night." He took the case from the coffee table. "I'll send for some things now that I know I'm staying. Or I might just buy some new clothes."

Burgess stood at the door and shook their hands with enthusiasm, that same boyish smile on his face. "It's been a pleasure meeting you both, and I look forward to working with you. I don't know about you two, but *I* think this is going to be *fun*."

CHAPTER TWO

Shortly after three in Karen's fourteenth-floor office in Century City, she poured scotch into a couple glasses on the sideboard. "You take ice?" she said.

"Nope."

"Me, I like ice." She'd brought a bucket of ice from the refrigerator in the break room. She dipped two fingers into it and scooped out a couple cubes, dropped them into her glass. The ice tinkled as she swirled the whiskey around in her glass. She took Keoph's drink to him.

He was seated in the swiveling black leather-upholstered chair in front of her desk. Karen went to the matching couch, kicked off her shoes, and sat on the end of the couch with her feet tucked under her.

"I don't usually drink this early," Keoph said.

"Oh, neither do I." She lifted her glass. "And the check's in the mail."

Keoph raised his drink. "To vampires."

"To vampires."

They drank.

"No offense, Keoph," Karen said, "but you look like you really needed a drink."

"No offense taken. I'm exhausted. There was a lot going on at my office yesterday, my ex-wife has been on my ass for more money, and I only got a couple hours of sleep last night. Then I had to fly here. It used to be such a simple, quick trip, but now, with all the security, it takes forever, and it's exhausting."

It was a comfortable chair, and for a moment, Keoph thought about how good it would feel to fall asleep there. He looked around at the office, done in a lot of black, white, and chrome, with a big, black, angular glass-topped desk. The windows behind the desk looked out on a small rose garden on the roof of the building.

"Nice place you've got here," he said.

"Thank you."

Karen stood and took her drink to her desk. She sat down and reached over to a small console of buttons on her desktop. She pushed a button and closed all the white blinds on the windows that looked out into the hallway and beyond to a group of desks in the next room. She opened a drawer and removed an ashtray, a pack of Winstons, and a Bic lighter. "I'm afraid my employees and colleagues don't approve of my smoking. And technically, it is against the law, but . . . do you mind?"

"Only if I can join you," Keoph said as he reached a hand under his coat and removed a cigarette and a brass Zippo lighter.

"You smoke, too?" she said.

"Now and then."

"Smoke 'em if you got 'em."

He lit up, and his lighter made a solid *chuck* sound when he closed it, then put it back under his coat.

"We smokers have to stick together," Karen said with a smile. "They're trying to snuff us out."

"If we don't snuff ourselves out first," he said, with smoke coming from his mouth and clouding before him.

"Look, Keoph," she said, "I'm not used to working with anyone, either. If you want to know the truth, I took the job for the money, and maybe to find out why that *Times* reporter would write such a thing for the *Post*. I mean, he must have believed it to be true. Also, I have . . . personal reasons for taking it. Anyway, I just wanted to let you know I've never done this before."

"That makes two of us," Keoph said. He looked at her a long moment, took her in. She had short auburn hair and a very attractive, heart-shaped face, with large brown eyes. She was dressed in a simple black-and-grey business suit. Keoph guessed her age to be between thirty-seven and forty, but she looked youthful and obviously took good care of herself. She stood about five feet, seven inches tall with a shapely figure. To a certain extent, Keoph was sorry they would be working together—he had wanted to ask her out when he first saw her on the elevator. "What's your personal reason for taking the job?" he asked.

She smiled and took a swallow of whiskey. "When I was a little girl, my uncle Arty used to babysit us. He was my mom's brother, and he was a cool guy, always fun to be with. He collected comic books and loved horror films. So whenever he took care of us, which was often, my brother, sister, and I had to watch whatever *he* wanted to watch on TV, and it was usually a horror film. I remember the first one I ever saw—it was some Technicolor Dracula movie with Christopher Lee. When I saw that man with blood all over his mouth and realized that he'd been drinking that woman's blood, I was so disgusted, I almost threw up. I had nightmares for weeks after that, and Uncle Arty was instructed by my mother not to make us watch horror movies anymore. But that single image of Christopher Lee standing there with his fangs bared and blood all around his mouth—it's always stayed with me. To this day, I can't watch vampire movies because I just find the whole idea so repulsive."

"So now you're going to investigate vampires?" Keoph said.

"I'm doing it because I know Uncle Arty would want me to. That's all. Sounds silly, but I like Uncle Arty, and I'd like to be able to tell him the story, you know?"

"What does Uncle Arty do these days?"

She smiled. "He's a comic book artist. He's with Marvel at the moment."

Keoph nodded his approval. He drew on his cigarette, let the smoke out slowly. "Maybe it would help if you knew a little about me," he said.

She nodded. "Yes, we should at least trade resumes, or something."

"I'm not talking about my work, I'm talking about me. There are things you should know if we're going to work together. I always tell the truth. That means I sometimes offend people. I'm not what you'd call 'politically correct.' I'm just not wired that way. So if I say something that offends you, feel free to say so, and you won't hurt my feelings. Personally, I don't offend. It just doesn't happen. So, say what's on your mind, I can take it. But most of all, I need to know that you'll always tell me the truth. Should we find ourselves in a dangerous predicament, I need to be able to trust you, and believe everything you say. Not only that, but I expect full disclosure of all the information you gather on this case. The only way this will work is if we work as a team, not as if this is some kind of competition. Is that understood?"

Karen smiled. "I think we're going to get along, Keoph. We already have a lot in common." She took a drag on the cigarette and blew smoke. "I like people who speak their mind, because I don't hesitate to speak mine. I think we're going to get along just fine."

"What do you think of our client?" Keoph said.

"I tend to believe him," Karen said. "I think he's genuinely curious to know where things like vampires and werewolves come from. What about you?"

"I think he should probably be medicated, if he isn't already."

Karen laughed. "That's possible, but I don't think so. If I really thought the guy wasn't right in the head, I wouldn't take his money. I've read enough of his work to think Mr. Burgess has an honest interest in this."

"I suspect his problem is that he has too much money, and too much time on his hands."

"We're getting a nice chunk of that money," she said. "And that's only the first payment." Karen picked up the black phone on her desk and pushed a button. "Hello, Libby. I need you to do something for me. Farm out all my clients to other investigators for the next, oh, let's say the next month, for starters. And don't make—what? Yes, you heard me right. All of them. And don't make any new appointments for me until I say otherwise. Got that? Great. Thank you." She replaced the phone on its base. "That's taken care of."

"I need to do the same thing," Keoph said, taking a cell phone from his right suitcoat pocket. He called his office in San Francisco and gave his secretary the same instructions Karen had given hers. When he was done, he put the phone back in his pocket.

Karen said, "What do you say we get to those files?" She opened hers on the desk.

Keoph put his briefcase on his lap, opened it, and took out the file.

They spent the next hour silently reading and occasionally commenting.

Keoph read everything in the folder, starting with the piece by Walter Benedek, writing as Woodrow Hill.

Like Karen, Keoph was puzzled why a reporter for the *Times* would write an anonymous piece for a rival tabloid. Keoph had known a few reporters in his time, and they weren't the type to do anything so risky to their careers. There had to be a good reason behind it—unless he was just a nut.

The scrapbook was filled mostly with news clippings. There were several pages of notes by Burgess, most of which were written about interviews with so-called witnesses. As far as Keoph could tell, all of Burgess's witnesses were homeless people who had hung around outside Live Girls, some of whom were injured when the peepshow blew up.

There were a couple photographs, too. Both were of the same subject, and both were very blurry. The background was dark, and something dark and blurry was in the foreground—it looked like part of a fence. In the first photograph, a face was in the upper part of the picture caught in what appeared to be the beam of a flashlight—a pale, oval face with dark spots where there should be eyes, hollow cheeks, and an open mouth. From the direction of the blur, the face was moving downward. Part of that blur were two slender streaks that came down from the upper lip— long, curved fangs. In the second photograph, the face was lower and not quite as blurred, but still ghostlike, still with those fangs in the yawning mouth. The pictures were creepy as hell, but they did not prove a thing. They easily could have been faked. There was no source for the pictures to be found on the page, which made them anonymous, and useless.

He read all the way to the final article, a piece from the *Inquisitor* a few months ago.

When he was done reading, he paged backward and scanned a few articles a second time.

As he read the material from Burgess's scrapbook, he felt like he was getting to know the writer a little better. Keoph was certain that Burgess wanted the vampire story to be true. There was a good chance, Keoph was sure, that Burgess would not believe them if they told him there was nothing to it.

"I think our client is going to be very disappointed," Keoph said.

"You think so?" Karen said.

"I don't think this is going to lead anywhere."

"We'll know more after I talk to Benedek."

"If you can get him to talk. What if he refuses?"

"Well, if necessary," Karen said, "I'll pay him for his story." She stood. "I skipped lunch, so I'm hungry. Want to get a bite to eat?"

"Sure."

They went across the street to a small diner.

"Are you familiar with Los Angeles?" Karen asked after they ordered.

"No, I'm not. I don't like it here. I only come when the work leads me. I live in a walking city, and I like to walk places. Nobody walks in LA."

"That's true, but the clientele here is incredible. I'm not kidding, I'm either hiring out bodyguards or investigating divorce cases, and it's never-ending."

Keoph nodded once. "Sounds like prime territory. But I couldn't live here. I love San Francisco too much."

"I like it, too. I enjoy visiting your city."

After a moment, he said, "What shall I do while you're in New York?"

"Just sit tight. I don't expect to be there overnight—I'll be there and back. Do you have a hotel yet?"

"I've got a room reserved at the Chataeu Marmont on Sunset, but I haven't been there yet to check in." He put a hand over his mouth and yawned.

"Why don't you go to your hotel room, take a nap," Karen said.

"I think I'll do that."

They exchanged cell phone numbers.

"You should take in some of the sights while you're here," she said. "You know, see a movie at the Chinese theater, or something."

"I think I'll sleep, mostly. Then I'll read this file

again." He put the manila folder back in his briefcase, then stood.

"While I'm gone, my office is yours," Karen said. "I'll tell Libby. You can come and go as you please."

"Thank you."

"I'll call a cab for you," Karen said as she picked up the phone. "Call me when you wake up."

"Will do."

The cab showed up out front a few minutes later, and took Keoph to the Chateau Marmont. He checked in, got his key, and went upstairs to his room. He kicked off his shoes, removed his clothes and hung them in the closet, then got into bed and fell asleep almost immediately.

CHAPTER THREE

In his robe and slippers, Walter Benedek started a pot of coffee, then reached into a plastic container on the counter and removed a handful of garlic cloves. He put the cloves on a cutting board and used a large knife to cut each of them in half. While the coffee brewed, he took a fistful of the clove halves and went to the two windows behind the small table and chairs in the kitchen. Holding the cut ends of the halves downward, he ground them into the sill of the first window. He went all the way around it, scrubbing the garlic into the wood. He did the same thing with the other window.

Benedek slowly wandered around the inside of his house and rubbed the garlic around all the windows. His tiny black-and-brown chihuahua, Bruno, followed him the whole way. Now and then, he went back to the kitchen for more clove halves. The whole house smelled of garlic, but Benedek had been doing it for so long, he hardly smelled it himself anymore.

He was a tall, slender man of sixty-four who was slightly stooped from a lifetime of self-consciously trying to appear shorter. He still had a thick crop of silver hair, for which he was very grateful, and he still watched what he ate and exercised to stay trim. He went for a long walk every day, and rode a stationary bike three times a week. He wasn't the type to overdo it.

Benedek lived in Honeoye, in upstate New York. It was a town of about five thousand people on the northern shore of Lake Honeoye, one of New York's Finger Lakes. The town was nestled in a valley near the Bristol Mountains, and consisted of a good-sized grocery store called Shurfine, two auto parts stores, a video store, a few other shops, a few restaurants, and a run-down old manufacturing facility, long closed, with a huge, ugly, peeling sign on its facade that read, "United We Stand."

On his way through the living room, he passed the portrait of his late wife, Jackie, over the fireplace and muttered, "Good morning, love." His heart always felt a faint clenching sensation whenever he looked at the portrait. It had been painted by Jackie's brother, and he had done an excellent job of capturing her smile. She'd been a beautiful woman whose full, wavy hair had gone white very early—instead of trying to hide it, she'd embraced it. Jackie had not been the sort to hide anything.

When he was done with the garlic, he fed Bruno and changed his water. Bruno's paws made clicketing sounds on the kitchen's tile floor as he walked over to his bowl and began to eat.

Benedek showered and dressed in jeans and a pale-blue shortsleeve shirt. He returned to the kitchen and poured a cup of coffee. He drank his coffee black because all of the things typically added to coffee were bad for him. So was the coffee, but it was the one thing he refused to give up. He had three cups every morning, and had no plans to change that routine.

He put his coffee on the table, then got more cut garlic cloves and went out the front door. He kept a ladder leaning against the front of the house by the picture window. He scrubbed the garlic along the bottom of the window, then up both sides. He got on the ladder and methodically rubbed it into the top edge as well. He had to move the ladder once to get the other half of that edge.

Benedek heard a familiar yipping behind him as he came down the ladder. He turned to see Mrs. Captree, a stout old woman who walked her two white toy poodles by Benedek's house every day, strolling down the street with her dogs on leashes.

"Hello, Mrs. Captree," he said with a wave.

"Hello, Mr. Benedict," she said. She'd never gotten his name right. "Nice morning," she said.

"Yes, very nice."

She walked on after her little dogs.

Benedek wondered if Mrs. Captree was ever curious about what he was doing every morning. He would happily explain the whole thing, if he didn't think she would write him off as an old loon. He didn't talk about it anymore, not like he used to, back when he thought he could make a difference. His story contained a truth that most people did not want to believe, even refused to believe.

He went back inside and got more garlic. Bruno followed him out and around the house as Benedek made his way to each window. At the windows, there was always something for him to step up on to get the tops—a step-ladder, a big rock, a stack of wooden crates. He hit every window, then rubbed the garlic cloves around the outside of the back and front doors, and that night around sundown, he would do it all again. Benedek went through a lot of garlic every day.

As he came back around to the front of the house, a battered old blue Chevy pickup pulled into his driveway. Pete Etchel killed the engine and got out of the truck.

"Hey, Pete," Benedek said with a smile as he picked the newspapers up off the lawn. He subscribed to four. "How's it hangin'?"

Pete laughed. "Hangin' is about all it's doin' these days."

"Come on inside."

"What are you doin' out here?"

Benedek held out his hand, which held the remains of the garlic cloves he'd used. He turned and went in the house, with Pete right behind him.

Pete stood five feet, ten inches tall, with a beer gut that tightened the front of the overalls he wore. He was sixty-eight and limped slightly when he walked because of a bad hip. Under the overalls, he wore a shortsleeve red-plaid shirt.

"Do you have any idea how . . . *antisocial* that is, Walter?" Pete said, smirking.

"Yeah, but I don't really care. I never have company, except for you, and I know you can handle it."

"Gotta keep them vampires out, huh?" Pete laughed.

That's what Pete always said. Of course, he knew nothing about Benedek's past. He was just joking, just poking a little fun at Benedek for his strange habit. He had no idea he spoke the truth.

"You know, I've never really asked you," Pete said in the house, "why *do* you do that?"

Benedek wasn't sure what to say. He could always tell him the truth and then joke about it—Pete would never believe that particular truth—or he could make something up.

"I'm very superstitious," Benedek said. "It's an old superstition, a habit I got into many years ago."

"It's a nasty habit, is what it is," Pete said, smiling. "Why don't you take up smoking again? I think that would be less annoying. Oh, well. To each his own, I guess. That's what my grandma always used to say."

"Oh, yeah?" Benedek said. "You know what *my* grandma always used to say? 'If you don't have something nice to say about someone, come over here and sit next to me.' You want some coffee?"

"No, I can't stay. Just wanted to see if you'd like to go fishing tomorrow morning. I feel like taking the boat out on the lake. You up for it?"

"You know I never say no to fishing, Pete. What time?"

"I'd like to go out around six."

"I'll be there with lures on my toes."

"Maggie said she'd fix us breakfast burritos to take with us, so don't eat before you leave. I'll bring the burritos, you bring the coffee."

"You got a deal."

"Then you're in." Pete turned and went to the door. "I'm going to get out of here before that smell gets into my clothes."

Bruno barked at Pete as he left.

Benedek smiled and said, "Don't let the garlic hit you in the ass on the way out."

"Don't bring any with you tomorrow," Pete said. "See you in the morning."

Benedek stood at the screen door as Pete limped back to his pickup. He noticed the lawn had been neglected long enough. He decided to mow it that morning after he read the papers.

He poured himself a fresh cup of coffee, poured nonfat milk on a bowl of Grape Nuts, and sat down at the kitchen table to read the news.

CHAPTER FOUR

Karen drove her rented Ford Taurus down Main Street through Honeoye, which was actually Route 20A, with no idea where she was going. Burgess's New York private eye had determined that Benedek lived in Honeoye, but that was all he knew. Karen had looked him up in the book, but his number was unlisted. She told herself she should have known it wouldn't be that easy.

She pulled over and parked at the curb in front of a bar called the Oasis, a little place with a window filled with neon advertisements for beer. She got out of the car and went inside. It was a rectangular bar, dark inside, with the bar on the right and four booths against the wall on the left. There were two pinball machines and a jukebox in the back. The jukebox played something blue and boozy.

It was just past one in the afternoon, but there were

a few sad-looking people with bad posture seated at the bar. Karen went up to the bar and took a seat far from the nearest person.

The bartender was a woman in her early twenties with honey-blond hair pulled back in a ponytail. She wore a shortsleeve white blouse and a short black skirt. She had a nametag, but Karen couldn't read it in the bad light.

"What can I get you?" the bartender said.

"I'd like a cup of coffee, please."

"That's it?"

"I'm afraid so."

The young woman looked at Karen suspiciously, but got her coffee and put it on the bar.

"Excuse me," Karen said as the young woman started to walk away. She came back and Karen said, "What's your name, by the way?"

"Suzi."

"Oh, Suzi, I have a sister named Susan. Look, Suzi, I wonder if you could help me with something. I've come here looking for a man named Walter Benedek. I know he lives here in Honeoye, but I don't know where. Would you happen to know him? The name's Walter Benedek."

Suzi slowly turned her head back and forth. "No, I don't know anybody by that name."

"He's a retired reporter," Karen said. "For the *New York Times*. You don't know anyone like that?"

"No. I'm sorry, I don't. But hold on a sec." Suzi pushed away from the bar, lifted her head, and shouted, "Okay, everybody, listen up."

The three other heads at the bar lifted and turned to Suzi. Karen realized there were people in a couple of the wooden booths along the wall when heads peered out from behind the dark dividers.

Suzi spoke loudly when she said, "Anybody here know a guy named— " She looked down at Karen. "What's his name again?"

"Walter Benedek," Karen said.

"Anybody here know a guy named Walter Benedek?" Suzi said to her patrons.

After a moment, the heads at the bar turned down again, refocusing their attention on their drinks and their problems.

Suzi looked at her and said, "Looks like you're outta luck."

"Well, thanks, anyway," Karen said with a smile.

Someone else came in and took a seat at the bar, a middle-aged man wearing a baseball cap. Suzi went to wait on him.

Karen was prepared to go into every bar in town if she had to, but she tried to think of something more efficient.

Benedek was a journalist. What kinds of things would a retired journalist do? *Maybe he rents movies*, she thought—she would check the local video stores.

Books, she thought. *Journalists are readers*.

When Suzi walked by, Karen said, "Excuse me, Suzi. Does Honeoye have a public library?"

"Yeah, it's just up the street a ways," Suzi said

"Thank you." She stood and paid for the coffee and left the bar.

Back in her car, she drove farther up the street, but slowly, looking for the library. It was a one-story 1950s red-brick building with a flat roof. Karen parked in the small lot in front and went in.

Inside, the library smelled like a library. Karen had noticed that all libraries smelled the same. It was the smell of books, probably, but she liked to think of it as the scent of knowledge.

She went to the front counter where a black woman in her late sixties stamped a card, slipped it into a book, and handed the book over to a little girl. Karen waited until the girl was finished, then stepped forward and gave the woman her biggest smile.

"Hi, my name's Karen," she said.

The old woman smiled at her and nodded once. "My name's Margaret."

"Well, Margaret, I'm looking for someone who lives here in Honeoye, his name is Walter Benedek."

"Oh, yes, I know Walter," Margaret said. "He comes in here often."

"Could you tell me where he lives?"

Margaret's smile faltered. "Does he know you?"

"No, I'm afraid not." Karen slipped a hand into her purse and produced a business card, which she handed to Margaret. "My name's Karen Moffett, I'm a private investigator from Moffett and Brand Security in Los Angeles. I just need to ask Mr. Benedek some questions."

Margaret's smile fell away. "A private investigator. I don't know."

"Mr. Benedek's not in any kind of trouble, or anything. I just need to ask him a few questions about a case I'm working on. It has to do with an article he wrote back in 1987."

"Well, I don't mean to seem suspicious of you," Margaret said, "but Mr. Benedek is a very private kind of person. That's why I hesitate. I have an idea, though. Why don't I give him a call and tell him you want to speak with him?" As she spoke, she picked up the phone, then reached over and flipped through a Rolodex, found his number, and punched the phone's buttons.

Margaret smiled when she said, "Hello, there, Mr. Benedek. This is Margaret, down at the library. You know, those Sidney Sheldon books are all overdue. All four of them. *Shame* on you for reading that trash." She listened a moment, then laughed. "That's not why I'm calling, though. There's a young woman down here looking for you. She says she's a private investigator and her name is—" Margaret checked the business card. "— Karen Moffett. She says she wants to ask you some questions about an article you wrote back in 1987." She looked up at Karen. "Yes." She nodded her head. "All right then, that's what I'll tell her. And you better bring those books in, young man." She laughed, then said, "All right, bye-bye, Mr. Benedek," and hung up the phone.

Karen smiled. "What did he say?"

"He told me to tell you to please go away."

Karen nodded. "Okay. So . . . you're not going to tell me where he lives?"

"I'm afraid I can't. Mr. Benedek doesn't want me to. I'm sorry, Karen, but I can't help you."

As she left the library, Karen remembered that Burgess had said his New York investigator had gotten no more than a post office box. She wondered if she was going to have the same luck.

Back in the Taurus, she drove through town looking for a video store. She found one a couple blocks up, a place called Movieland Video. She found a parking space along the curb, dropped a quarter into the parking meter, and walked back the way she had come to the video store. If this didn't work, she'd look for other video stores, and if there were none, she would look for used bookstores.

There was a gangly teenage boy at the counter, talking on the phone as he wrote something down on a sheet of paper attached to a clipboard. Quickly, before he turned to her, she reached up and unfastened a couple buttons on her shirt, just enough to reveal a touch of cleavage. As he hung up the phone, she approached the counter and smiled.

"Hi, my name is Karen," she said, holding out a hand to shake.

The boy smiled and shook her hand. "Hi, Karen. I'm Nate." He had pimples on his cheeks and wore a retainer.

"Maybe you can help me, Nate. I'm looking for an old friend of mine. I know he lives here in Honeoye, but I don't have his address. I'd call him, but I want to surprise him. His name's Walter Benedek."

Nate tipped his head back. "Oh, yeah, I know Mr. Benedek. He comes in here all the time. He always rents widescreen DVDs, never any full-screens, unless the movie was shot that way."

"Would you happen to know where he lives?"

"Sure, he lives just up the road from me. Sometimes I drop by his house on the way to work to pick up videos. He always appreciates that. I don't think he gets much company."

"If you could point me in the right direction, I'd sure appreciate it, Nate."

"Sure, you just go up Main here another two blocks and turn right on Sycamore. You go out Sycamore past the 7-Eleven, until you get to a short bridge over a creek. Just a ways past that, you turn right down Wells Street. His is the third on the left."

"Oh, I can't thank you enough, Nate, you saved my day."

"Sure. No problem." Nate blushed.

She went back out to her car and drove a couple blocks till she got to Sycamore, where she turned right.

Karen's spirits had fallen a little when Margaret told her Benedek wanted her to go away. But she was certain she could win him over in person.

She started to button up her shirt, but changed her mind and left it open.

CHAPTER FIVE

On Wells Street, Karen parked in front of Benedek's ranch-style house with a covered porch and a big, well-groomed yard. The yard smelled of freshly mown grass. Briefcase in hand, she went up the flagstone walk, climbed the porch steps, crossed the porch, and rang the doorbell. Her nose wrinkled when she got a whiff of garlic.

Karen had reread the file on the plane. She could imagine someone believing it all. If one were open to that sort of thing—which she tended not to be—she could understand taking it seriously and wanting to find out the truth. Unlike Keoph, she did not think Burgess had a screw loose, but she agreed with him that Burgess was likely to be very disappointed in their findings.

There were footsteps on the other side of the door.

It opened on a tall, slightly stooped, but trim and fit man in his mid-sixties with thick white hair. He wore small round glasses beneath his bushy eyebrows. His long, rubbery face reminded Karen of that of an old basset hound.

"Hello," he said.

"Are you Walter Benedek?" Karen asked.

"Now, why would an attractive young woman like yourself want to know that?"

The way he said it, as if he'd been waiting for her to arrive so he could deliver the line, made her smile. "My name is Karen Moffett. I'm a private investigator. I've come to ask you some questions."

"You found me, anyway, huh?"

"I'm afraid I'm tenacious. I'm looking into the incident in Times Square in the winter of 1987," she said. "The explosion in a place called Live Girls. Does that sound familiar?"

His jowly face fell a little and he stood up a bit straighter. But he said nothing in reply.

"You *are* Walter Benedek, aren't you?" Karen said.

"Who wants to know?"

"I do."

"Who hired you?"

"I'm sorry, but that's priveleged information."

He looked beyond her at the road out front. "Are you alone?"

"Yes."

"You're sure you weren't followed?"

"No, I wasn't. Why do you think I would be?"

He ignored the question. "Are you a reporter?"

"No, I'm a private investigator."

"Can you prove it?"

She removed her wallet from her purse and opened it to show him her license.

"Moffett and Brand Security. California, huh?"

"Los Angeles."

"Are you working for a reporter? Do you want this information so you can publish it?"

"Absolutely not. My client is not a journalist, and this is not for publication." Karen hoped that was true—Burgess had said nothing of writing about it. "Anything you tell me will go only to my client, and will remain completely confidential."

He nodded once. "What do you want to know?"

"I have a number of questions. Would it be all right if I came inside?"

Benedek thought about it awhile as he looked beyond her at the road. Finally, he sighed and stepped back so she could enter. His living room was to the left, and he led her there.

As she entered the living room, she smelled garlic again. It wasn't just a whiff this time, but a strong odor.

"Have a seat," he said. "Can I get you something to drink?"

"I'd appreciate a glass of ice water." She sat down on the couch.

"Sure, no problem."

While he was gone, she looked around. There were books and magazines everywhere. The couch and recliner faced the flatscreen plasma TV on the wall above a bank of electronics—a DVD player, a VCR, and a stereo system. Over the fireplace was a painting of a beautiful woman with long silver hair.

A wriggly little black-and-brown chihuahua rushed into the room and came straight to Karen. The dog hopped into her lap, put forepaws on her chest, and licked her face. Laughing, she pulled her head back and held the excited dog at arm's length a moment before putting him back on the floor.

Benedek returned with a glass of ice water, which he handed to Karen. He went to the recliner and sat down.

"That's Bruno," he said. He snapped his fingers once and said, "Bruno, not now. Not now." Bruno went over to the recliner and curled up at Benedek's feet. "Now, you stay there."

"Bruno seems to be a very happy dog," Karen said.

"Spoiled rotten," he said with a smile. "How did you find me?"

"My client hired a New York private investigator to track you down several years ago. It wasn't easy, but he did. He determined you were here in Honeoye. I found out where you lived by asking around."

"I've tried hard not to leave a trail, but these days, it's impossible." He reached down and scratched the top of Bruno's head. "For awhile, I considered changing my name."

"Why?"

"Because I didn't want them to find me."

"Who?"

Benedek frowned at her a moment, thinking. "How much do you know?" he said.

"Enough to know that you're probably referring to vampires. I read your Woodrow Hill piece. As well as every article ever written about it over the last seventeen years."

"Yeah, the *Inquisitor* loves that story, don't they? They keep going back to it, time and time again. I think they've got someone making that shit up, because it's all crap."

"I'd like you to tell me the truth, Mr. Benedek," Karen said.

"What's your client's interest in my story?" Benedek said.

"I'm not at liberty to—"

"Well, if you want me to talk to you, you're going to have to bend the rules a little. You don't have to tell me who your client is, nothing like that. Just tell me what this person's interest is in my story."

She thought about it a moment. She was uncomfortable with it, but it seemed to be a deal-breaker for Benedek.

"I won't talk to you otherwise," Benedek added.

Karen tipped her head back slightly and said, "My client's interest is simple curiosity. My client wants to know if vampires really exist."

Benedek pursed his lips as his eyebrows rose. "That's it?"

"That's it. My client has followed this story since it happened."

"Then he doesn't know anything because most of what's been written since my article has been complete nonsense."

"Well, that's his interest in your story," Karen said.

"And you took the job?"

"My partner and I, yes."

"Where's your partner?"

"He's in Los Angeles boning up on vampire mythology."

There was a can of soda on the small table beside the recliner, and Benedek took a couple swallows from it, then crushed it in his hand as he stood. "You can forget the mythology, most of it's wrong." He tossed the soda can into a brown paper bag half-filled with crushed soda cans. He stepped into the kitchen for a moment and returned with a cup of tea, which he took back to the recliner. "I hope your client's paying you a lot of money," he said.

"As a matter of fact, my client is paying us a great deal of money."

"Because you're going to be risking your lives if you plan on looking into vampires. They don't like to be looked into."

"What can you tell me about them?" Karen said.

"Didn't you hear me, Miss Moffett? I just said your life will be in danger if you pursue this investigation."

"I heard you."

"That doesn't bother you?"

"I'm not sure I believe it to be true. You haven't told me what I'm supposed to be afraid of yet."

"Why tell you?" Benedek said with a shrug. "You'll listen to every word, you might even take a few notes down in a little notebook, or whatever it is you do. But you won't believe it. You won't believe a word of it. And you'll go on not believing it until one of those things comes out of the dark and sinks its fangs into your throat."

Karen found the casual way he said it vaguely disturbing.

"Does it matter to you whether or not I believe your story?" Karen said.

"You're damned right it matters. Because if you don't believe my story, then you probably think I'm crazy. I don't like it when people think I'm crazy, when all I'm doing is telling the truth. That's why I haven't discussed this with anyone in eighteen years."

"But you're discussing it with me."

"I'm considering discussing it with you. I'm discussing whether or not I want to discuss it with you."

"Which way are you leaning?"

"I seldom have company, and it's never as pretty as you. I may tell you just to keep you around for lunch. I may tell you to impress upon you the gravity of what you're doing, the danger involved. On the other hand, I might just send you on your way with nothing. I haven't decided yet."

Karen took a drink from her glass of ice water. "Any idea when you'll know for sure?"

Benedek frowned as he stared down at Bruno for several seconds. "Have you eaten, Miss Moffett?"

"I skipped breakfast," she said. "I could use something to eat."

"Drive down to the corner and turn right. Four or five blocks down, you'll come to the Coffeepot Café, on the right. The food's terrible, but they make an okay omelette or burger. Before I tell you anything, there's someone I have to call first. As soon as I'm done, I'll come join you. We can talk then."

"Deal," Karen said.

They both stood and she handed him the glass of water. "Thanks for the drink."

Karen got back into her car and drove to the Coffeepot Café.

Benedek went down the hall to his bedroom and found his address book in the top drawer of his bedstand. It was old and falling apart—he'd never gotten around to replacing it, although he would have to soon because some of the pages were falling out. He carefully opened it to O and ran his forefinger down the page until he found the name Davey Owen. A few numbers had been crossed out under Davey's name, but the one at the bottom of the list remained untouched. He picked up the cordless and punched in the number.

CHAPTER SIX

Davey Owen heard the phone's chirping as if through a layer of mud. It was garbled at first, but slowly grew louder, clearer. He finally lifted his head from the pillow, eyes closed, and listened. The phone sounded again.

He lay in bed with his wife Casey, both of them naked. The black vertical blinds on the bedroom windows were all closed, and the room was dark.

Davey groped for the phone on the bedstand and finally closed his hand on the reciever. He put it to his ear.

" 'Lo," he said.

"Davey? It's Walter Benedek."

"Walter? Hey, Walter." Davey sat up in bed, slowly put his legs over the edge.

"You okay, Davey?" Benedek said.

"Woke up from a sound sleep."

"Yeah, I was afraid of that. Look, I've got something important to talk to you about. You want me to call back in ten minutes, give you a chance to wake up?"

"Yes, I'd appreciate that, Walter. Give me . . . fifteen. In fact, I'll call you. It's the same number, right?"

"Yep."

"What's this about?"

"Someone's asking questions."

Davey took a deep breath and let it out through puffed cheeks. "I see. I'll call you back in about fifteen." He replaced the receiver, then rubbed his eyes as he yawned. He stood and stretched his arms.

Someone's asking questions.

Benedek's words began to sink in. Someone knew, or thought he knew.

Davey walked around to the other side of the bed and sat on the edge. Casey was sleeping on her right side. He gently put his right hand on her shoulder.

"Casey? Case, honey. Come on, wake up." He shook her slightly.

She awoke suddenly, with a gasp, and sat up.

"Sorry," Davey said. "I didn't mean to startle you."

"What'sa matter?"

"I'm not sure."

"What do you mean?"

"Let's go to the kitchen and make coffee. I'm going to call him back in a few minutes."

"Call who back?"

He went to the closet and got his gunmetal-gray robe, slipped into it. "Walter. Put your robe on and come with me."

Downstairs in the kitchen, Davey quickly started a

pot of coffee brewing. Casey came in, her strawberry-blond hair, which fell halfway down her back, in a tangle.

"What did Walter say?" she said.

He recounted the phone call to her.

As soon as the coffee was ready, Davey poured some into two mugs. He put some sugar in Casey's, a little cream in his. They took their coffee to the kitchen table and sat down. A phone was on the wall above the table, with a speaker beneath the keypad.

"What do you think Walter meant when he said someone was asking questions?" Casey said, still sleepy-eyed.

"I'm assuming it's someone asking around about vampires in general or us in particular."

"It's not necessarily us."

"No. But we won't know till I call him."

Casey reached over the table and poked him in the ribs playfully. "Then what're you waiting for?"

Davey hit a button on the phone, then punched in Benedek's number.

"Hello?" Benedek said.

"Walter, it's Davey. I've got you on the speaker. Casey's with me."

"Hello, Walter," Casey said.

"It's good to hear your voice, Casey," Benedek said. "It's been too long."

"You sound good, Walter," she said.

"Thank you, dear. I wish I could say I was just calling to catch up," Benedek said, "but that's not it."

He told them about Karen Moffett.

"Are you pretty confident she's not a reporter?" Davey said.

"I can tell she's not a reporter. She's too well-dressed, for one thing, and she didn't ask the right questions. A reporter would've started asking questions right away. I believe she's not a reporter. I believe she's a private investigator working for someone, but I don't know who that someone is, and that's what worries me."

"What are you afraid of, Walter?" Davey said.

"What if it's a vampire? From 'eighty-seven. One who just got tired of hunting for me and decided to hire a private eye to do it."

"That's not their style, Walter," Davey said. "I've told you before, I think they've given up looking for you, or they would've found you by now. Maybe they're just not interested anymore."

"I'm not so sure," Benedek said.

"What do you want us to do, Walter?" Casey said.

"I'd like you to talk to this woman. When I tell her my story, I know she's going to want to meet with you."

Davey and Casey exchanged a frown.

"Why, Walter?" Davey said.

"I wrote that article eighteen years ago, Davey, and it was dismissed by everyone, laughed at, ridiculed. I was hoping I could create an awareness of those predatory vampires, that I might be able to save a few lives. But nobody believed me. Now, this woman comes along, and she's taking me seriously. Finally, someone wants to hear my story. I just want you two to corroborate it for me."

"But that would involve revealing ourselves to this woman," Davey said.

"She claims the information she gathers goes only to her client and remains completely confidential. Her client's only interest is to find out whether or not vampires really exist. I just don't want to tell my story if I'm going to be the only one telling it. Do you understand? I don't want her to look at me with that condescending, pitying look when I tell her what happened in New York eighteen years ago. Unless I can send her to you. Then she'll *have* to believe me."

Davey said, "I don't know, Walter."

"Think about it," Benedek said. "You know what they're doing. Not you, not others like you, but the . . . what do you call them?"

"The brutals," Casey said.

"Yeah, the brutals. Think of what they're doing, night after night. Think of the people they prey on and kill. Maybe Miss Moffett's client is someone who can *do* something about that. That's all I ever wanted to do—warn people, let them know. Maybe I can still do that."

"That would involve exposure, Walter," Davey said. "In order for something to be done about the brutals, it would be necessary to expose vampires everywhere."

"Not necessarily everywhere," Benedek said. "People like you wouldn't need to be exposed. It would be the predators who would be exposed, the murderers, the child-nappers. You could easily keep your cover."

"Unless talking to your private investigator shines a light on us," Casey said.

"I don't think that'll happen."

"But you can't be sure," Davey said.

Benedek sighed. "Okay, a risk exists. But not a very big one, I don't think."

The long silence over the line was finally interrupted when Davey said, "I don't know, Walter."

"I didn't want to do this," Benedek said. "I really didn't. But I feel it's necessary."

"Do what, Walter?" Casey said.

"I didn't want to call in a favor," he said, "but you both owe me. I went into Live Girls after you. I've never asked you for anything in the eighteen years I've known you. Please. Do this."

Casey looked at Davey and shrugged. The movement said, *He's right, we owe him.*

"We'll do it on one condition, Walter," Davey said.

"What's that?"

"She comes to us, we answer her questions, then she leaves us alone after that, okay? She leaves us completely alone."

"Fine," Benedek said. "If that's the way you want it, fine."

Another silence stretched out over the line.

"How've you been, Walter?" Casey asked.

"I'm getting by. Arthritis in my hips makes me hobbly early in the morning or when it rains, but it always feels better after I go for a walk. This business of aging is for the birds."

"Are you seeing anyone?" Casey said.

"Oh, Lord, no. I don't think I'll ever be seeing anyone, Casey. I had the love of my life. There won't be anyone after Jackie. I still miss her terribly. It's never gotten easier."

"You need to come spend some time with us here in California, Walter," Davey said.

"That would be nice," Benedek said. "I might do that someday. Are you going to do this for me, or not?"

Davey and Casey laughed at Benedek's abruptness. Davey gave Casey a questioning look, and she nodded.

"Okay, we're going to do this, Walter," Davey said, "but on a one-time-only basis."

"Understood."

"Send her over here for lunch tomorrow," Davey said. "If she wants to meet with us, she'll have to come here."

"Lunchtime?" Benedek said. "You're sure you want to do that? You're pretty groggy about this time of day."

"Don't worry, we'll be fine."

"Okay, I'll do that, Davey," Benedek said. "I can't thank you enough."

Afterward, Casey said, "What do you think?"

Davey said, "I think that somebody who can afford to hire private investigators just to find out if vampires really exist or not is probably somebody with too much money and time. What do *you* think?"

"I don't know," Casey said. "Do you suppose someone finally *believes* Walter? After all these years?"

"Could be," Davey said. "We'll see."

CHAPTER SEVEN

"I haven't told my story to anyone since I wrote that piece for the *Post*," Benedek said. He sat across from her in a booth at the Coffeepot Café.

Karen had just been served her omelette and hash-browns when Benedek had come into the diner and joined her. He knew the waitress by name—Gladys, who had the lined and sagging face of a woman in her late fifties, but hair that had been dyed jet-black. Not a single white hair was visible, and Karen had found the look unsettling. Benedek had ordered an English muffin with margarine on the side.

"If you've read the *Post* piece," he said, "then you know the story. What more do you want me to tell you?"

Karen opened her briefcase on the seat beside her and retrieved a microcassette recorder. "I hope you don't mind if I record our conversation. It will be played only for my client, and no one else."

"Can I get that in writing?"

Karen smiled. "I'm afraid I don't have a copy of that particular form with me at the moment."

"I suppose I should just be grateful that someone finally wants to listen to this story, to take it seriously."

"I'm not out to laugh at you, Mr. Benedek. Neither is my client. I'm taking this investigation very seriously." Karen put the small recorder in the center of the table and pressed a shiny silver button with a red dot on it. "How did you become aware of the vampires, Mr. Benedek."

Gladys brought Benedek's English muffin and he slowly spread the margarine on each half as he talked. "My sister was suspicious of her husband. He was coming home late, way too late, and he didn't look well. I was on vacation at the time, so I agreed to tail him for a little while, see what he was up to. He went straight to a little peep-show in Times Square called Live Girls. While he was there, he was bitten by a vampire. He was forced to exchange blood with a vampire, and he was turned. Into a vampire. Then he slaughtered my sister and niece."

He took a bite of his muffin and chewed slowly.

Benedek said, "I knew there was something up with that peep-show joint, so I kept an eye on it. That's how I met Davey."

"Who's Davey?"

"Davey Owen. A friend of mine now, although he was a stranger at the time. He went into Live Girls looking fine, then limped out looking drained. I struck up a conversation with him, got his confidence. He changed right before my eyes, Miss Moffett. He died, but his body kept on living. Technically, he should be dead, but he's not, see. I put him through a little test. We found out that crucifixes had no affect on him. He had a reflection in the mirror. But he couldn't stand garlic, had an immediate reaction to it."

Karen said, "You're telling me your friend became a vampire?"

"Yes. He had a relationship with one of the performers from Live Girls, a beautiful vampire named Anya. She also worked at the Midnight Club, which I investigated myself, by the way, and it was not only run by them, but they were storing up great quantities of blood in the back. That's where I found my brother-in-law."

"You found him?" Karen said. "What did you do?"

He took another bite of the muffin and took his time chewing it. "I found out they heal very quickly . . . but they can be killed if you do it right."

A silence fell over them for about twenty seconds.

Karen said, "In your article, you mention mutated vampires that were being kept in the basement of Live Girls."

Benedek nodded. "I've learned the story behind those things from Davey. They were vampires who had gone out on their own a little too early, without the guidance of someone older and wiser. Without a sponsor, you might say. They leave the nest too early and don't know enough to avoid drug addicts, or people with possible diseases of the blood, and they are mutated by that bad blood. It happened to Davey—he lost the use of his left hand."

Frowning, Karen said, "That's fascinating. What about Davey? What became of him?"

"Oh, he's very happily married now. His wife Casey is one, too. She was held captive at Live Girls and turned."

"Your friends are living a . . . normal life?"

"Oh, sure. They live in Los Angeles now, and they're successful screenwriters. They write romantic comedies, of all things."

"And no one has a clue."

"Now you do. I hope you meant what you said about confidentiality."

"This is for my client's eyes only."

"They're not alone, either, Davey and Casey," Benedek said. "There are plenty more just like them, living among us as if they *were* us, when they're not. Not at all. I'm not saying there's one on every street-corner, because there's not, but they're around. They manage to blend in quite well. According to Davey and Casey, they tend to be urban, although there are some in the suburbs, as well. In rural areas, too."

"Are they organized in any way?"

"They own a chain of blood banks all over the country—a kind of co-operative—from which they get most of the blood, which is sold by the bottle in the backs of shops run by vampires. You know, small grocers or antique shops, something with a front like that, and then in the back, they sell blood to vampires."

"So, they drink . . . bottled blood?"

"Not all of them. I'm talking about only one specific segment of the vampire world. There are many who do *not* drink bottled blood. They like to get their blood the old-fashioned way. They prey on people. These predators are very dangerous. Some are monsters. Most vampires fall into that category. And yet, some of the people being preyed upon aren't even aware they're victims, only that they feel a little tired and worn out, more fatigued than usual."

"They don't remember being bitten?"

"These vampires are very powerful. They can cloud the mind, fog up the memory. I think it's a kind of hypnosis. Some victims are simply drained and discarded. Some are held in captivity and fed on over a period of time. It's frightening to think how many unsolved murders or missing persons out there are the work of vampires. They never get caught. That's why I want to tell my story to you. Maybe your client is in a position to *do* something about it."

Karen said, "Your friend is in the minority, then?"

"I'm afraid so."

"What would happen if vampires were exposed?"

He nodded as he chewed another bite of his muffin. "I've often thought about that. I can imagine the fear and paranoia that would break out. People would start suspecting their neighbors of being vampires, maybe even their own family members. They would also commit acts of violence against real vampires when they found them. Those who've managed to blend in and make peaceful lives for themselves would probably be weeded out and killed. And I'm sure a number of innocent people would be killed because they were mistaken for vampires. It would be awful."

"You paint an ugly picture," Karen said.

"I have great faith in the human race, Karen. Whenever possible, it will probably do the wrong thing."

"Why have you decided to talk to me?" Karen said. "Do you think something can be gained by it?"

"To be honest . . . there's a part of me that wants

them to be exposed. Then everyone else would have to live with the fear I've lived with for the last eighteen years. No one would go out at night, and they would rub crushed garlic around their windows and doors. I do that, you know."

"I *thought* I smelled garlic at your house."

"It's not a very sociable thing to do, but I never want to see one of those things come to my window again."

"When did that happen?"

"One of them came to our bedroom window and dragged off my wife. Back in New York." His eyes narrowed, and his jaw flexed. "Took her away from me. I found her in the basement of Live Girls later. They'd . . . *fed* her to those . . . *things* in that basement."

Benedek took off his glasses and put them on the table while he wiped his eyes with a knuckle.

"Sorry," he said, and his voice broke on the word.

"You didn't include that in your *Post* article, Walter. Why?"

"I couldn't write about it yet. I tried, but couldn't. It had just happened. I was distraught."

"Wait. You're saying one of these things dragged off your wife and fed her to mutant vampires?"

"Yes. That's what I'm saying."

"What did you tell the police?"

He shrugged. "That I woke up in the morning and she was just gone. They investigated, found no signs of foul play. She's still . . . missing. Now, maybe you understand why I'm reluctant to tell my story. It's still very painful. I wrote the article for the *Post* in a fit of hubris. I was righteously indignant and thought ex-

posing them was the most important thing I could do.
I thought about the lives I'd save simply by letting
people know they were out there, to beware of them.
I was an idiot. The only people who paid any attention to that piece were the tabloids. I've lived in fear
ever since that article was published. A rumor circu-
lated at the *Times* that I'd written it, but no one ever
knew for sure if I had or not. But that wasn't what
worried me. If the rumor was flying around at work,
then was it possible that the *vampires* knew who really wrote that article? I retired early a couple years
later and got the hell out of the city. I moved here, as
much for my health as the fishing. I needed peace and
quiet. I needed to relax."

"And have you? Relaxed, I mean?"

"For the most part, yes, I have. But there's a part of
me that can never relax, can never let down its guard.
It's the part of me that knows they're out there. After
a lifetime of thinking of them as nothing more than
mythological figures at best, I find out they're real,
and they're living among us. That's a tough thing to
get over."

Karen cocked her head. "You say all this as if it's
just . . . I don't know, an everyday thing."

"It *is* an everyday thing for me. Every day, I go
around the windows and doors with garlic cloves,
crushing them into the wood. Every day, I wonder if
this will be the day they finally find me and decide to
pop up and make me pay for writing that piece.
Every day."

Karen noticed Benedek's hands were trembling.
They were big hands, with prominent blue veins
mapping their backs. She reached across the table

and put a hand on top of his. "Walter, I'm going to ask something of you, and when I do, I want you to think about it before you answer. Really think about it and ask yourself what harm it could do."

Benedek nodded as he pulled his hand away and said, "You're going to ask me to introduce you to Davey and Casey."

Karen put her hands flat against the table on each side of her plate. "All I'm asking for is a lunch. Let me buy them lunch so I can talk to them. I'll take it from there."

"I've already arranged for you to meet with them. You'll have to go to their house."

"That's it? It's that easy?"

"I knew you'd want to talk to them, so I called them, got their okay. If they hadn't agreed to meet with you, I wouldn't have told you anything. I wanted Davey and Casey to back me up, and they've agreed to do that."

"Thank you for arranging that. I expected you to say no."

Karen realized she had not touched her cheese omelette and hashbrowns. As she ate, she experienced a feeling of gratification—it was her first day on the investigation, and already it seemed she'd tracked down some "vampires."

As Karen ate, Benedek said, "What do you make of all this, Karen? I know it's your job to gather information about vampires—" He always lowered his voice when he said that word. "—but what do *you* think so far?"

"Frankly, I'm fascinated."

"Good. Your job may be dangerous, but at least it's not boring you."

CHAPTER EIGHT

Keoph sat at the computer in Karen's office. He had spent the day searching the Internet for everything he could find about vampires. His knowledge of the nocturnal bloodsuckers did not extend beyond the horror movies he'd seen about them. He found numerous Web sites run by people who claimed to be vampires and had vampire names like Midnight Moonglow or Vladimir Gaunt. Many of them were involved in elaborate role-playing games about vampires. Many of them, Keoph imagined, were simply lonely people desperate for some attention.

He found scholarly articles about vampires, and about the movies and literature that kept them alive, and he found a few vampire entries in encyclopedic sites about fantasy and mythology. He read of a few vampire myths from other cultures. But he found little he didn't already know about them.

Keoph already knew vampires rose at night to suck the blood of the living, that they could not tolerate sunlight, they were repulsed by crucifixes, holy water, and garlic, and the only way to kill them, besides beheading or purifying fire, was to drive a wooden stake through the heart.

How do I know all that? he thought.

He had never sought out information about vampires before. He had, instead, absorbed it over the years. The vampire rules had been as solid as facts in his mind by the time he was ten years old. Who, in a million years, would guess that he would turn to them again now, as an adult, without so much as a smirk on his face.

His cell phone played a pinched trumpet fanfare—dah dah-dah *daaah!*—and he took it from his coat pocket.

"Keoph."

"Hello, Keoph. Karen here."

"Where are you?"

"I'm at the airport, on my way home. Guess what?"

"I don't have a clue."

"Tomorrow, you and I are having lunch with two real-life, honest-to-God vampires."

"Are you drunk, or am I?"

"Neither nor. It's all set up."

"You mean, I'm going to have to spend my lunch tomorrow listening to a couple loons talk about death and eternal life and the power of blood? If it's a couple of those weirdo goth kids—"

"It's two successful screenwriters, Keoph, not a couple of wackos. I think it's important we both attend this interview."

"How serious are you about this, exactly?" Keoph said.

"I'm very serious. Benedek is setting us up with two close friends of his, a man and a woman, married, living a perfectly normal life. And they're vampires. They were both turned by vampires from Live Girls in Times Square, the place that blew up."

"Well, I guess we'll see about that," Keoph said with a chuckle.

"I'll give you all the details when I get back. I think we should sit down and carefully discuss tomorrow's interview. We need to agree on our goals, yes?"

"Yes, I agree."

"I think the two most important things we can do tomorrow is gain their confidence and start a relationship with these two, and then get more names from them."

"More names?"

"The names of more vampires. I want to get an idea of how many there are out there, how common they are."

"Wait a second, hold it," Keoph said. "Your mind is already made up, isn't it? You've already decided these people are vampires."

"Wrong, Keoph. I'm assuming *they believe* they're vampires, and taking it from there. If these are the vampires Burgess wants us to find—a bunch of delusional people who believe they're immortal vampires—then I think we should learn as much about them as we can. Maybe it's some kind of cult, I don't know. Anyway, he's paying us a lot of money, so I think we should produce."

"Are you questioning my work ethic?" Keoph said with a smirk.

"Don't be a boob, Keoph. Of course I'm not. I'm just saying, this is probably the closest thing we're going to get to real vampires, so we should use them to do our job."

"I can't argue with that."

"Are you at my office?"

"Yes."

"Stick around. I'll see you there when I get back."

Keoph turned back to the computer and clicked on another link in his search. A photograph opened up of Christopher Lee as Dracula, surrounded by four gorgeous, voluptuous women with blood on their mouths. The caption below read, "Dracula and his brides."

Keoph made a "hmph" sound and muttered, "Dracula always gets all the great women."

Karen sat waiting in a terminal of the airport in Rochester, New York. She thought about the upcoming interview. She had been asked by Benedek more than once if the information they were gathering was for publication. She wasn't sure *what* Burgess had in mind for these so-called vampires once they'd been found.

She took her cell phone from her purse again. She had already programmed Burgess's cell number into her phone's memory. She pushed a couple buttons, then put the phone to her ear.

"Hello," Burgess said.

"Mr. Burgess, this is Karen Moffett calling."

"Miss Moffett. Is anything wrong?"

"Well, I'm not sure. I need to know something from you. I've found two people who *claim* to be vampires, and we'll be talking to them tomorrow. They only ask one thing—that none of this sees publication. Are you planning to write about these people?"

"Uh, well, to be honest . . . I'm not sure *what* I'm going to do if you should find some real vampires out there. My only concern so far has been the hunt."

"Look, Mr. Burgess, I have to be able to tell these people you're not going to publish what you learn about them. And I won't tell them that if it's not true."

"I see. Well, I can tell you this—I have no plans to publish any of it. I never have. Remember what happened to that horror writer who claimed to have been abducted by aliens? He went public with it and wrote a book about it—a few, actually—and now he's not known for being a good writer anymore, which he is, because he's known as the nutjob who was anally probed by aliens and got rich off writing books about it. I'm doing this to satisfy my own curiosity, not to take some kind of exposé to the press, or anything like that. Tell them they have nothing to worry about."

"Thank you. I'm glad to hear that."

When she had finished talking to Burgess, Karen stood and went into a small cocktail lounge. She took a seat in a small booth by the door.

"Scotch on the rocks," she said to the waitress, then smiled.

Karen and Benedek had returned to his place after lunch. Benedek had called his friends again and Karen had talked to them briefly.

"Would you like to have lunch with us?" Casey Owen had said.

"Sure, that would be fine. I'll be with my partner."

"Partner?" Davey had said. "I thought it was just you."

"No, I have a partner. We've been hired together to investigate this . . . well, whatever it is. We both work for the same client."

"Oh," Davey had said. "Well, I guess that will be okay."

Now, sitting in the cocktail lounge, the thought of having lunch with a couple of "vampires" gave Karen a vague chill. But she shook it off quickly, telling herself the Owens probably had nothing more menacing than a kinky blood fetish. Maybe they had blood-drinking orgies with their fellow fetishists, but it probably wouldn't get more exciting than that.

But something had frightened Walter Benedek, something that had stuck to his soul. She had seen the fear in his eyes, heard it in his voice. Davey and Casey Owen seemed to be good friends of his, but he feared other vampires. Nothing about him gave her the impression that he was delusional or manic, or anything other than a frank, reasonable, down-to-earth man who was genuinely afraid of *something*.

Karen wondered if they would frighten her, too.

CHAPTER NINE

Benedek made spaghetti for dinner and ate it in front of the TV while watching a nature documentary on the Discovery Channel. It was a warm evening and he had the air conditioner on as dusk darkened to night.

Bruno sat up on his haunches in front of Benedek and watched him eat. It was the dog's way of begging for a bite.

"I've got nothing you want, Bruno," Benedek said. "I just fed you. The good stuff, too. Go eat it."

Bruno did not move and continued to stare up at him with big puddly eyes, so Benedek ignored him. He watched the documentary, but didn't really see it.

Talking with Karen Moffett had stirred up a lot of old memories. He found himself thinking about things that hadn't crossed his mind in years. Worst of all, it made him relive, in his mind, the horrible night he'd lost Jackie, as well as finding her again in that basement with all those hideous, hungry things.

Karen Moffett had said her client had no intention of publishing his findings, but this was not the kind of story that stayed secret. Benedek thought he would feel tremendous relief if the vampires were exposed. Maybe *then* he could sell his story. Benedek had spent most of his journalistic career looking for a chance to sell out, but he'd been unable to find any buyers. Now he had a story that would make a great book, but no editor he knew would take it seriously for a moment. Of course, if it were backed up by the revelation that vampires walked among them, they'd probably fight each other for it.

"Listen to me, Bruno," Benedek said as he got up to take his dish back to the kitchen. "Thinking about book sales while that nice young Karen is putting herself in so much danger, all because some clown wants to know whether or not vampires really exist."

He went to the sink and washed his plate and fork clean, then put them on a drain rack to dry. He dried his hands on a hand-towel tied to the handle of the refrigerator door. He opened the refrigerator and took out a bottle of Heineken.

Bruno barked a few times, paused, then went into a fit of yipping. He stood in the center of the living room and barked loudly, upset. Between the barks, Bruno growled.

"S'matter, Bruno?" Benedek said. He put the beer down on the end table beside his recliner, then went to the front door. Bruno followed him, still barking. He opened the door and turned on the porch light.

Bruno put his forepaws up on the heavy screen in the security door as he yipped even more furiously.

Benedek could neither see nor hear anything outside, but something had set Bruno off. He bent down and picked the dog up in his arms and held him close.

"What's up your little butt, huh, fella?" He closed the door and locked it again. Bruno squirmed in his arms eager to get back to his barking.

Benedek bent down to put the dog back on the floor, and he heard something. He quickly went to the recliner, got the remote, and muted the television.

He heard it again. It was a creaking, thumping sound. At first, he thought it was coming from inside the house, but the second time he heard it, it clearly came from overhead.

Someone was on the roof.

He heard a different sound, this time something that was not connected to the house. It was a flapping sound, but it only lasted briefly. It was immediately followed by more movements on the roof.

"Oh, my God," Benedek whispered. A cold explosion of fear in his chest spread throughout his body and made him tremble, made his heartbeat increase. He hurried into his bedroom and got the 12-gauge pump-action shotgun that leaned against the wall beside his bed. It was loaded and ready. He took the gun back up the hall to the living room.

He had decided many years ago that he would fight to the very end, that if possible, he would take one or more of them with him when he went. Benedek had no intention of going out easily.

The front window that looked out on the lawn exploded inward, and a pale figure flew through and hit the sofa, bounced off, and landed in a heap on the floor. He was naked, and he was a mass of muscle, bleeding from several cuts sustained while going through the window. He had long black hair that fell past his shoulders and a dark, trimmed beard and mustache. The cuts were already healing when he got to his feet and began to cough and gag. The garlic was getting to him.

Bruno rushed up to the man, barking and showing his teeth.

Benedek aimed, and fired.

Most of the man's head disappeared in a splatter of red and black material. Bits of his skull and some of his teeth chittered over the hardwood floor as his body collapsed.

Benedek walked over to the body and put the barrel of his gun to what remained of the creature's skull, and fired again, destroying it.

A shudder passed through the naked body on the floor, then it convulsed for several seconds before falling still.

Looking at the broken window, Benedek wondered how many were out there. The one on the floor had been willing to risk a reaction to the garlic to come through that window. Would the others?

Benedek looked down at the vampire's body on the floor. It had gone from a pale white to a greyish-yellow hue, and it was beginning to peel. The smell that rose off the rapidly decaying corpse was sweet and awful.

He bent down, picked up Bruno, and carried him down the hall to his bedroom. He closed the door and locked it, then put Bruno on the floor. He went to the phone on his bedstand, put the gun on the bed, picked up the receiver, and pressed 911.

"Nine-one-one, what is your emergency?" the woman on the line said.

"I'm being attacked," Benedek said, his voice hoarse and dry. He was a little winded as well.

"Who's attacking you, sir?"

"I don't know. I shot one of them. He broke into my house, he came through the window. He came through and tried to—"

A thunderous slam against the bedroom door created a crack that started at the top and went halfway down the center of the door. Just outside the bedroom, he heard more coughing and gagging and hacking.

Benedek dropped the receiver, got his gun, and raised it.

A few things happened then, but they happened so fast that all Benedek knew was that the gun had been taken from his hands. What happened was this: The door exploded inward and a svelte, naked female came in. She became a blur as she moved from the door to Benedek. She took the shotgun from him and slammed the butt into his face. It caught him right on the nose—it broke both lenses in his glasses—and for a moment, he felt dizzy. He felt a dribbling warmth coming from his left nostril and knew his nose was bleeding. Benedek stumbled backward and dropped onto the bed. The room tilted around him as he lay back on the bed, his feet still on the floor.

Another figure entered the room, this one big, male.

"I found this in the yard," the male said.

Benedek lifted his head just enough to see, through his cracked lenses, that the vampire held a chain. It was the chain Benedek used to tie Bruno up when he went outside. He didn't want Bruno to run loose so he could go out in the road and get hit by a car, so he tied him to a post on the porch on a long chain for awhile, with food and water nearby.

The vampire doubled the chain up, wrapped some of it around his hand. The chain made a small whooshing sound as the vampire brought it down on Benedek like a whip. The end of it bit into his face and opened an inch-long cut beneath his eye.

"No!" Benedek cried as he rolled over onto his stomach.

The chain came down hard on his back again and again.

Benedek shouted his anger and pain. He wanted to kill the vampire whipping him. He knew that wasn't going to happen, but he wouldn't take anymore whipping.

He rolled over as the chain came down again, but this time, he caught it and jerked it hard. The vampire stumbled forward to the edge of the bed.

Benedek clenched his teeth and growled, "Knock it the fuck off." He pulled himself up into a sitting position, and tried to stand.

The woman slammed the butt of the gun into his head again, this time across his temple. In a flash of white, Benedek found himself lying on the bed again.

The naked woman got up on the bed and straddled him. She had short red hair and an angelic, freckled face. She coughed a wet, hacking cough and her eyes looked puffy and glistened with tears.

Benedek felt weak, unable to resist.

She bent down and said, "This is for writing that fucking article." She bent his head to the side and plunged her fangs into his neck.

The pain of the bite was intense, but it was soon

overwhelmed by the sucking he felt. The woman's lips smacked against his neck. The tip of her tongue was on his skin.

A small electrical current seemed to run from Benedek's neck to his genitals, and he became aroused.

"Don't get carried away," the naked man said. "I get half, remember."

Benedek fought to think clearly. They had found him, and he was sure it was no coincidence that they found him on the same day Karen Moffett had stopped by for a visit. They had been following her—she needed to be warned.

But he wouldn't be able to do that, he knew, because they were going to bleed him dry.

She kept sucking and sucking, and Benedek felt as if his soul were leaking out of him. He was being drained of all energy and will to live.

The room grew dark.

The woman pulled away from him, licking and smacking her lips as she got off the bed.

"Okay," she said, "the rest is yours."

Benedek felt a bite in the other side of his neck, but wasn't able to pay it much attention because he could not concentrate.

The sucking sounds continued and Benedek felt himself draining away.

The room became very dark, and Benedek drifted off for the last time.

The woman's name was Polly, and she had been nineteen years old for fifty-eight years. She felt sated and a little sleepy—she could do with a nice nap. But it would have to wait until she got back to the city. There was no way she could sleep with all that garlic in the house. It made her eyes sting, made them puffy and teary, and made her throat swell. She kept coughing, which became gagging.

"We have to bring the head back with us, remember," Polly said. Her voice was hoarse and raspy.

Her partner's name was Woody. They'd lost Jack.

"I remember," Woody said. "I suppose you want me to cut it off."

"You know I can't handle the messy stuff, Woody. Get a good butcher knife from the kitchen. Or a cleaver, if you can find one. And hurry—this garlic is getting to me."

Woody left the bedroom. While he was gone, Polly wandered around looking at things.

The top of one dresser was covered with framed photographs. She did not understand the mortals and their memories—they seemed to spend half their lives in the past, in one way or another. They had to photograph everything, then they showed the photos to others, who usually weren't really interested in any photos but their own. They made baby books and scrapbooks and yearbooks—they were all so wrapped up in their pasts that they didn't see what was going on around them now.

Polly lived for the moment. She'd decided decades ago that if she was going to live forever, she wasn't going to clutter up her life with things like memories and nostalgia. The moment was all that mattered— and at the moment, she would much rather be out dancing in a club.

Woody returned with a large butcher knife, coughing into a hand. "I couldn't find a cleaver," he rasped.

"Try to be quick, okay?"

Woody went to the body and wasted no time. He began cutting all the way around the neck.

Polly left the room and stood out in the hall. She did not have a strong stomach—unless she was feeding, in which case blood and violence did not bother her in the least—and she could hear the sound of Woody cutting the head off. The sound was not audible out in the hall.

"Okay, I'm done," he said, and Polly returned to the bedroom. "I wish I had something to carry it in," Woody said.

"Well, let's see what we can find," Polly said as she went to the closet. "Ah, he was a bowler." She bent down and unzipped the blue-and-white bowling bag, and removed the ball, put it on the floor. She turned around and handed the bag to Woody. "Here, use this."

"Perfect," he said.

"Now, can we get the hell out of here?" Polly said before coughing several times. "This garlic is really bothering me. And these small towns give me the creeps."

CHAPTER TEN

Davey and Casey lounged on lawn furniture and watched *Jimmy Kimmel Live* on the flat roof of their poolhouse. Casey had a laptop open on her thighs. Applause arose from the small plasma TV as the late-night talk show broke for a commercial.

It was a warm summer night and the sky was clear. Stars twinkled through the filter of pollution in the air. From the poolhouse roof, they could see the lights of Perry Stabler's house across the canyon— Perry was a cinematographer who threw a lot of parties.

Casey's fingers moved rapidly over the keyboard, then she said, "Oliver says, 'You know, sometimes you remind me *way* too much of my mother.'"

A small table with a round top stood between their lounge chairs, with a plate of grapes and sliced apples in the center and a glass of blood on each side. Davey chewed on a grape as he considered her line. Then he said, "Rachel says, 'I'm not surprised I remind you of your mother—that's what you're *looking* for!'"

Casey's fingers clattered on the keyboard, then she said, "Oliver says, 'Don't analyze me! I pay someone very good money to do that, and once a week is enough.'"

Davey laughed, "Hey, I like that."

Casey smiled. "Yeah, me, too." She picked up the tall glass on her side of the table and first sipped from it, then took a couple big gulps before putting it down.

Davey saw her staring at the television. He knew she wasn't watching the commercials—she was lost in thought and something was bothering her.

"Is tomorrow worrying you?" he said.

"Doesn't it worry you? Just a little?"

"Of course it does. More than a little. I'm doing it more for Walter than any other reason."

"Yes, but if Walter's story gets out, *our* story gets out."

"I know, and I've talked to Walter about this a number of times. I've always told him that if he does it, I want him to do it without outing us personally. He understands. I don't want to be the poster children of the big vampire outing."

"But he's already identified us to someone," Casey said. "To this Karen person."

"That's why I believe she's not media-related, because obviously Walter believes that, and I trust him."

It was true. He knew Walter would never set him up in such a way—Walter knew something like that would destroy their friendship. They didn't have much in common, but they were like war buddies. They had gone through a powerful, life-changing experience together, and it had created a great bond between them.

"If you say so," Casey said. "Rachel says, 'You should get your money back, it's not working.'"

Davey said, "Hm. Not too sure about that one."

"Me, neither."

"'You should get your money back,' I like," Davey said. "But it needs something punchier at the end."

They were silent for awhile as they sipped their drinks.

"You're afraid of what might happen, aren't you?" Davey said.

"I don't understand why you're not," Casey said.

"Who said I'm not? I'm just as afraid as you are."

"Then why are we doing this?"

"Because if the story is going to break, we're at least in a position to control our involvement in it. Hell, if I have to, I'll give them money to keep us out of it."

They stopped talking to watch Jimmy Kimmel interview a beautiful young contortionist.

"They're so brazen now," Casey said, her voice little more than a breath. "It's almost like they're not even trying to hide anymore. You read about them every week in the paper—people disappearing, an attack that was foiled or aborted. It's never identified as a vampire attack, of course, but we know better, don't we?"

"That's another reason I don't want to be at the center of this story if it breaks. I want to be *behind* it. Don't worry, they won't come after us. We're too high profile, now. They're a lot bolder, but they're still careful about press, and about getting attention."

"True, they don't like any attention at all." Casey rubbed her left temple with her fingertips. "I'm getting a headache from worrying about this so much."

Davey said, "Casey, think of all the people they kill. They've got to be stopped. The truth has to come out about them eventually, or they'll just go on slaughtering people."

"I know, I *know*. I just didn't want to be this close to ground zero."

"I understand, and I agree. But we'll do everything we can to stay out of it, and the first step is to talk to these detectives. We can point them in the right direction and then we can step back into the shadows."

"All right." She squeezed his hand and smiled.

"Can I get you something for the headache?" Davey said.

"I'll get it," she said. She got up and put the laptop down on the lounge chair and went to Davey. She bent down and kissed him, then said, "Be thinking about that line. It needs to be fixed."

She walked over to the ladder and climbed down.

Davey settled back and tried to watch Kimmel, tried not to worry about whether or not they were doing the right thing.

CHAPTER ELEVEN

The morning of their interview with the Owens, Karen took Keoph clothes shopping. He had sent for some clothes from home, but they had not arrived yet, and Karen was tired of looking at that gray suit. She convinced him to dress more casually, and by the time they left the store, he was wearing a light gray sportcoat over a pale blue T-shirt and a pair of charcoal slacks. He carried his gray suit, and some other clothes he'd bought, in shopping bags.

Karen drove them to the Laurel Canyon address Davey Owen had given her over the phone. Their large, two-story house at first looked deceptively small—most of it was hidden away under a canopy created by a couple sprawling oaks, two willows, and a big silk tree.

Karen parked her Lexus in the driveway, and they got out and walked up the front steps. She was about to ring the doorbell when the front door opened. A petite woman stood back in the shadows and said, "Are you Karen Moffett?"

"Yes, and this is Gavin Keoph," Karen said with a smile.

"Please, come in."

The first thing Karen noticed when she stepped inside was that it was very dark and cool. Casey led them from the foyer, down a hall, and into a large dark dining room. The rectangular table was set for four at one end, and soft golden light came from a chandelier above it, and the four candles set up on the table.

"Give your eyes a minute to adjust," Casey said. "We keep the sunlight out during the day. We're usually sleeping right now. You'll have to forgive us—we aren't exactly at our best this time of day. I'm Casey Owen, by the way." She reached out a hand to shake, and Karen took it. Casey's hand was cold.

Karen's eyes adjusted quickly and she took in Casey Owen. She wore a black blouse with yellow daisies on it and a pair of bluejeans. She was very pretty, with a youthful face.

"I hope you're hungry," Casey said, "because lunch is ready. Conchata made her famous salmon patties."

"I'm ready to eat," Keoph said with a smile.

"Come sit," Casey said, "right here." She seated them across from each other at the head of the rectangular table. Casey sat down next to Karen. "Davey's on the phone, he should be here any minute. I'll go tell Conchata we're ready to eat." She got up and left the dining room.

Keoph leaned toward her. "Does this look like a vampire's lair to you?"

"I don't know," Casey said. "I've never seen a vampire's lair before."

"If you'd told me a week ago that in a week I'd be doing this, I would've laughed in your face."

Casey returned with a tall, slender man, handsome with dark hair and a well-trimmed goatee. Both he and Casey looked very tired, with drawn faces.

"You must be Karen," the man said, smiling.

Karen shook his hand and said, "And you must be Davey. This is Gavin Keoph." Davey's hand was cold, too.

"Nice to meet you both." He shook Keoph's hand. Davey wore a shortsleeve white shirt with a broad black stripe down one side, and a pair of black shorts and tennis shoes. He wore a black glove on his left hand, which was curled up in a half-fist. Karen remembered what Benedek had said about Davey's left hand. "I hope you found your way with no problem," he said as he sat at the head of the table.

"You give excellent directions," Karen said with a nod.

The salmon patty lunch was served by a heavyset Mexican woman. When she was gone, Karen said, "Is your maid . . . is she . . . like you?"

"Yes, she is," Davey said with a nod. "All our employees are. It only makes sense. See, this thing about us that's brought you here—it's not something we typically talk about to anyone, unless it's someone like us. In order to keep our secret, we have to hire others like us who are as discreet and responsible as we."

"What do you mean, 'responsible'?" Keoph said.

Casey said, "We don't prey on people. But there are

plenty who do. It's in our nature as vampires to hunt down and attack, to take blood straight from the vein, the artery. That's what we mean by 'responsible'— vampires who don't prey on people."

"It's what we do," Davey said. "It's in our blood. We choose to resist those urges. We get our blood through safe channels, no one gets hurt. We do our best to live normal lives. We're very private people, a close-knit group. We fear not only being discovered by mortals— who, if they knew the truth, would probably hunt us down and kill us—we're also pretty frightened by those of our own kind who choose to live differently than we. They're as much a threat to us as they are to you. We've known others like ourselves who were killed by the brutals for little more than sport. They hate us. And we're not too crazy about them."

"Who are the 'brutals,' Davey?" Karen said.

"They're predatory vampires," Davey said. "They refuse to drink bottled blood. They do their feeding the old-fashioned way. A lot of them are millionaires because they're ruthless, and they have all the time in the world. They're soulless people, Karen, without conscience, people who have actually lost their souls, I think. They're going full-speed ahead without a rudder."

"I hope you're not expecting me to feel sorry for them," Keoph said.

"Not at all," Davey said. "They're called brutals for a reason. I'm simply trying to make you understand that they're very different from us. There are a lot of different kinds of vampires out there. We tend to adjust to our environment. Many want to blend in and live comfortably with the mortals, like us. We don't want to hurt anybody. We simply want to be left alone."

Karen looked across the table at Keoph and he winked at her with a smirk.

Karen said, "Mr. and Mrs.—"

"Please," Davey said, "just Davey and Casey. And I don't know if Casey mentioned it or not, but this is a bad time of day for us. We're usually sleeping, because our energy is at its lowest in the middle of the day. We don't normally look this wiped out because we're usually in bed now."

Karen nodded. "Why should we believe that you're vampires?"

"You're going to have to believe sooner or later," Davey said. "As they get bolder and braver, the brutals will stalk and attack mortals more and more often. Did you know that, as we speak, there are mortals being bought and sold by vampires, right here in this country? No doubt right here in this city. Most of them are illegal aliens, some are runaways, others are people who've been plucked from their lives and stripped of everything. And no one knows it, except for us vampires. People like Casey and me are stuck in the middle. We think what they do is wrong, and we think they should be stopped and punished. But if we expose them, we expose ourselves, and I'm not sure people would make the distinction, know what I mean? We don't want to be exposed, Karen. Do you understand?"

Karen exchanged a look with Keoph, who reflected her frown.

"I'm not sure I do, Davey," she said.

"I'm saying that we'll give you the information you

want," Davey said. "We'll tell you whatever you want to know. As long as you leave us alone. If you want to go after brutals, be my guest, kick some ass for me, but we can't be seen as your informants. If we are, we'll be killed. Do you understand? We'll talk with you today as long as you'd like, and we'll give you the information you're after, but only if, having given you that information, we can disappear back into our lives again, unexposed and totally anonymous."

Keoph said, "I'm not so sure we can make that promise."

"Why not?" Karen said.

"We can't promise you won't be exposed," Keoph said. "That will be out of our hands. The information you give us is completely confidential, and you will both remain anonymous. That's the best we can do for you."

"We appreciate that," Davey said. "I believe you because Walter believed you."

There was something about Davey and Casey that Karen tried to isolate. Even though they were tired and weak, they both had a great deal of presence, in much the same way some movie actors and most politicians have presence. They were—she searched for the right word—charismatic. They spoke quietly, but something about them—their bearing, perhaps, or body language—made Karen listen closely to everything they said. They were . . . different somehow from Karen and Keoph. Just different.

"Before we go any further," Keoph said, "I need to see something that proves to me you are what you say you are."

"Maybe we should let them go at their own speed,

Keoph," Karen said. She did not want to rush or bully them—she had a feeling they were going to be very useful allies.

"No, that's all right," Davey said. He turned to Keoph and opened his mouth wide. Two pale, narrow, snakelike fangs descended from above his canines and curved downward slightly when fully exposed. Then Davey closed his mouth, and they were gone.

Karen felt a chill the moment she saw the fangs. But she reminded herself that this was Hollywood, and there were some pretty elaborate make-ups out there.

"Could you lift your upper lip, please?" Karen said.

Davey closed thumb and finger on his upper lip and pulled it back. There was a small lump in the gum above each canine, with a tiny hole through which the fangs extended and retracted. Davey opened his mouth wide again and the fangs came out of the small lumps, then disappeared in them again.

Karen gulped back a gasp. There were no make-ups *that* elaborate. And it didn't seem to be the kind of thing that could be accomplished by even the best orthodontist.

"My turn," Casey said. She took the knife from beside her plate in her right hand, and slashed the blade across her left palm. "Ow, that hurts. But only for a second." She held out her hand so they both could see her palm. The cut was open and blood was bubbling up from the wound. But before it even had time to bleed much, the cut closed up and the skin stitched itself back together, until there wasn't so much as a faint scar remaining. Casey wiped up the smear of remaining blood with a napkin.

"Oh, my God," Karen breathed. She looked at Keoph—he still stared at Casey's hand. "Oh, my God," Karen said again.

To Davey, Casey said, "I don't think they were expecting this."

"We . . . weren't," Keoph said. His eyes were a bit wider than usual when he looked at Karen. "Were we?"

"No," Karen said, "we were not. I . . . I don't know what to say."

"What were you expecting?" Casey said.

"Delusional people," Karen said. "At best. We weren't expecting anything so . . . authentic."

Karen felt a little light-headed and fought to regain her composure. What she had just seen flew in the face of everything she knew to be true. There was no such thing as vampires—they didn't exist, they were boogey men, the stuff of imagination and legend.

Davey and Casey Owen smiled pleasantly at Karen and Keoph, who sat with their mouths hanging open.

"You okay?" Davey said.

Karen nodded once, but she felt as if the breath had been punched from her lungs. She was afraid to speak because she did not trust her voice. As her eyes moved back and forth between Davey and Casey, a shudder moved through her from the top down.

"Are you okay?" Keoph said.

Karen turned to him and said, "Don't are-you-okay me, Keoph. You're the one who thought this whole thing was a joke. At least I had an open mind."

"Can I get you something to drink, Karen?" Casey said. "We have liquor."

"Do you have any scotch?" Karen said. "I could use a little scotch on the rocks. Maybe more than a little."

"Be right back," Casey said.

As she headed out of the room, Keoph said, "I'll have some, too, while you're at it." Then he smiled at Karen and said, "It's refreshing to see a woman handle stress with alcohol. I like that about you, Moffett."

Karen said, "What can I say? I need a drink."

"I think we could all use a drink," Casey said as she returned with a tray holding four glasses, a bottle of Chivas Regal, and a pair of tongs in a bowl of tiny ice cubes. "I hope Chivas is okay with everybody," Casey said as she dropped a few ice cubes into one glass and poured.

Karen took a couple gulps of the whiskey and enjoyed the warmth of it going down. She closed her eyes as she drank and wished she were at home in a hot bubble bath. Opening her eyes, she looked at Davey and Casey and told herself, *These people drink blood to survive.*

She took a couple more gulps and poured some more Chivas into her glass.

"Now that we're past the hard part," Davey said, "what would you like to know?"

CHAPTER TWELVE

How and where do you meet?" Karen said. She'd set her small cassette recorder on the table and pressed the RECORD button.

"In different ways, different places," Davey said, "I belong to a garden club. I keep a flower garden in the backyard—you should see it before you go—"

Casey laughed and said, "Don't get him started on his garden."

Smiling, Davey said, "Anyway, that club is made up of vampires. We get most of our blood through that group. Occasionally, we buy it from a small deli that's vampire-owned and -operated. We sometimes go to a club that's by and for vampires. We go there for drinks now and then."

"How do you find out about all these places if they're secret?" Keoph said.

Davey said, "It's usually easy for us to spot other

vampires. None of them advertise that they're vampire-friendly. Word gets around from one group to the next."

"Do you go out at all during the day?" Karen asked.

"Occasionally, we have to, for a meeting or a business lunch," Casey said. "When that happens, we use a powerful sunblock, wear dark shades, and take big umbrellas for portable shade. It's not that weird—plenty of people, *besides* Michael Jackson, use umbrellas for shade in the hot sun. It's not unheard of."

"And no one has suspected?" Keoph said. "You've been writing screenplays how long?"

"Since 1992," Davey said. "We've written five movies, and now we get a lot of work doctoring scripts. We haven't had a movie out there for awhile, but we're working on a new one."

"Why romantic comedies?" Karen said.

Davey and Casey looked at each other a moment and smiled, then shrugged.

"I'm not sure," Davey said. "It just worked out that way."

"We found out we were good at them," Casey said. "We didn't know until we tried."

Karen sipped her Chivas. Her trembling had stopped and she felt quite relaxed, thanks to the scotch. The lunch dishes were removed by Conchata, and Karen folded her arms on the table. "We need to get some sense of the structure of . . . well, your people. How do they live? How do they find people like themselves without giving themselves up to others?"

"Like I said," Davey said, "we can usually spot each other easily enough. There's just—I don't know, something *different* about vampires."

"There is," Karen said with a nod. "I noticed it as

soon as I met you. You have a powerful presence, both of you, even though you're not feeling up to speed. I'm not sure I can explain it in any other way than that. You fill a room."

"Look," Davey said, "*our* people aren't the ones you should be worried about. We just want to live our lives and be left alone. You should be concerned about the brutals. You should do something about them."

Karen said, "It's not our job to *do* anything. We're just gathering information for our client."

"Who should we talk to to learn as much as we can?" Keoph said.

"We'll take you to someone later," Davey said. "From her, you can learn just about everything you need to know. But I've got to warn you, the brutals do *not* want to be exposed. They prey on people now with impunity. They don't want anyone to know they're out there. And they'll do anything to see that it doesn't happen. If you're going to ask questions and snoop around, you need to know you'll be putting yourselves in danger."

Karen said, "Is there any way we can do this *without* putting ourselves in danger? Because I would prefer that."

"I'm afraid not," Davey said.

Karen turned to Keoph and said, "I'd rather do things without danger."

"But it comes up in the job now and then," Keoph said.

"Yeah," Karen said. "So we'll deal with it. And we'll be as discreet as possible."

"Don't expect a lot of people to talk to you," Casey said. "We have one person lined up to talk to you later, but beyond her, you may find no one willing to talk."

"What about the brutals?" Karen said. "How do *they* live?"

"They live in the shadows," Davey said. "Trust me, they would never talk to you. If they knew what you were doing, they would only kill you."

"But what do they do?" Keoph said. "What kind of work do they do? How do they make a living?"

"The city's full of night jobs," Casey said. "They still work a lot in the adult entertainment business, too. They have nightclubs and strip joints and peep-shows. The average guy out to look at naked girls is an easy mark. They may only be drunks and perverts, but drunks and perverts are people, too. They're feeding on them. Some get sick and die. Some become addicted to the feedings, to being bitten by the beautiful vampire."

Karen wrinkled her nose and said, "Addicted to being bitten?"

"Vampires do more than just bite," Davey said. "The predatory vampire possesses the victim, if only for the duration of the relationship. Their vampirism is psychic as well as physical. It makes the vampire irresistible to the victim. I'm a little rusty because I don't use the ability, but with a little effort, I could make either one of you feel a sudden urge, a need, to go to bed with me, if I wanted. But, as I said, we don't do that. We choose not to."

A phone trilled somewhere in the house, and Casey stood. "I'll get that," she said as she left the dining room.

They were silent at the table for awhile as Casey's muffled voice came from the kitchen.

"Are you two sure you want to continue this investigation?" Davey said. "If I were in your position, I'd tell my client to go to someone else."

Keoph said, "We've already committed ourselves to this investigation."

Davey shrugged. "If you say so. But you're going to be putting yourselves in—"

Casey came back into the dining room near tears and said, "Walter's been murdered."

Davey's eyes widened. "What? Who called?"

"It was Kenny Weller, Walter's chess buddy," Casey said. "He lives down the street from Walter, remember him?"

Davey nodded, frowning. "What happened?"

"Walter called 911 last night and said he was being attacked by someone. He was killed during the call. By the time the sheriff's deputies got there, Walter was dead. Kenny said he was bled to death and . . . beheaded. His head was missing."

"Oh, my God," Davey whispered. He turned to Karen. "They followed you."

"What?" Karen said. "Who? What do you mean?"

"They've been looking for Walter all these years," Davey said. "And they followed you to him."

"Wait a second," Karen said. "Why would they be following *me*? *How* would they be following me?"

Casey said, "They must know about your client."

Davey scrubbed his right hand down his face as he said, "Oh, God. Poor Walter."

"What about my client?" Karen said.

Davey said, "Has your client been investigating this himself? Has he done some poking around on his own before hiring you?"

Karen turned to Keoph and they both nodded. "Yes," Karen said, "he's been looking into it himself."

"Then he got their attention," Davey said. "And they've been watching you. That's how they found Walter."

"*Who's* been watching me?" Karen said.

"The brutals," Davey said. "They've been tailing you. Which means they know you're here. You've put us all in danger."

"Wait, wait just a second," Karen said with a hand on each side of her head. She lowered her hands and took a deep breath. "Why would they take his head?"

Davey said, "As a trophy. As proof to others that they'd killed Walter Benedek, the man who tried to expose them with an article in the *Post*."

"That was eighteen years ago, and it didn't work," Keoph said.

"They don't forget, Gavin," Davey said. "They're very vindictive."

As she went back to her seat at the table, Casey said, "Kenny said there was another body in Walter's house. A mostly headless, naked, decayed corpse."

Davey smiled a little. "Then he got one. Good for you, Walter."

"What do you mean?" Keoph said.

"When a vampire is killed," Davey said, "the body immediately begins to decay to its natural state. For example, if I were to die, my body would do eighteen years' worth of decaying, because I was turned eighteen years ago. Walter obviously killed one of the vampires that came after him. He always said he wouldn't go out alone."

Keoph turned to Karen and said, "We need to call him and let him know."

Karen knew he was talking about Burgess. The only possible reason the vampires could be following them was that they had been keeping an eye on Burgess. He needed to know. She stood and took her cell phone from her purse, put the purse on her chair. "I need to make a call," she said. "Is there someplace I can go for some privacy?"

"Right through that door to the kitchen," Casey said, pointing. She still had a stunned look on her face from the news of her friend's death.

Karen took the cell phone into the kitchen.

Davey needed to talk to Casey. He stood and said, "Would you excuse us a minute, Gavin?" He turned to Casey and said, "Come on."

They went into the living room.

"What are we going to do?" Casey said.

"First of all, we're not going to panic," Davey said. "If they wanted us dead, we'd be dead by now. So they're watching us. That's *all* they're doing so far."

"But what about those two detectives?"

"What about them?"

"We can't just let them go out there knowing the brutals are following them. It would be a death sentence."

Davey covered his face with his right hand and sighed into his palm. He thought of how good their life had been since they had come to Los Angeles. Over the years, he'd often felt suspicious of his good life, waiting for the other shoe to drop. Whatever it was, he'd always known it would have something to do with vampires. They were like a shadow that was always cast over him and Casey. It had been only a matter of time before they came back into their life.

He dropped his hand and said, "You're right. We have to get them out of this. Come with me."

Davey headed down the hall to the kitchen, with Casey right behind him.

"Mr. Burgess, I'm trying to tell you that you're in danger," Karen said.

"How am I in danger?"

"When you personally investigated this, you got the attention of some particularly nasty vampires. They don't want to be exposed, and for all they know, that's what you're planning to do."

Davey and Casey came into the kitchen, and Davey reached for the phone.

"Is that your client?" Davey said.

Karen nodded and said, "Yes."

"Let me speak to him, please."

She hesitated, but Davey asked again. She handed the cell phone to him.

Davey put the phone to his ear and spoke sternly. "You have to call this investigation off right now. Both of your detectives are in danger because of it, and so are you. You have to call them in and stop this investigation immediately."

Davey's eyes met Karen's and she felt a chill. Beneath his dark frown, his eyes were concerned as they looked at her. His eyes looked like they meant business, and they worried Karen. She suddenly felt a sense of urgency about what he said—that she and Keoph were in danger. She was still in Los Angeles, a city she knew well, but suddenly she felt alone in some foreign land where she did not speak the language.

"Your only option," Davey said, "is to stop this investigation." He listened for a moment. "My name is

Davey Owen. I was a friend of Walter Benedek. He's been killed because of your investigation. Your detectives will be next if you continue, I have no doubt about that." He listened again, then said, "All right," and handed the phone back to Karen.

She put it to her ear and said, "It doesn't really matter if you call the investigation off or not, I'm stopping it. I'm sending Keoph home to San Francisco, and we're going to forget about this."

Burgess sighed. "All right. Call it off. Keep your first payment, and discontinue the investigation."

"Thank you, Mr. Burgess," Karen said. "Now, here's what you need to do—cut some garlic cloves in half, then grind them into the wood all around your windows and doors. Do it every day. Do you understand me?"

"Are you serious?"

"I'm very serious, Mr. Burgess. You're in danger. Rub the garlic around all your doors and windows. Will you do that as soon as we hang up?"

"I . . . I can't believe you're serious. So . . . they really exist?"

"Mr. Burgess, you're the one who wanted to know if there were really vampires. Well, now you know there are, and some of them are pissed off at you for looking into them. They don't *want* to be investigated."

"I . . . I see. Garlic. Around the doors and windows. Will that work?"

"It won't hurt."

"What *else* should I do?"

Karen turned to Davey as Keoph joined them in the kitchen.

"What's going on in here?" Keoph said.

Karen said to Davey, "He wants to know how he can protect himself."

Davey reached out for the phone and she handed it to him. "Do what she said, rub garlic around your doors and windows—a *lot* of it. And it wouldn't hurt to rub it on your body, as well. That's about your best defense. We have a terrible allergic reaction to garlic." He listened a moment, and nodded. "Yes, that's right, I am. Yes. . . . Yes, we do, we really drink blood. . . . No, crosses don't work at all. Most of the mythology is nonsense. But not all of it. . . . No, my wife and I drink only bottled blood. No one gets hurt. We don't prey on people like the vampires you've stirred up."

Karen rolled her eyes and took the phone from Davey. "Mr. Burgess, I'll call you later, all right?"

"Yes, please do."

"As soon as you hang up, get that garlic and get to work."

"Oh, I will, I will."

She closed the cell phone as she turned to Davey. "You convinced him. He called it off. I guess we'll be leaving you alone."

"No," Davey said. "It's not that easy. Somehow, we've got to get word on the street that you've canceled the investigation. You can't just walk away from this. They'll only follow you. They need to know you're no longer a threat to them."

"How do we do that?" Karen said.

"We'll worry about that," Davey said. "Like I said, we lined up someone for you to talk to tonight, and now it's even more important that you meet with her. We'll take you to her tonight. In the meantime, you stay here."

CHAPTER THIRTEEN

Martin Burgess's wife Denise was out playing tennis with a friend. He wore a blue T-shirt that read, WHEN IS THE WIZARD GOING TO GET BACK TO YOU ABOUT THAT BRAIN?

There were a lot of doors and windows in their Topanga Canyon house. He wasn't going to be able to do it alone. He went into the kitchen and found his cook putting dishes in the dishwasher.

Mrs. De La Pena was a rotund Mexican woman of fifty-one, and the best cook Burgess had ever had. Her English was clumsy, but it had never been a big problem.

Mrs. De La Pena turned to him and smiled.

"Garlic?" Burgess said.

She pointed to two silver bowls suspended by thin chains from the ceiling; the top bowl contained red and green peppers, the bottom was filled with cloves of garlic. Burgess hurried to the bowl, reached up and took a handful of cloves and put them on the counter. He turned to Mrs. De La Pena again and said, "I need a sharp knife."

She went to a diamond-shaped block of wood on the counter with a dozen or so knives in slots. She removed one and handed it to Burgess.

He quickly cut the cloves in half.

"Mrs. De La Pena, here's what I want you to do," he said. He reached up to the window over the sink, removed a couple potted violets from the sill and put them on the counter. He took the halved cloves in a fist and rubbed them back and forth on the windowsill vigorously, ground them into the wood. "I want you to do this, Mrs. De La Pena, around every window. Do you understand?"

Mrs. De La Pena stared at Burgess as if he had just sprouted a bill and quacked like a duck.

"See? I want you to do this all the way around the window." He scrubbed the garlic over the sides, then the top of the window.

"Yes, yes, I understand," Mrs. De La Pena said. "But . . . why?"

"Just do it, okay, Mrs. De La Pena? Please?" He smiled.

Frowning, Mrs. De La Pena shrugged and picked up some garlic cloves.

"All windows?" she said.

"All the windows on the ground floor. I'll get the doors."

Mrs. De La Pena went across the kitchen to the window that looked out at a vine-covered embankment beside the house.

Burgess cut some more cloves in half and put them

in a Tupperware bowl. He left the kitchen and hurried around looking for Nita, the housekeeper. He wasn't even sure she was in the house. On his way up the stairs, he called her name.

She leaned out of a bedroom into the upstairs hallway. "Yes?" Nita Coolidge was a wiry black woman in her mid-forties. Burgess had no idea how he would explain this to her, but he needed her help.

"Nita, I'm going to ask you to do something that's going to sound crazy," he said as he went down the hall to join her in the open doorway of one of the guest rooms, where she'd been changing the sheets. She held a pillow in her right hand and a pillowcase in her left.

"What's that?" Nita said.

"See these garlic cloves? I've cut them in half. I want you to rub them into the wood around all the windows on this floor.

Nita frowned as she looked from the garlic to Burgess. "No disrespect, Mr. Burgess," she said, "but have you gone off your nut?"

Burgess went into the bedroom and to a window. "Like this," he said as he scrubbed the garlic back and forth on the sill. "On the sides and tops, too. You'll need a step-ladder for some of them."

Nita put her hands on her hips. "Let me get this straight. You want me to rub that garlic inta the windas."

"Yes."

"Well, if you want me to, I will. But I'll tell you right now, Mr. Burgess, I ain't cleanin' it up."

"Don't worry about cleaning it up right now, Nita, just get it done. I've got to do the doors downstairs, and then I'll come up here and help you."

"Whatever you say."

Burgess hurried downstairs, where Mrs. De La Pena was in the living room rubbing garlic around the windows. He went into the kitchen and cut up some more garlic. He took it to the front door, went outside, and rubbed it around the doorway. He went back inside and did the same there.

In the next hour, he managed, with the help of Mrs. De La Pena and Nita, to cover all the windows and doors in the house. He wondered if he should rub it around the garage doors as well, but decided that would be impractical. He did go out and get the windows in the garage, and he covered the door that led from the garage into the kitchen.

The house reeked of garlic.

Denise was a neat freak. She was probably going to have a fit. But he couldn't worry about that yet. He had one more thing to do.

Burgess gave Mrs. De La Pena and Nita the rest of the day off and saw them out. Then he cut up some more garlic cloves—he'd used up nearly all the garlic in the bowl, and made a mental note to buy more, preferrably at bulk rates—and took them upstairs to his bedroom. He took his clothes off and tossed them onto the bed. He stood in nothing more than briefs and a pair of white socks. He rubbed the garlic all over his body.

He had written three books about vampires. The fact that they really existed at once excited and frightened him. That some of them were out to get him made his stomach cold with panic.

When he finished rubbing it all over himself, Burgess put the garlic cloves on the bed and put his clothes back on. He picked up the cloves and took them downstairs with him.

In the kitchen, he heard Denise drive up in her BMW Z4 Roadster convertible, heard the garage door open. He put the remaining garlic cloves on the counter and then washed his hands at the sink with liquid handsoap.

Denise entered the kitchen from the garage wearing a white-and-pink tennis outfit and carrying her raquet. She put her purse on the counter and her racket on the kitchen table.

"Hi," she said in that cheerful way she had. It usually made Burgess want to get her down on the nearest flat surface and make mad love to her, but he was preoccupied.

He returned the smile and said, "Have fun?"

"Yeah. I think Micha and her husband are getting a divorce." Micha was the friend with whom she'd been playing tennis.

"Did she say that?"

"Not in so many words, but she's making noises. She said—" Her nose wrinkled. "What's that smell? Is Mrs. De La Pena cooking something?"

"I sent her and Nita home early today."

"Why? And what's that smell? Is that *garlic?*"

"Yes, it's garlic."

"Where's it coming from?"

"Let me explain."

"I have to take a shower first. Hold that thought." She hurried out of the kitchen, and Burgess heard the muted thumps of her footsteps going upstairs. From the hall, she shouted, "It's up here, too! What *is* it?"

Burgess left the kitchen and went to the foot of the stairs. "I told you, it's garlic."

"But why does it smell so strong up here?" She appeared naked at the top of the stairs, a towel in one hand.

Burgess's eyes took a snapshot of Denise standing there on the landing, her posture casual, completely naked. So beautiful, so blond . . . and so young. He often wondered if he'd made a mistake in marrying her. She was always telling him he was crazy.

"You know," she'd said in bed only a few weeks ago, "sometimes I read your writing, and I wonder if you're crazy."

"Oh, come on, now," he'd said. "You know we have the kind of relationship where, if I were crazy, I'd tell you."

"No, I mean it. The things you come up with in your books—well, some of them are completely insane. Don't you think sometimes that maybe you are a little crazy? Just a little?"

"To tell you the truth, I wonder that almost every time I look at you."

"Huh?"

"I wonder if I was crazy for marrying you. I'm worried you'll get tired of me, that eventually, I'll just bore you."

She'd laughed as she rolled over on top of him, then kissed him. "Oh, baby, you know that's not true. If I thought for a moment that I might get tired of you, I wouldn't have married you."

When he explained the garlic throughout the house, she might very well call him crazy again, and this time, she might really mean it.

"Take your shower first," he said.

She disappeared from the landing, went to the bathroom, and closed the door.

Burgess paced in the hall, wondering how he was going to explain the garlic to Denise. He went into the kitchen and ate a banana. He planned to order pizza for dinner later—with extra garlic. If it helped to have garlic on his outside, it wouldn't hurt to have some inside, too.

Denise did not take long in the shower. She came downstairs wearing a white bikini bra, a pair of denim cut-offs, and thongs on her feet. The patch of skin between her eyebrows was wrinkled vertically. But it disappeared briefly as she smiled at him and said, "Did you miss me today?"

She went to him and he put his arms around her. "Terribly. I always miss you terribly."

She pulled away from him abruptly and said, "My *God*, Marty, you *reek!*"

"Look, honey, there was something I *had* to do."

"Something you—Marty, why does this whole house stink of garlic?"

He went to her and put his hands on her upper arms. "Listen to me. I hired—"

"Get away from me," she said, pushing him back. "You smell like you've been lying in a *vat* of garlic."

"Well, that's not too far off the mark."

"Not too far off—what the hell is going on? *Who* did you hire?"

"Remember that scrapbook I showed you?" he said. "The one that started with that article in the *New York Post* about vampires in Times Square? Do you remember that?"

"Yeah, I remember. What's that got to do with anything?"

"I hired some private investigators to investigate the story. A man, Gavin Keoph, and a woman, Karen Moffett."

"The more you talk, the more confused I get," Denise said, putting a hand to the side of her head. Those vertical creases were back between her eyebrows.

"Just listen," he said. "They investigated it. For just a couple days. And they found . . . well, it turns out . . . vampires really do exist."

Her reaction was very slow—her eyes slowly widened and her mouth slowly opened as she took a step back from him. "What . . . what are you telling me, Marty?"

"I got a phone call from Karen Moffett. Before I hired them, see, I'd done a little investigating on my own. Well, Miss Moffett tells me I attracted the attention of some very, uh, unpleasant vampires. It seems I've, um, pissed them off. We could be in some danger, according to Miss Moffett. I actually talked to one of the vampires, Davey Owen. But he's not like the vampires that are pissed at me. He and his wife, they don't attack or kill or prey on people like these other vampires do. Anyway, he told me the best thing I could do to protect us was to rub garlic all around the doors and windows. So I had Nita and Mrs. De La Pena help me, and while you were gone, we hit every single window and door in this house."

"You . . . rubbed garlic . . . around the doors and windows?"

"Well, only the doors on the ground floor that go outside. This Davey Owen guy also told me it would be a good idea to rub garlic on my body, which I've done." He stepped toward her again and put a hand to the side of her face. "I think to be safe, you should, too."

Denise pressed a hand to her chest and said, "You want *me?* To rub garlic? All over my *body?* Martin . . . are you crazy?"

"*Dammit,* I wish you'd quit saying that." He turned away from her and walked across the room. "You married me for my money, didn't you?" he said as he slowly walked back.

"What?"

"Because that's not the way you talk to someone you love."

"Honey, what're you . . . what're you *talking* about?"

"Did you not hear me? What have I been saying?"

"And you're . . . serious?"

"I know it sounds crazy, and I know I've never really explained my interest in this before, how great it is, but I'm telling you now, Denise, and you *have* to believe me."

A look of deep concern battled with a look of sadness on Denise's face. "Sweetheart, you said the new book wasn't coming along very smoothly, but I had no idea you were—"

"This has got nothing to do with my writing."

"I think we should call and make an emergency appointment with Dr. Van Wyck."

"Dr. Van—why would I call him? He can't help us."

"He might be able to recommend someone who could give you the help you need."

"You want me to see a *shrink?*" Burgess said. He was afraid this was going to be more difficult than he had anticipated. "Denise, there's nothing *wrong* with me. Look, you want me to get one of the detectives on the phone? You can talk to Karen Moffett. She'll tell you that I hired her and her partner, and that they've found vampires—*real* vampires—living here in Los Angeles. You want me to do that? I'll do it."

Denise slowly turned her head from side to side. "You wouldn't let me get Mom and Dad a car for their anniversary, but you can afford to hire *two* detectives? How much is this costing?"

"Hey, a car would've been fine, but you wanted to get them a Hummer. Denise, what on earth would your parents do with a Hummer, besides menace other drivers? As far as I'm concerned, I've already gotten more than my money's worth out of this investigation, because they found vampires. Can you believe that, Denise? I mean, *vampires*—you know, Dracula—'I vant to drrrink your blood.' All that's *real!*"

Denise said nothing. She continued to stare at him, but the look in her eyes had changed. Now she looked suspicious, wary.

Burgess blinked a few times when a crisp, vivid image of his ex-wife Sheila materialized in his mind. He felt heavy with sadness when he realized that, if Sheila were standing in front of him now, she would believe him. She would not only believe him, she would want to know what she could do to help protect them. He found himself, for a moment, missing Sheila.

"You don't believe me," Burgess said.

Denise stared at him awhile longer, then said, "Maybe it's . . . I don't know, some kind of mid-life thing."

Burgess had met Denise in a creative writing course he'd taught at UCLA. He remembered how she used to look at him in the classroom—as if he were some kind of god. She hadn't looked at him that way since they'd married.

Now she looked at him as if he'd just written on the wall in his own feces.

Denise had come early to class one night with a box containing every novel and short story collection he had written. She'd said she was a big fan and wondered if he would sign her books for her. He signed them. From the bottom of the box, she took a thin manuscript.

"I'm sure people do this all the time," she'd said, "and it's probably rude of me to ask this of you, but I'm going to anyway, because I'm desperate to know if I'm any good. Would you read this for me, please?"

"You understand," he'd said, "that if I read that, I would only be giving you my opinion, which doesn't really mean anything. I mean, if I say you're great, that doesn't mean you are. Just as if I say you're awful, that's not necessarily true. Do you understand?"

Her face had burst into a broad grin that showed all her beautiful teeth, and she'd said, "Your opinion is the only one I want."

The thing was, she'd turned out to be talented. Her story had him laughing out loud—the piece was genuinely funny, and the laughs came mostly from her intelligent, witty, rapid-fire dialogue. She was good, and she'd caught him completely off guard. He'd told her he wanted to send her story to his agent, Elliott Farber, in New York. Elliott was quite impressed, and suggested that Denise try her hand at a novel, which she'd been working on ever since. He and Denise had started up a secret telephone flirtation. Burgess had started staying up later—he'd waited till Sheila was asleep, then went to his office and called Denise on a prepaid cell phone. The phone calls led to meetings, and one thing, as they say, led to another.

Burgess still regreted hurting Sheila. That had never been his intention. She'd found a pair of black panties in the glove box of his Porsche. She'd asked him if he were seeing another woman, or was he a cross-dresser, and he could not lie to her, not to her face. When he said yes, he'd been seeing someone, she'd said, "Move out. I want a divorce."

After Sheila kicked him out, Burgess was certain Denise would break it off with him, and he would be completely alone. Marriage had not crossed his mind for a moment, and when that was where their relationship ended up, no one had been more surprised than Burgess.

Only ten months of marriage, and already he was wondering if he'd made a mistake.

Sheila would have believed him, he was sure of it.

"Marty," Denise said. She stepped forward and snapped her fingers in front of his face.

"Sorry," he said. "I got sidetracked for a second."

"Marty, you're not well."

"Oh, for God's sake, will you stop that. I'm perfectly fine, there's nothing wrong with me."

"Have you been drinking?"

"*No,* I haven't been drinking. I can get one of those detectives on the phone right away." He took his cell phone from his pocket, flipped it open, and triggered the programmed number. "I'll just have them tell you what they told me."

Karen Moffett answered.

"Miss Moffett, Martin Burgess here. I need you to do something for me."

"What's that?"

"I need you to tell my wife everything you told me."

"Mr. Burgess, we really don't have time for that right now. We're—"

"You don't understand, my wife doesn't *believe* me. If she doesn't believe me, it makes it difficult to properly prepare for—look, she doesn't believe my story, all right? You need to convince her, Miss Moffett."

"Convince her of what?"

"That we're in danger from vampires."

Karen Moffett sighed, then said, "All right, Mr. Burgess. Put her on."

He turned to Denise and held the phone out to her. "This is Karen Moffett, one of the two detectives I hired. She's going to tell you that I'm not crazy."

Denise took the phone. "Hello?" she said. "Yes, this is—no, it's *Sykes*-Burgess, my name is Denise Sykes-Burgess. Yes, go ahead." Denise listened for a long time. She slowly turned her eyes toward him. "Okay, wait. Who are you, again?" Denise held the phone in her left hand, and raised her right hand to her mouth so she could chew on the nail of her index finger. She had a bad habit of chewing her nails when she was nervous or anxious—there was very little left to chew. "You're serious." She turned away from Burgess. "No, really, I mean it, you're *serious?*"

Burgess smiled, confident that Karen Moffett was explaining everything to Denise.

Suddenly, Denise held the phone out to Burgess and said, "This isn't funny."

Burgess could hear Karen Moffett still talking on the phone, unaware that no one was listening.

"This isn't *meant* to be funny," Burgess said. "Listen to her, she's telling you the truth."

"I don't know who you put up to this, Marty, but it's not funny and I'm not laughing." She turned the phone off and severed the connection with Karen Moffett. She handed the phone back to Burgess and put her hands on her hips. "That smell, I can't stand that *smell!*"

"Well, I'm sorry, but you're going to have to live with it for awhile, because it's the only thing that's going to protect us from those vampires." He put the phone back in his pocket.

"Vampires!" Denise snapped. "What's *wrong* with you, Marty?" Her face screwed up and she started to cry.

"Please don't cry, honey," Burgess said as he put his arms around her.

She pushed him away and said, "You *stink.*"

Burgess stepped back and sighed, exasperated. "Why didn't you listen to what Karen Moffett had to say?"

"Because this is *ridiculous!*" she said before a great sob made her shoulders hitch. "You're scaring me, Marty. All this talk about vampires—that's *crazy.* There's no such *thing* as vampires."

"If you would've listened to her, you would've learned that—"

"I'm *leaving!*" she shouted, her fists bunched at her sides. She left the kitchen and went back upstairs. When she returned, she was buttoning up a red blouse over the bikini top. "I'm going to my mother's. Before I get back, you'd better do something about this damned *smell.*"

She snatched her purse up off the counter and went to the garage door.

"Please don't go," Burgess said. He grabbed her

arm and turned her around to face him. "Listen, honey, can't you see that I'm *serious* about this?"

"That's what scares me so much," she said as she opened the garage door in the kitchen. "Martin, I can deal with just about anything, but if you're going to have mental problems . . . well, I'm just not cut out to handle that kind of thing."

She went out into the garage. Standing in the doorway, Burgess said, "Get back before dark. That's when they come out."

Denise started the Roadster as the garage door slowly began to open. She had the car's top down.

"Did you hear me?" Burgess said. "Get back before dark."

She ignored him as she backed out of the garage, then drove away.

CHAPTER FOURTEEN

Shortly after dark, Karen and Keoph got into the backseat of the Owens' Mercedes C240 sedan and Davey drove them into North Hollywood, in the San Fernando Valley.

As they started out, Keoph leaned over to Karen and said just above a whisper, "Aren't you worried about what this will do to your professional image?"

She nodded. "The thought has crossed my mind."

"Because I'm sure as hell worried about *mine,*" Keoph said. "If word gets out that you and I have been out vampire hunting, we're liable to become laughingstocks. I mean, I'd hate for it to get out to prospective clients. It could be very bad for business."

"I won't be putting this job on my resume, that's for sure," Karen said.

When Davey started talking, Karen and Keoph leaned forward and listened.

"Mrs. Dupassie is a very old vampire," Davey said as he drove. "She's also very old physically."

Casey said, "She was an old woman when she was turned—kind of a cruel trick, no doubt performed by some sadistic vampire with a sick sense of humor."

"She's different than other vampires," Davey said. "For one thing, she's psychic. That's how she makes her living, doing consultations for people, mostly vampires, but some mortals, as well. Her customers also include many brutals. She's more plugged into the vampire underworld than anyone I know. You want to find out what's happening among vampires on the street, you talk to Mrs. Dupassie. You want to *get* something out on the street, you talk to Mrs. Dupassie."

"We need to get the word out that you've called off your investigation," Casey said.

"So we're going to talk to Mrs. Dupassie?" Keoph said.

Davey said, "Yes, we are."

They stopped at a run-down, pink stucco apartment complex with a faded sign out front that read Hollywood Palms Apartments. It was a U-shaped building with two levels of apartments, with a wrought-iron railing on the top, all the way around. In the center of the complex was a worn old fountain that hadn't seen any use in a long time.

Karen whispered to Davey, "I thought you said most vampires were rich."

"Mrs. Dupassie owns this apartment complex," Davey said, "along with a lot of prime real estate all over southern California. She doesn't *have* to live here—she chooses to."

"Are all these apartments occupied by, uh . . ." Karen still had trouble saying the word out loud.

"Yes," Davey said before she finished, "they are."

Davey and Casey led them to a ground-floor apartment to the left, number 106, near the corner. The door was open with a screen door closed, and a television played loudly inside. Davey knocked on the edge of the screen door.

The television went off and a small, frail-looking, chocolate-skinned old woman came to the door. They stepped back so she could open it.

"Come in, come in," Mrs. Dupassie said.

As soon as they entered the small living room, three cats scattered and hid.

"Come to the table," Mrs. Dupassie said. She led them to a table in a small dining area. "I've made some coffee. Would you like some?"

Karen and Keoph both said yes, and Mrs. Dupassie poured coffee into two cups and brought them to the table. She went back for her own. There were four chairs at the table. Mrs. Dupassie went to a chair against the wall, scooted it over, and sat down with them.

Karen wondered how old Mrs. Dupassie had been when she was turned. The woman looked ancient—Karen guessed she'd been somewhere in her eighties. She had papery skin and a sunken, skull-like face. Her thinning silver hair was pulled back in a bun and she wore a simple green-and-white housedress that seemed too big for her small frame. Karen wondered how someone like old Mrs. Dupassie could end up being the informational center of the vampire underworld.

To Davey and Casey, Mrs. Dupassie said, "I haven't seen either of you in awhile. How the fuck are ya?"

"We're working on a new script, Mrs. Dupassie," Casey said, smiling. "It's coming along well."

"Ah, that's fantastic, fanfuckingtastic," the old woman said as she reached over and patted Casey's hand enthusiastically. She smiled and revealed only a few teeth remaining in her head. Karen thought of the extra fangs she had tucked away in her upper gum. She turned to Karen and Keoph and said, "And who might you be?"

"Mrs. Dupassie," Davey said, "this is Karen Moffett and Gavin Keoph."

Before Davey could continue, Mrs. Dupassie reached across the table and put her hand on Keoph's. She said, "You're worried you'll do damage to your professional reputation. Don't worry. You don't have a fucking thing to worry about, Gavin." She patted his hand a couple times, then sat back in her chair.

The color left Keoph's face. He turned to Karen with a look of shock.

"How can I help?" Mrs. Dupassie said. "What's the story?"

Davey said, "They're private investigators, and they were hired by someone to investigate vampires. Prior to hiring them, their client had done some investigating of his own, and he got the attention of the brutals. One man has already been killed, and we're afraid that Karen and Gavin might be in danger."

Mrs. Dupassie clicked her tongue and shook her head. "So much violence everywhere. That's a fucking shame."

"Well, they've called off their investigation," Davey said. "It's over, off, they're no longer looking into the vampire underworld. We need to make sure word gets out about that, do you understand?"

"Of course, of course," Mrs. Dupassie said, "that's perfectly understandable." She turned to Karen and Keoph. "You know, I believe I've heard word about you two. Recently. Yes, you'd be much better off investigating something else, if you ask me. Anything else."

"Well, the important thing," Karen said, "is that we're not investigating *this* anymore."

Mrs. Dupassie nodded. "That's very wise. I think you should—"

Someone knocked at the screen door with a rattle. Mrs. Dupassie stood and headed for the door.

"Hello, Norman," she said as she unlocked the screen door.

The man who came in had to duck to get through the door. He was almost too wide to get through, as well. Norman towered over the petite Mrs. Dupassie. He carried a grocery bag in the crook of his arm, but it looked quite small next to him.

Mrs. Dupassie took the grocery bag from him and went to the kitchen. She put the bag on the counter. She waved toward the table and said, "Norman, you've met Davey and Cascy. This is Karen and Gavin. Everybody say hello to Norman."

They all said hello at the same time, then laughed.

Norman smiled at Davey and said, "Hey, Davey."

"Hey, Norman, how's it going?"

"What have you been up to, Norman?" Casey said, smiling.

Norman blushed. "Oh, hi, Casey, um, I been helping Mrs. Dupassie a lot lately."

He kept looking down, as if embarrassed. Norman was clearly very shy. He was in his twenties and wore a black T-shirt and jeans. He had a belly, but his shoulders and arms were very muscular, and enormous. He stood over six and a half feet tall.

As Mrs. Dupassie put the groceries away, Norman reached into his pocket and pulled out some one-dollar bills and a five.

"Here's your change, Mrs. Dupassie," he said.

"You keep the change, honey. That's for being nice enough to go get this stuff for me."

"Oh, thanks, Mrs. Dupassie." He put the money back into his pocket, smiling. Then he turned to Karen and Keoph and said, "It was real nice to meet you." Then to Mrs. Dupassie, "I gotta go."

"Where you off to, Norman?" Mrs. Dupassie said.

"I gotta go serve soup at the homeless shelter."

"You tell Madge I said hello when you get there."

"I sure will," Norman said as he walked back to the front door. "Madge'll like that." He ducked again on his way out.

"That Norman is a real sweetheart," Mrs. Dupassie said as she returned to her seat at the table.

"Is he for real?" Karen said. "I mean, is he really going to go serve soup at a shelter?"

"We try to keep someone working the homeless shelters as regularly as possible," Mrs. Dupassie said. "That's often the first place a new vampire will go, usually confused and scared. We like to have someone there to bring them in, get them help adjusting to their new lives. It's our way of preventing the creation of any more of those fucking brutals."

"Where else do you keep a lookout for new vampires?" Keoph said.

"Bus stations, train stations, airports," Mrs. Dupassie said. "We have shelters of our own, halfway houses where novices can be educated about their new condition, and hopefully encouraged not to prey on mortals. But my Norman—he's such a good boy, he'd probably do it without being taught. That's just the kind of person he is."

Karen said, "Has Norman ever dealt with the brutals?"

"Oh, yes," Mrs. Dupassie said. "Poor Norman lost a good friend to the brutals, a young woman he'd taken under his wing. They became very close. This was just last year, not all that long after Norman had been turned. I think Norman was pretty sweet on this girl. I don't know how she felt, but I know she liked him and appreciated his help. Then one night, she was out walking, and she was taken, and raped, and bled dry."

Karen said, "The brutals feed on their own kind?"

"They don't consider us their own kind," Mrs. Dupassie said. "Those fuckers despise us. They see us as weak and vulnerable. They don't understand the strength it takes to go against our nature as vampires and drink only bottled blood. They don't understand that because they are either incapable of or unwilling to see anything from somebody else's fucking point of view."

"What did Norman do when his friend was killed?" Keoph said.

"Well, I wasn't there, so all I know is what I heard," Mrs. Dupassie said. "But the story goes that he got ahold of some brutals, and he tore them up with his bare fucking hands. Took them to pieces. Broke them in half. For the life of his friend, he took three of theirs, and he did it, as the story goes, without a weapon. Now, I suppose that tale has been exaggerated some, but I have no doubt he's capable of such a thing. Normally, he's a kind and gentle soul. But he has his limits. And he doesn't like the brutals, not one bit. He's a strange fuckin' case, Norman is. He still lives with his parents, and they don't know he's a vampire. He was changed by some mean-spirited woman. Most vampires are just assholes, you know that? Anyway, Norman doesn't know how to tell his parents, or even if he should. At the moment, they think he's lazy for sleeping so late, and they seem to think he's gay but won't admit it to himself or anyone else. He's frustrated and confused, and I try to give him a little guidance whenever I get the chance. Norman is a little slow, but he's no fucking dummy. He's a smart boy. See, he once thought people just didn't like him. I had to point out to him that, because of his size, most people were just fuckin' *afraid* of him. That made perfect sense to him, he'd just never thought of it that way. Ever since then, he's been very soft-spoken and unfailingly polite, he never raises his voice, he's a perfect gentleman. He goes out of his way not to frighten people, and if they are frightened by him, he does his best to put them at ease." Mrs. Dupassie shook her head. "But you don't want to piss him off. No, not Norman."

"I'm glad he's on our side," Keoph muttered.

Mrs. Dupassie leaned forward and said, "Now, let's get back to your situation."

There was an explosion of sound from the living room. Karen turned to see four people rushing into the apartment. Everything after that was a blur. She heard Casey cry out. Then something came down hard on the back of her head, and Karen lost consciousness as she fell out of the chair.

* * *

Davey was caught completely off guard. One moment, Mrs. Dupassie was talking, the next someone was rushing the table. He was knocked over backward in his chair, and before he could get up, he was kicked in the stomach. Then a foot came down hard between his legs and smashed his testicles. He rolled onto his side and vomited.

He heard Mrs. Dupassie say, "Well, I sure fucking didn't see *this* coming."

Keoph saw the blur of movement coming from the door, but only had time to stiffen his back before he took a great blow to the side of his head. He went over backward in his chair, and the back of his head slammed into the wall. He rolled off the fallen chair and got to his hands and knees, but the floor tilted sharply and he fell over on his side.

In what seemed like seconds, the commotion was over and the apartment was silent.

Davey righted the chair and leaned on it heavily as he got to his feet. He looked around. Keoph was on the floor on his hands and knees, still dizzy, but slowly getting up. Mrs. Dupassie remained seated at the table, untouched.

Casey and Karen were gone.

"Oh, shit," Davey said as he ran to the door. He still felt nauseated from the kick in the nuts, but he tried to push it from his mind. The screen door had been kicked in and ripped off its hinges and lay on the floor in the living room, bent out of shape. Davey looked all around the courtyard, but saw no one, nothing. "Oh, God," he muttered as he ran across the courtyard to the front of the complex. He saw no cars pulling away—there weren't even any driving by on the street. "Oh, Jesus," he said as he looked up and down the street, and saw nothing.

Davey turned around to find Keoph limping toward him. "What happened?" Keoph said. "Where's Karen? Where's Casey?"

Davey's voice broke when he said, "They're gone. They've been taken."

"Oh, my God."

Davey felt hot with anger. Part of him wanted to punch Keoph right in the face—it was his stupid investigation that had gotten them where they were. The nausea he felt now was only partly due to being kicked in the testicles—part of it was fear for Casey. Karen, too, but it was Casey he worried about most. He knew how cruel they could be, how sadistic. They wanted something in return for Casey and Karen, and Davey knew they would let him know what that was. He was prepared to give them anything they wanted. But even if he did, that was no guarantee that Casey and Karen wouldn't be tortured or harmed in some way. The brutals had no conscience. They were not burdened by morals. They took delight in the suffering of others.

He clenched his fists, his jaw. He had to get her back. Davey was not sure he could function without Casey. Panic gripped his lungs as one thought repeated itself over and over in his mind: *The brutals have her. The brutals have her.*

"Who were they?" Keoph said. His voice was breathy with tension. "Where did they go?"

Davey put his right hand over his face a moment, then pulled it backward, pulling his face tight on the right side as he released a sigh. "They were brutals.

They've taken Casey and Karen, and will probably hold them until we can assure them that your investigation has stopped. I don't know, they may want more than that now. They're very unpredictable in many ways, and in others, they're like Pavlov's dogs."

"You're saying they've been *kidnapped?*" Keoph said.

"No, no. Kidnappers would be much easier to deal with. These are vampires. Very angry, bitter, mortal-hating vampires." Davcy went back into Mrs. Dupassie's apartment. She was standing at the short bar between the kitchen and the dining area, talking on an old-fashioned wall phone with a rotary dial and a long, curly cord connecting the receiver to the base. She held the phone in her right hand, while her left was on the bar, bunched into a pale, blue-veined, knobby fist.

"No, *you* listen to *me*, Castlebeck," Mrs. Dupassie said. Her little old lady voice was gone, and now her voice sounded low and smoky, filled with controlled rage. "They broke into my fucking *home*, do you understand that? I carry some fucking weight in this community. I've been in it a lot fucking longer than you. Longer than *most*, in fact. I know how you fucking clowns operate. I turn a blind eye to a lot, Castlebeck, and a lot of it trails right back to you in one way or another. This was brought into my *home*, you fucking moron. Maybe I'll start paying more attention to what's going on around me, you know what I mean, Castlebeck?"

As soon as she saw Davey, she smiled and waggled her stiff fingers at him in a girlish wave. She listened for a moment, then said, "That's not enough, Castlebeck. Bring those young women back here immediately. Right fucking now." She said nothing for a moment, then shook her head. "Not enough, Castlebeck, not enough."

"Who's Castlebeck?" Davey whispered.

"Don't forget," Mrs. Dupassie said, "I know where all the fucking bodies are buried. And which ones have been dug up and moved. You hear me, Castlebeck?"

"Does he know where Casey is?" Davey said.

Mrs. Dupassie held up a hand with her forefinger sticking up straight in a wait-just-a-second-I'll-be-right-with-you gesture.

Keoph came in and joined them in the kitchen. "What's going on?" he said.

"You have until midnight," Mrs. Dupassie said. "I want them brought back here to my apartment, *untouched*. Don't fuck with me, Castlebeck, because I'm one of the few people in this town who can fuck with you right back. I might, anyway, for what happened here tonight." She slammed the receiver down on its hook. She opened a cigar box on the bar and took from it a big fat cigar. She took a butane lighter from the counter and turned the cigar around and around in her mouth with her left hand while holding the flame to the end with her right. She puffed on the cigar awhile, then picked up the box, opened the lid, and offered it to Davey and Keoph. They declined.

"Well, if it's him," she said around the cigar, "we'll know pretty fucking quick."

"Who's Castlebeck?" Davey said.

"A big-shot in adult entertainment—a pornographer, really, might as well be honest about it—with connections to the brutals. They provide him with much of his talent—enslaved mortals, to be humiliated, mortified."

"You think he might be behind it?" Davey said.

"It's possible. If he is, like I said, we'll know pretty fucking quick. That fat fuck is terrified of me. And on top of that, he owes me money, and a lot of interest. If Castlebeck did it, he'll have your friends back pretty soon. But he sounded genuinely flustered. My suspicion is, he's not behind it."

"Then who?" Davey said.

Mrs. Dupassie shrugged and puffed.

Keoph said, "I thought you were supposed to be psychic."

Mrs. Dupassie removed the cigar from her mouth. "*Supposed* to be psychic? Who told you I was *supposed* to be psychic."

"I'm sorry, Mrs. Dupassie, he's just unfamiliar with you." He turned to Keoph. "Mrs. Dupassie *is* psychic."

"But that doesn't mean I *know* everything," she said. She moved an ashtray from the bar to the table and sat down again. "Hand me their purses."

Their purses hung from the corners of the backs of their chairs. Davey got Casey's while Keoph got Karen's, and they put them on the table in front of Mrs. Dupassie.

She put her cigar in the ashtray, reached out both arms, and pulled the purses to her chest in an embrace. She turned her head and rested it on the purses. Ten seconds later, she sat up in her chair and pushed the purses away.

"I'm not getting anything," she said as she put the cigar between her remaining teeth again and puffed. "It's possible they're unconscious. I can try again in awhile."

"That's it?" Keoph said. "That's the best you—"

"Gavin, please," Davey said. "Let me handle this."

"I'm psychic," Mrs. Dupassie said to Keoph, "but I don't do magic, okay? I'll try again in awhile."

Keoph ran a hand through his hair as he paced.

Davey sat down with Mrs. Dupassie at the table. "Do you have any idea at all who might have taken them?" Davey said.

"Well, obviously, they were brutals," Mrs. Dupassie said. "Beyond that, I've got no fucking idea. There's a chance Castlebeck is involved, we'll see. If he is, then Barna's involved."

"Who?" Keoph said.

"Victor Barna."

"The real estate mogul?" Keoph said.

"One and the same."

"He's a vampire?"

Mrs. Dupassie waved a hand dismissively. "He's a sadistic monster, and an arrogant prick."

Davey felt as if his entire body were vibrating. He could not bear the thought of Casey in the hands of brutals. He understood Keoph's impatience, and felt it, too. But he couldn't afford to alienate Mrs. Dupassie. Davey leaned toward her. "Mrs. Dupassie, would you mind if we stuck around for awhile?"

"Sure, that'd be just fine." Mrs. Dupassie stood. "Can I get you a beer? Some blood?"

Davey realized he was feeling the nagging pangs of hunger that were especially strong at night. He asked for a bottle of blood, which she got from the refrigerator.

Keoph asked for a beer and she gave him one.

Mrs. Dupassie went back to the phone and made a call. "Hi, Norman, honey. I know you're on your way to the shelter, but I thought I'd tell you this before you went to work. Not long after you left, a few fucking brutals busted into the place and roughed everybody up, then took Casey and Karen." She puffed on her cigar as she listened. "That's right. . . . No, they didn't touch me. Don't worry about it now, honey, but we'll handle it later tonight, when you're done at the shelter. Okay? All righty, bye-bye now."

When she hung up the phone, Mrs. Dupassie caught Keoph staring at her.

"You use Norman?" Keoph said.

"We use what we have, Gavin," she said. "And as you pointed out earlier, Norman is, fortunately for us, on our side. He's as big as a fucking house. We use what we have."

Mrs. Dupassie went out to the living room with her cigar and sat down in a recliner facing the television. She took the remote from the arm of the chair and turned the television on as she said, "I'm missing my fights."

Davey went into the living room with his bottle of blood in hand and found her watching professional wrestling.

"Have a seat, boys," Mrs. Dupassie said. "Watch the fights with me. I'll see if I can pick something up from Casey and Karen in a little bit."

Davey sighed heavily as he sat down on the couch with Keoph. For the time being, they had nothing else to do but wait.

CHAPTER FIFTEEN

Karen remembered bits and pieces, but only vaguely: Being thrown into a van, her hands being tied together behind her back, being blindfolded. There were male voices, too.

"This one's hot."

"They're both hot."

"How much time we got?"

"No fuckin' way, not with these two. They're to be delivered untouched."

Her head ached. She floated in and out of consciousness for awhile before finally drifting off.

When she finally opened her eyes again, she could see nothing but blackness. At first, she thought she was blind, then she brought her hand to her face, and when it was close enough—about an inch from her eyes—she could see it, a shape in the darkness.

She sniffed. All she smelled was some kind of industrial cleaner with a pine scent.

She felt around herself with both hands and determined she was lying on a cot with a thin blanket over her. She sat up on the edge of it and swept the blanket aside. The only light in the room came from under a door, just a thin slit of light. Karen realized she was no longer wearing her clothes; she was naked.

"Hello?" she said.

A whispered voice came out of the dark: "Oh, you're awake, Karen."

"Who's there?" Karen whispered, too.

"It's Casey. How do you feel?"

"My head hurts."

"Mine, too."

"Where are we?" Karen asked.

"I don't know, but from the looks of the room, we're in some kind of dormitory."

"You can see the room?"

"I have very good night vision, Karen. Much better than yours."

"One of the advantages of being a—" Karen cleared her throat. "—a vampire?"

"Yes, it is. But the truth is, I'd rather be mortal."

"Really?"

"Oh, yeah," Casey said wistfully. "I'd be forty-four. Imagine that. Middle-aged. Davey and I would have a few kids. They'd be in high school by now. We'd have a dog, a couple cats." She laughed a breathy laugh and said, "Listen to me go on."

"What are they going to . . . do to us?" Karen said.

"I don't know, honey. I honestly don't. But I can promise you one thing: It's going to be very unpleasant."

Karen gulped. "Thanks for cheering me up."

"I'm not going to sugarcoat it, Karen. We're in trouble. If they wanted us dead, we'd be dead already. They're keeping us alive for something, and whatever it is, it's not going to be good. We need to be prepared."

"Well, I'm *not* prepared. How the hell do you *prepare* for something like that?"

"Whatever you do, don't fight them, don't resist. I'll look for an opening, any opening."

"An opening for what?"

"For me to get us out of here."

Mrs. Dupassie hugged the purses to her again, rested her head on them. She stayed that way for several seconds.

"They're afraid," she said. "Very afraid. Both of them." Almost a full minute passed before she spoke again: "They're . . . together. But . . ." Another thirty seconds of silence passed. "That's all I can get. There's nothing else right now. It's all dark."

The phone rang. It was an old-fashioned ring from a real bell, not the electronic chirping that came from most phones.

Mrs. Dupassie got up and went to the phone over the bar. "Hello? . . . Castlebeck. Why aren't you here with those two young women?" She looked at Davey and Keoph as she talked. "All right, Castlebeck, all right. Calm down before you have a stroke, you fucking sperm whale. Do you know anything about them? Who took them?" She puffed on her cigar as she listened. "You hear anything, you'd fucking well better call me, you understand, you fat fuck? I don't suppose I have to remind you that you still owe me a lot of fucking money." She smiled and nodded her head. "Well, it's about time. Now you remember, you hear one fucking word about those two women—what? . . . One is a mortal, one is a vampire. The vampire has strawberry-blond hair, the mortal auburn hair. They've been taken. You hear one fucking word about them, you call me. If I find out you didn't, I'm gonna sic Norman on you, understand?"

She hung up the phone and turned to them. "Well, Castlebeck doesn't have them. If he did, he would've sent them back already." She giggled like a little girl. "I love putting the fear of God in him. I make him shit his pants."

"What do we do, Mrs. Dupassie?" Davey said.

"We should go to the police," Keoph said.

"Lotta vampires in the police department," Mrs. Dupassie said. "They work the night shift all over town. You go to the cops, you're liable to get somebody who covers for the brutals. There are quite a few of them, in fact. You might end up getting yourself into trouble."

"Well, we can't just stand around *waiting!*" Keoph said, almost shouting.

"You don't have much choice at the moment," Mrs. Dupassie said. "You don't know who took them. You may hear from them, you may not. If they were taken by brutals, and we know they were, they'll be letting us know what they want soon."

"Will you keep trying to pick something up again?" Davey said.

"Sure I will, Davey," she said. "I'll call you the second I come up with anything."

"Thank you," Davey said. "I've got a couple people I can talk to. Come on, Gavin, let's go."

"Where are we going?"

"To see someone I know."

They left Mrs. Dupassie's apartment, went back to the Mercedes, and got in.

"I was researching a script about five or six years ago," Davey said as he started the car. He eased out of the parking spot and drove away from the apartment building. "One of the characters was a car thief, and he had to sound like he knew what he was talking about. We wanted him to be as authentic as possible, so I started asking around among my friends—did anybody have a car thief in the family, or know someone who might know a car thief? Well, someone put me in touch with someone who put me in touch with Isaac Krieger. He was a retired car thief, among other things. Actually, I shouldn't be so glib about the other things. This guy also did time for arson and serial rape. A registered sex offender. I had a very tense dinner with him one evening, my treat. He seemed . . . well, intense, and I was always afraid I was going to say something to offend him, maybe set him off. But once you start him talking, he comes out more, and—well, to be honest, he comes off like a nice guy. Comes *off* as one. Which is, you know, a little suspect if you take into consideration his record."

Davey turned right on Ventura Boulevard, and they left North Hollywood.

"So this guy Isaac talked to me," Davey said, "and answered all my questions about being a car thief. Then he started asking me questions about writing movies. He was very curious about the business. 'I've seen a lotta shit,' he said. 'I could write me a movie, I think—if I knew how.' In exchange for talking to me,

I offered to acquaint him with the screenplay form and give him a few tips about writing within it. So I helped him, and he told me stories about his life of crime. He hung out with what I suspected to be brutals—although he was a mortal—because his friends were more vicious and sadistic than he was, judging by some of his stories. I asked him about his friends once, and he smiled and said, 'They're vampires.' He acted like he was joking, but I knew he wasn't. I'd seen it before—he knew what they were, and that was part of the reason he hung out with them. He found them to be *cool*. I'm surprised one of them hasn't turned him yet, or at least bled him dry. They have no loyalties, no boundaries. The brutals, I mean. Anyway, I don't know what Isaac is up to because we haven't talked in a couple years, but he's very connected and seems to know a lot about what goes on at night. He might have heard something, or he might hear something, that could be helpful in finding them."

Keoph put his right elbow up on the edge of the door and put his hand over his mouth, tapped his fingers on his cheek, stroked his chin.

"If it's any consolation," Davey said, "I'm sure Casey will do everything she possibly can to protect Karen."

Keoph nodded. "That's true. I'd almost forgotten she's a vampire, too."

"She can deal with them a lot better than Karen can, and that gives them both a better chance of surviving."

"What, uh, what are the chances they'll kill them?" Keoph said.

"If their intention is to kill them," Davey said, "then they're already dead."

CHAPTER SIXTEEN

Burgess called Denise's cell phone again.

"Marty, stop calling," she said when she picked up.

"*Please* come home, Denise," he said. "The sun is down."

"Marty, if you don't stop talking like that, I'm *never* coming home."

"Come on, Denise, don't say that."

"Did you do something about that smell?" Denise said.

He sighed. "Not yet. The smell is necessary, Denise. I'm very disappointed that you refuse to believe what I'm saying."

Burgess heard Denise's mother in the background: "The stuff he writes, it's no *surprise* he's got mental problems."

"Is that what you've been doing over there?" he said. "Sitting around talking about my *mental* problems?"

"Look, I'll be home soon, okay?" Denise said. Then she severed the connection.

Burgess made himself a screwdriver—it was his third. He usually only drank the hard stuff on weekends, but he was on edge.

He sat around and watched television for almost an hour. Shortly before ten o'clock, he heard the Roadster pull into the driveway. He got up, went through the kitchen, and out to the garage, just as the door slowly began to roll up. Denise's headlights hit him and made him squint. There was a light mounted above the garage door outside that was activated by a motion sensor, and the car had set it off. It's light washed over the Roadster.

As she started to drive into the garage, Burgess heard a flapping sound growing closer, louder. Something big and dark swept down on Denise from above and plucked her from the convertible. It was something as big as a man, but with large dark wings. The creature pulled her from the car as if she weighed nothing. She screamed, but it was cut off abruptly as she was carried away. Burgess heard the flapping of wings fade into the night.

The Roadster continued to roll slowly forward into the garage with no driver. Burgess hurried over to the car, got in, and parked it in the garage. When he got out, he rushed out of the garage and looked around outside.

"Denise?" he called. *"Denise!"*

The only sound was the chirping of crickets.

Burgess said, "Oh, my God."

Isaac Krieger had not changed since Davey saw him last. He was a short man with a deep tan, and his face had been badly scarred by acne. His eyebrows were faintly joined above the bridge of his nose, his eyes deepset beneath them. He wore a T-shirt with the sleeves torn off, showing off the tattoos up and down his muscular arms. His brown hair had thinned out a little on top. He was in his late forties.

Davey had decided to check the Corner Pocket, a pool hall in Sherman Oaks where he had first met Krieger. Sure enough, Krieger was there, playing pool. Davey and Keoph waited for him to finish his game.

"Remember me, Isaac?" Davey said.

Krieger smiled and said, "Course I remember ya. 'Sup?"

"I wanted to ask you some questions," Davey said. "Can I buy you a beer?"

"I never turn down free beer." He turned to the bar and shouted, "Hey, Cam, Pabst for the three of us." To Davey and Keoph, he said, "Let's go to a booth and sit down."

They went to one of the booths against the wall and Krieger sat across from Davey and Keoph. Davey introduced Keoph, but said nothing more about him.

Krieger said, "I was thinking about looking you up, Davey."

"Oh? What for?"

"I finished my first script," Krieger said. "I was wonderin' if you'd take a look at it and tell me if it's any good."

"Sure, Isaac, I'd be happy to."

"Really? That's great. But I want you to be honest. I won't learn anything unless you're honest."

Davey smiled. "Don't worry, I'm always honest. Isaac, we have a problem. My wife and Gavin's partner have been kidnapped. We have reason to believe it might have been pulled off by people like . . . well, like your friends. Have you heard anything about it?"

The waitress brought their beers, then Krieger leaned forward and said, "No, haven't heard anything. What makes you think it was vampires?"

"Gavin and his partner were investigating them."

"*You're* the one doing that?" Krieger said, turning to Keoph. "I've heard talk about it. They've been upset lately because someone was investigating them. That's all I knew about it, though, until now."

"Who is *them?*"

Isaac shrugged. "Vampires. They talk. No one in particular, just the word on the street. The, uh . . . what's that word? *Zeitgeist.*" He smiled proudly. "Yeah, it's just been in the zeitgeist."

"Isaac, can you keep an eye open for me? I'd appreciate it if—"

Keoph's cell phone went off in his pocket. He pulled it out, unfolded it, and put it to his ear. "Keoph," he said. He frowned as he listened. "Please, Mr. Burgess, calm down, I can't understand what you're saying."

Davey heard the voice at the other end come sharply from the earpiece.

"I don't know, Mr. Burgess, I don't know what—no, don't do that, don't call the police. It's not safe. . . . Okay, give me your address."

A minute later, Keoph folded the phone up and put it in his pocket. "My client's wife has been taken," he said.

"Oh, God," Davey said. "This just keeps getting worse by the minute." He turned to Krieger again. "Isaac, will you do me a favor? If you hear anything about two women, Casey, a vampire, and Karen, a mortal, will you let me know?" He gave Isaac a description of each woman. "If you hear a *word* about them, will you call me?"

Krieger shrugged. "I might be able to do that, but . . . look, dog, I can't be gettin' myself into trouble with my friends."

"Don't worry, you won't." Davey took out his wallet and removed from it a business card and a twenty dollar bill. He took a pen from his shirt pocket and wrote his cell phone number on the back, then handed the card and the bill to Krieger. "Call me anytime, day or night. Have a couple more drinks on me."

"Yeah, yeah, okay, bro," Isaac said. "Thanks."

"We've got to go now," Davey said as he stood. "Thanks for talking to us."

They left the Corner Pocket and got into the Mercedes outside.

"Where does he live?" Davey said.

Keoph gave him the address in Topanga Canyon.

They said nothing as Davey drove, remaining silent with their own thoughts.

Davey felt ready to come out of his skin over the loss of Casey. He could not imagine life without her. He had to get her back.

"It's not safe to talk to the police, Mr. Burgess," Keoph said at Burgess's house.

Davey said, "Some of the police are vampires who cover for the brutals. Going to the police would be too much of a risk. Unless, of course, you did it during the day. That might not be as risky."

They stood in the living room, where Burgess paced, wringing his hands.

"They took my wife, too," Davey said. "And his partner, Karen."

"They've got them all?" Burgess said.

Davey and Keoph nodded.

"Jesus, what am I going to do?" Burgess said breathlessly.

"There's nothing you can do at the moment, Mr. Burgess," Keoph said. "We're going to do all we can to find them."

"That's it? I mean, that's all you've got to *tell* me, that you're going to do all you *can*?"

"Mr. Burgess," Davey said, "do you have something that belonged to your wife? A personal item she usually kept with her?"

"Her purse was in the car," Burgess said as he turned and led them into the dining room. Denise's purse was on the table.

"We've got a psychic working on this," Davey said, "and it would help to have something of Denise's to give to her, so she'll have something to work with."

Burgess went to the table, rummaged through the purse, and finally pulled out a red hairbrush. "How's this?" he said.

Davey took the brush. "This is perfect." To Keoph, he said, "Let's go back to Mrs. Dupassie's."

Keoph turned to Burgess and watched him pace. "I'm very sorry about this, Mr. Burgess."

Burgess stopped pacing and turned to Keoph. "Find her and bring her back to me, and I'll pay you the full amount I was going to pay you before the investigation was canceled."

"I'm going to try to find her, anyway, Mr. Burgess. I don't need money for that."

* * *

Mrs. Dupassie held the brush in her left hand as she hugged the purses to her on the table. Her eyes closed, she sat there for a minute before speaking. She frowned above clenched eyes.

"I'm getting . . . *some*thing, but . . . it's all dark. There's definitely a connection, but nothing's coming through but fear, the same fear I felt before." She released the purses, put down the brush, and leaned back in her chair. "I'm still not getting anything. But I'll keep trying, Davey."

Davey said, "Thank you, Mrs. Dupassie."

CHAPTER SEVENTEEN

The lights came on and a moment later, someone came into the room. The light was blinding to Karen at first, and she raised her hand to cover her eyes.

"All right, let's go, ladies," a large woman said. She was tall and big-boned, with frizzy dark hair and a skillet-flat face.

Karen and Casey were led out of the room naked. They went down a hall of doors, and each door was numbered. Karen wondered if the building had been a hotel at one time—it looked like one.

Karen felt groggy as she shuffled down the hall. The woman led them to an elevator. In the car, she pushed a button, and the elevator started going down. She did not speak. Karen was afraid to speak. She covered her breasts with her upper arms, and held both hands together over her pubis.

Casey stood with her arms at her sides, frowning. She looked angry but tired, with heavy-lidded eyes.

When the elevator reached the basement, the door opened and the big woman led them out into a concrete corridor with grey walls. Overhead, exposed pipes ran along the corridor.

The woman turned right, opened a door, and led them into a grey room that contained what looked like two dental chairs and a large couch. There was a round drain in the center of the room's floor.

"Wait in here," the woman said. "Sit in the chairs."

The woman left the room and closed the door.

Karen and Casey sat down in the chairs and looked at each other for a long time without speaking. Finally, her voice thick, Casey said, "I'm afraid they're going to torture us."

"Why?" Karen said. "For what?"

"I don't know. Prepare for the worst."

Karen leaned forward, put her face in her hands, and cried quietly.

"Please don't fall apart now, Karen," Casey said. "I need you to hold yourself together, okay?"

Karen sniffled and tried to stifle her crying.

The door opened and a tall, slender man in a black turtleneck, black slacks, and black shoes, carrying what looked like a black doctor's bag, entered the room. He had longish shiny white hair, and pink eyes in his deathly pale face. He was followed by the big woman who had led them to the room earlier.

"Secure them," the man said. He had a German accent and it came out, *Secure zem*.

The chairs had straps on them, and the woman fastened them, first across Karen, then Casey. She strapped their arms to the armrests.

The man put his bag on a small stainless steel table and opened it. He removed a pair of garden sheers. He squeezed the handle and the blades hissed together a couple times, snapping closed with a sibillant metallic *snick*.

"I am going to ask you a question," he said to Casey. "If you do not tell me the truth, I will cut off your little toe. I will make my way through all your toes unless you tell me what I want to know. And then I'll start on your fingers."

Karen was unable to control herself. She began to shiver in her restraints and tears rolled down her cheeks.

The man said, "Now, with whom do I start?" He smiled and his pointed finger moved back and forth between them as he muttered, "Eenie meanie minie mo . . ." He ended on Karen.

"No," she whispered.

The man rolled a small stool over to Karen's chair and sat down on it. He picked up her right foot at the ankle and put the clippers to her little toe. Karen tried to pull her foot free, but his grip was iron.

"Whom have you told?" he said.

"What?" Karen tried to stop crying. She coughed a few times and took a deep breath. "What did you say?"

"Whom have you told?"

"About what?"

"About us. About your investigation. Whom have you told?"

"No one. I've told no one."

The albino squeezed on the clipper's handles and the blades closed on Karen's little toe.

Karen screamed.

CHAPTER EIGHTEEN

Hold it just a second," a fat man said as he burst into the room. He spoke with firm authority. "Whatever you're doing, stop."

"I beg your pardon?" the albino said as he stood and turned to the fat man. "Oh, it's you, Mr. C."

"I haven't *seen* these two yet, do you have any idea why?" the fat man said.

"No, Mr. Castlebeck, I have no idea," the German-accented albino said. "I'm just following orders."

"Well, let me take a look at them, at least, before you mark them up."

Karen surprised herself when she had to bite back a laugh, which she was sure would lead to an hysterical fit of laughter. What struck her as funny was Castlebeck's suit—it looked like a big balloon that had been over-inflated. Above his bloated double chin was a fat face that seemed in the process of consuming itself. He was of average height, had thick brown hair, and a bulbous nose.

Castlebeck apparently had hurried because he was a bit winded. It was possible, Karen decided, that he was always a little winded, as fat as he was.

He stepped toward Casey and looked her over, then turned and did the same with Karen.

"This one's a little long in the tooth," Castlebeck said of Karen. "But she's nice. A nice MILF." He turned to the albino. "You know what a MILF is, Malcolm?"

Malcolm shook his head.

"M-I-L-F. A MILF is a Mom I'd Like to Fuck." Then he laughed. He turned to Casey again and said, "This one's a beauty. Yes, I'll able to—" He frowned as he looked Casey over again. He reached down and lifted her upper lip. When he saw the lumps above her teeth, he turned to Malcolm and said, "She's a vampire."

"That's right, Mr. Castlebeck."

Karen watched Castlebeck as he stroked his chin, then tugged on the roll of fat beneath it.

"I want 'em," Castlebeck said. "Both of 'em."

"You will have to take that up with Mr. Barna." He pronounced it, *You vill hoff to take zat up wiss Mr. Barna.*

Castlebeck took a cell phone from his pocket. "I will, then. Don't damage them. Not yet." He punched in a number and put the phone to his ear. He frowned after a while and said, "No answer." He pushed the Off button, then turned it back on and punched in another number. "Hello, this is Frank Castlebeck."

As he listened, his eyes moved over Karen's body

and one half of his mouth curled up in a smile. She felt his stare on her, even when she closed her eyes. They made eye contact for a moment.

He said, "Yeah, you've got a couple women here in Room B who I'd like to use, if that's all right with you." He nodded his head slowly as he listened. "Ah, I see. I didn't know that. But I'd still like to use them in—oh, of course. Yes, I understand." He winked at Karen. "Well, in that case, if you leave them to me, I'll do my best to get what you want out of them. The humiliation alone—yes, I understand. Thank you, thank you very much." He folded the phone up and put it back in his pocket as he grinned at Karen, then at Casey. "Looks like you ladies are in my care." He turned to Malcolm. "Put them back in their room for now. I'll get to them in a little while."

Malcolm began to unfasten Karen's straps first, then Casey's. "Come on," he said. "Back upstairs."

Back in their dark room, Karen sat on the edge of her bed and faced Casey, who sat on the edge of hers.

"I feel groggy," Karen said.

"Me, too," Casey said. "It's possible they drugged us, but it's more than likely just them. Vampires are capable of doing some serious mental damage if they want. Or they can just make someone groggy and pliant, like us. Since I don't prey on people, I've never exercised most of my abilities. I mean, I have no reason to make someone groggy and pliant, you know?"

"You've . . . never done that?"

"Never had a reason to. Most vampires like Davey and me, they don't use most of their abilities as vampires. We're more interested in being human than in being vampires. As a result, though, my abilities are rusty, and I can't do much to fight off whatever the brutals are doing to me."

"What are they going to do to us?" she whispered.

"I don't know, but it's not going to be pleasant. If that Castlebeck guy hadn't come in when he did, you would've lost at least one toe."

"They want to know who we've told," Karen said, "but we haven't told anyone. The only people Keoph and I talked to were Walter Benedek, you and Davey, and that old woman, Mrs. Dupassie. We haven't told anyone anything."

"But how do we convince *them* of that?" Casey said.

"I wonder who Mr. Castlebeck is."

"I wonder who that creepy albino is," Casey said. "He made me feel cold. Hell, I feel cold now. Is it just me, or is it chilly in here?"

"It is," Karen said with a nod. She crossed her arms and scrubbed her upper arms with her hands. "I don't know about you, but I'm getting into bed." She got up, pulled the blanket on the cot back, and slid beneath it. She propped herself up on her left elbow and faced Casey, who had gotten into her own cot and covered up. "I wish they'd give us something to wear," Karen said.

Several seconds later, Casey said, "I've never had a problem with nudity. My parents were—well, they weren't exactly nudists, I mean, they didn't meet with any other people or go to nudist camps, or anything— but they were naked a lot. So was I when I was a kid. When no one else was around, we wandered around naked a lot. Mom and Dad taught my brother and I that it was only appropriate at home, and never when there were guests. I became more modest when puberty struck, though, and started covering myself up. But as an adult, I have no problem with nudity. In fact, before we started hiring help, I used to do housework in the nude."

Karen shook her head and said, "I don't think my parents were ever naked. I think they were *born* with clothes on. I come from a very buttoned-up family. Buttoned up in more ways than one."

"Ah. They weren't very affectionate?"

"No, not at all. When a parent hugged and kissed kids on TV, I was always uncomfortable with it. It felt inappropriate to me, because my parents never hugged or kissed me. By the time I reached high school, though, I'd figured out that it was *very* appropriate, and that the problem was with my parents. They were incredible. They were so uptight, they didn't even voice their opinions unless asked. As an act of rebellion, I became the exact opposite of them. I always said what was on my mind, I wore my feelings on my sleeve, and I showed a lot of affection to *them*. Drove them nuts."

Casey laughed. "My parents were hippies," she said. "They smoked pot. Never in front of me, but I could smell it. I didn't realize what it was until I was, like, in high school. Once I found out, I hunted down their stash and helped myself to it. They figured out I was pinching some now and then, and we had a talk. They told me they didn't think there was anything wrong with pot, but it was illegal. If I wanted to smoke it, fine, but only at home with no one else around, and I could tell no one. In other words, I could only get stoned with my parents. Well, there was no way I was going to do *that*, so as it turned out,

I ended up, for the most part, clean and sober in my high school years. Drugs were no big deal—not if my *parents* were doing them—and they held no interest for me, maybe *because* my parents did them. For me, drugs didn't have the appeal of forbidden fruit like they did for others. I'm glad of that, too. I know people who went too far with drugs. They're a mess now. I'd much rather be carried away by a good book."

Karen sighed. "Yeah, I like to read, too."

Casey said, "I keep telling Davey to write his novel. It's something he's always wanted to do, and I keep pushing him to do it. But he hasn't started it yet, as far as I know."

"What kind of novel do you think he'll write?" Karen said.

Casey thought a moment, then said, "Something sad."

They stopped talking and just lay in the dark, thinking. Karen's thoughts were a swift jumble of fear, and she could not slow them down. She kept feeling again the cold blades of the clippers on her little toe, and realized over and over—each time was heart-clenching, as if it had never occurred to her before—that she was being held captive by vampires.

After several minutes of silence, as upset as she was, Karen drifted off to sleep.

The lights came on with a horrible shrieking sound, and Karen was torn from sleep so hard, she fell off the cot. She got up quickly, shaking, and looked at Casey, who had plunged off the cot and stood beside it now.

Karen covered her ears with the heels of her hands and had to shout to be heard: "What *is* that?"

Wincing at the sound—an impossibly loud blend

of sirens, all of which clashed terribly with each other—Casey said, "I don't know. Maybe a fire alarm. Maybe not."

After a full minute, the sound stopped and the lights went out again.

While the lights were on—the overhead light and both bedstand lamps—Karen had gotten a look around at the room. Aside from their beds and the bedstand beside each, it was completely empty—even the walls were bare.

Seeing the room for most of that minute had given her a feeling of emptiness, and hopelessness. They were like animals in a cage.

Casey said, "That will probably go off at regular intervals to keep us from sleeping."

Karen released a long breath of relief as she sat on the bed.

"Did you get a look at the room?" Casey said.

"Yes. No windows."

"Just the door."

Karen heard Casey move around in the room.

"What are you doing?"

"I'm checking the door." The doorknob rattled. "It's locked." Casey sighed.

"I'm not surprised."

Casey's cot creaked when she sat down on it again. They had nothing to do but wait.

CHAPTER NINETEEN

Frank Castlebeck was usually a very happy man. He had a good life. He had money—most of the time, if not lately—he got plenty of pussy whenever he wanted it, and he was able to spend much of his time working around beautiful women who were either taking their clothes off or putting them on at any given time. He was a naturally upbeat man, something he'd developed back in school when others had picked on him for being fat. He'd found that if he was cheerful and optimistic, people were less likely to insult him. Of course, there were those who mocked him anyway, and his cheerfulness was a good way to conceal how much they hurt him.

Lately, though, things had gone downhill. Castlebeck liked to play the horses, and they had wiped him out two years ago. He'd been trying to get back on his feet ever since. In doing that, he'd made a terrible mistake: He had borrowed money from Mrs. Dupassie.

A horse called Norma Dune had been his downfall. He'd been so sure, his gut had never had a stronger feeling, and all the signs were right—the weather was sunny (he never bet on rainy days), and his horoscope in the *Los Angeles Times* had told him to be bold.

He'd bet it all on Norma Dune. The horse had lost the race. Didn't even place.

Castlebeck knew some mob guys, but there was no way in hell he was going into debt to them, or anyone like them. Then Christopher Parch, a vampire who managed one of Castlebeck's strip joints, had told him about Mrs. Dupassie. She loaned a lot of vampires money—even though Castlebeck wasn't a vampire, he worked with them, so maybe she would help him out.

He'd gone to see her, and had asked her for the loan. What could it hurt? She was a little old lady. A vampire, yes, but an old, frail vampire. She'd seemed so nonthreatening, even charming.

Castlebeck had managed to pay off a portion of the loan, but he still owed a great deal to her.

The vampires gave Castlebeck the willies. He did not like them, nor did he enjoy working with them. But he went where the money was, and they were rolling in it.

Back in 1985—back when he thought vampires were nothing more than characters in horror films—they had come to him. Very professional, spare with words. A Mr. Barna came to his office one evening—that was before Barna became well known—with what looked like a bodyguard, a broad-shouldered, deep-chested man whom Barna introduced as Stanley. Barna was Hungarian and spoke with the faintest touch of an accent. He and his "people" wanted to be Castlebeck's partner, and in exchange, they would provide him with all the talent he needed, not only for his strip joints, but for his adult film business as well, all for free. The only condition was that he turn a blind eye to a few things, and not talk about what he saw.

Castlebeck had refused at first. There was something very unsettling about Mr. Barna and his beefy associate Stanley. He'd wanted nothing to do with them.

He had been seeing a blonde named Mandy at the time. She was something. She had wanted to be in one of his movies, and in exchange for the role, she'd moved in with him and become his girlfriend for awhile. She was great in bed—she'd behaved like a slut and talked dirty, just the way Castlebeck liked it.

One night, he'd come home to find Mandy stretched out on the couch with her head in Barna's lap. Barna's silent, muscular friend was seated in a chair, but stood when Castlebeck came into the room.

"Hello, Mr. Castlebeck," Barna had said.

"Mandy?" Castlebeck said.

"Mandy is in an hypnotic state, Mr. Castlebeck. I've come here to show you why we are so seldom told 'no.'" Barna slid his arms beneath Mandy's upper body and lifted her toward him. "Mandy. You may open your eyes now."

Mandy opened her eyes, looked up at Barna, and smiled.

Barna opened his mouth and two deadly looking fangs slid down from beneath his upper lip. He bent forward as he lifted her toward him, and plunged the fangs deep into her neck.

Castlebeck started forward reflexively to help her, and in a heartbeat, Stanley was standing in front of him. He appeared so suddenly, Castlebeck slammed right into him.

Mandy squirmed in Barna's arms and made breathy sounds faster and faster. Barna made sloppy, loud sucking sounds.

Castlebeck could do nothing. He certainly wasn't going to get rough with Stanley, who stood six feet, four inches tall. After seeing Barna's fangs, his first instinct was to run out of the room, to get out of the building. He resisted the urge.

Mandy gasped and her whole body tensed tremulously, as if she were reaching orgasm.

Barna lifted his head and smiled at Castlebeck. Blood glistened on his lips and teeth, making his smile very red. The fangs were gone.

"I could drink every last drop of her blood and kill her right here," Barna said. "That would be difficult for you to explain to the police, no? But I'm not going to do that." He helped Mandy up into a sitting position, then he stood. "I simply want you to know that I'm capable of it. I could do just the same to you, if I wanted to." He stepped toward Castlebeck until he was standing close. He put his hands under Castlebeck's arms and lifted him off the floor with ease.

Castlebeck's blood ran cold. He weighed three hundred and thirty pounds, and yet Barna lifted him effortlessly and held him up high at arm's length.

"I don't like being told no," Barna said as he slowly lowered Castlebeck to the floor. "You can help us, and we can help you. I think we can work together well—

as long as you understand the situation. This is not an offer, Mr. Castlebeck. It's not open to negotiation."

Castlebeck had a chain of strip bars in Los Angeles and the San Fernando Valley called The Strip. He had a couple peepshows over on Western Avenue, along with a couple adult bookstores—one on Western, another on Hollywood Boulevard—and later, a few porn Web sites online. But his real money came from the porn movies he made. Barna and his vampires pulled it all out from under him. Once they got their claws into his business, he was nothing more than a figurehead who had to take orders from them.

Now, Castlebeck's business was nothing but a front for the vampires. They operated his two peepshows and fed on the customers when they stuck their dicks through the glory holes. They also took over his strip clubs and fed on the customers there, too. They owned the old hotel in North Hollywood called the Royal Arms, in which Castlebeck now stood, and they kept a lot of their victims there, all groggy and sleepy-eyed under whatever spell the vampires cast over them. It was from those women that Castlebeck was able to choose stars for his porn videos. He had to pay them nothing, which increased revenue considerably. They all had a bedroom air about them, thanks to their grogginess, and they looked good fucking on videotape. Some resisted, but only a little— the vampires had them under control.

Castlebeck had to pay his employees, of course, which included mostly vampires now. But they were in it for the blood, not the money.

He remembered watching a vampire movie on TV when he was a little kid—the old black-and-white original with Bela Lugosi as Dracula. It had frightened him badly, and his mother had taken him into her arms and held him as she reassured him that there was no such thing as vampires. He was forty-nine years old, and now he knew better. But instead of wanting to suck his blood, they wanted the business he'd spent twenty-two years building.

That, on top of his debt, was getting Castlebeck down. But now he had something Mrs. Dupassie wanted. She'd said one of the women who'd been taken from her home was a vampire, and one wasn't. Castlebeck knew Mrs. Dupassie was looking for them. He wondered if he could somehow use them to settle, or at least delay, the rest of his debt.

Driving home in his Porsche, Castlebeck called Mrs. Dupassie on his cell phone.

"I've seen them," he said.

"Seen who?" Mrs. Dupassie said.

"The women you're looking for. I know where they are."

"How do you know they're the women *I'm* looking for?"

"You said one was a vampire. She's got long strawberry-blond hair. The other one has short auburn hair and is older, a mortal."

"Where are they, Castlebeck?"

"Well, now, before I tell you, I'd like to know how this will affect my debt."

"Affect your debt?" She laughed. "It doesn't affect it at all."

"This is information you're interested in, I'm sure we can come to some agreement."

"What *kind* of agreement?"

"Well, you could knock some of it off, or you could give me more time to pay it back."

"Twenty-one fucking months isn't enough time? Look, Castlebeck, it's not my problem you got the hots for the ponies. Your time is up."

"In exchange for this information, I'd like to ask that you give me six more months."

"You'd *like* to, huh?"

"Yes."

She was silent for several seconds. "All right. You've got a deal, you fucking leech."

"Thank you."

"So, where *are* they?"

"At the moment, they're being held in the Royal Arms Hotel in North Hollywood."

"The Royal Arms, huh? I suppose you're going to use them in your movies."

"That's the plan."

"I don't suppose you'd be willing to help them escape, would you?"

"No, I'm afraid I can't do that. That would mean trouble for me. There's no way I could do that."

"I thought so."

"You could always talk to Mr Barna, Mrs. Dupassie."

"That wouldn't do any good. Mr. Barna and I don't get along, the arrogant rat-fuck."

"Well, I've provided you with all I have," Castlebeck said.

Mrs. Dupassie thought awhile, then said, "How would you like to lose some of that debt?"

"That's why I'm calling."

"Keep an eye on them for me. Try to keep them from harm. Will you do that?"

"Well . . . it won't be easy. It will endanger me and my position. I think it's worth at least twenty-five percent."

"Fifteen percent, take it or leave it. You do a good job and don't fuck it up, I'll knock off another fifteen when you're done."

"When will I be done?"

"That remains to be seen. Look, can you hold off using them in one of your movies for awhile?"

"All that for fifteen percent? I'm afraid not. They go into rotation with the others."

"You miserable cocksucker," Mrs. Dupassie said. "All right, twenty percent."

"Twenty percent before and after?" Castlebeck said.

"No, twenty percent before, fifteen percent after."

"I'll see what I can do, Mrs. Dupassie."

"I appreciate that, Castlebeck. So. Twenty percent up front, fifteen after, and you've got . . . four more months. I expect results for my generosity, Castlebeck. Don't fuck it up." She hung up on him.

Castlebeck smiled. He had no intention of keeping his promise. He could not wait to get the two women in front of the cameras.

CHAPTER TWENTY

Keoph had fallen asleep on the couch. Davey paced nervously in the kitchen. He had already called Mrs. Dupassie twice to ask if she'd picked anything up yet. She'd assured him she would call immediately when she did.

Davey had never felt so helpless. He wanted to pull on his hair and scream. His hands had not stopped shaking since the kidnapping in Mrs. Dupassie's apartment.

He took a bottle of blood from the refrigerator, unscrewed the cap, and drank half of it before stopping. He knew Casey would be getting hungry soon, and he worried that she would not be able to feed.

His cell phone chirped in his pocket and startled him. He took it out and opened it up.

"Hello."

"Davey, it's Mrs. Dupassie."

"Did you pick up something?" he said, eager and hopeful.

"Better than that. I got a call from Castlebeck. He knows where they are."

"Where *are* they?"

"Before I tell you, Davey, I want to shatter right now any notion you might have of going to find them. It would not only be dangerous, it would be suicide. They're in the Royal Arms Hotel in North Hollywood. The hotel is owned and operated by brutals. You do *not* want to go there. It's a fortress."

"Who stays there?"

"If you don't know, you don't want to know."

"I'm asking, Mrs. Dupassie. I need to know."

"You don't, really. Because you can't go there to get your wife, anyway. You wouldn't survive, and what fucking good would you be to her then?"

"Please tell me."

Mrs. Dupassie thought about it awhile. "The hotel houses victims, Davey. Mostly women, but some men. They are fed on there, and between feedings, they're used in pornographic films. They have no will of their own, so they do as they're told."

Davey's stomach rolled over at the thought of Casey being held there. "Who's in charge? Who's responsible?"

"You want nothing to do with him, Davey. He is a bad man, but very powerful."

"Do you know why they're holding Casey and Karen?"

"No, that's all I know. That they're at the Royal Arms. Don't go, Davey. It'll be the biggest fucking mistake you ever make. You don't use your mental abilities, but they sure as fuck use theirs. You've gotten rusty, while they've gotten strong. You would never survive an attempt to go in there and get her."

"But I have to do . . . *something*."

"I'll find out as much as I can from Castlebeck. He'll do his best to keep them from harm, for all the fucking good he'll be, and he'll keep me informed. They can't stay in that hotel forever—they have to come outside sometime, for something. I'll let you know as soon as I hear something."

When he finished talking to Mrs. Dupassie, he put his phone back in his pocket, and took his bottle of blood with him to the living room.

Keoph was awake and sitting up. "Who was that?" he said.

He relayed the information to Keoph.

Keoph said, "I take it you don't think it would be wise to go in."

"Every fiber of my being wants to storm that place and get Casey out. But Mrs. Dupassie's right—it would be suicide. The place is a vampire fortress."

"Then what do we—" Keoph was interrupted by his cell phone. He took it from his pocket. "Hello? . . . Yes, this is he." Keoph frowned suddenly. He held the phone away from his ear and beckoned Davey over to listen.

Davey walked over to the couch and sat down beside Keoph, who held the phone up between them.

"I'm calling about your investigation," the male voice said. He had a slight accent. "Stop it, and I might let your women live."

"We've already stopped the investigation," Keoph said. "We're prepared to walk away from it and forget it ever happened."

"That wouldn't be very satisfying to me," the voice

said. "I don't know whom you've told. I don't know how many people you've talked to. That's the information I hope to extract from Miss Moffett and her friend."

"We haven't told anyone," Keoph said.

"Forgive me if I don't believe you. I know you don't exactly have my best interests at heart. If you did, you never would have launched your investigation in the first place. I'm afraid I'm going to have to find out myself, in my own way."

"Please let them go," Keoph said. "They can't tell you anything."

"Oh, I won't be letting them go, Mr. Keoph, no matter what happens. The women are mine to keep, to do with as I please. That is the consequence of your investigation. This is not a negotiation, Mr. Keoph. I am simply calling to see to it that your investigation is called off. I appreciate the fact that you've already done that, but it doesn't change anything. The women are mine."

As he listened, Davey boiled with rage. He clenched his teeth. Whoever it was at the other end of the line, Davey wanted to throttle him, to pound him mercilessly with his fists.

"Is this Mr. Barna?" Davey said.

There was a long silence on the line. "My identity is not important. All that's important is how many people you've told. I won't be satisfied till I find out."

"The investigation is off, Mr. Barna," Davey said. "What's the point in keeping them?"

"I play for keeps, Mr. Owen."

A muted click severed the connection

Davey got up and paced. He finished off his bottle

of blood, walked back to the kitchen, and dropped it into the garbage can. He cracked his knuckles one at a time as he walked back to the living room.

"What do we do?" Keoph said.

"I'm not sure."

"I suppose I should call my client and tell him what's happened."

"You're a private investigator, right?"

"Right."

"I think the first thing we should do is find out everything we possibly can about Victor Barna."

CHAPTER TWENTY-ONE

Keoph awoke and realized he was sitting at Davey Owen's computer with his face on his arms. He lifted his head and looked around. He was alone. He stretched his arms, then looked at his watch. He'd slept for four hours. It was nine-thirty in the morning, but the room was still dark because of the black blinds on the windows.

He'd been able to find very little about Victor Barna online. The man kept a low profile. He was very wealthy and handsome, and the press liked him, but he seemed to avoid them. He was written about in gossip columns that speculated on his romantic life. He sometimes showed up in the society pages, attending parties and dinners, each time with a beautiful woman on his arm. Journalists were so infatuated with Barna's elligibility as a bachelor, they failed to write anything else about him.

Keoph looked at the picture of Barna currently on the monitor's screen. He seemed ageless—he could be in his twenties or his fifties—and was a favorite of the papparazzi. He had an olive complexion, dark hair combed straight back, an angular face with a firm jaw, and piercing blue eyes. He smiled in none of the pictures Keoph found, and usually wore sunglasses. There was one picture of him standing on a sidewalk with an unidentified woman out in broad daylight, holding an umbrella over his head. The caption read, "Real estate mogul Victor Barna shuns the sun on a hot June day in Los Angeles."

I know your secret, Keoph thought. No wonder he kept a low profile. He did not want anyone looking too deeply into his life.

Keoph got up and went downstairs. Davey was stretched out on the couch, eyes closed. As soon as he heard Keoph, he opened his eyes and sat up.

"I fell asleep and didn't get too far, but there doesn't seem to be much online about Barna," Keoph said. "More gossip about his love life than anything else."

Davey made a "hmph" sound and said, "If they only knew."

"I have an idea. I'm going to Karen's office. You need to get some sleep?"

"Yes, but don't you, too?"

"I've been asleep at the computer for four hours, I'm fine."

"Yeah, I think I'll go to bed and get some sleep," Davey said. "How long will you be gone?"

"I don't know. I'll leave my number—call if you hear anything."

* * *

Driving Karen's car to her office, Keoph got lost three times. He was distracted by the nagging worry that Karen's capture was somehow his fault. He regretted taking Burgess's offer. At the very least, he should have taken Burgess's story more seriously. But who would? It was a ridiculous story—*vampires*.

"Who knew?" he muttered as he pulled into the underground parking garage of Karen's building.

Upstairs in Karen's office, he went to her secretary, Libby, a fortyish woman with short blond hair and glasses.

"Libby, I'm afraid Miss Moffett is going to be unavailable for awhile," he said. "But she asked me to come here and do a couple things."

"Sure, Mr. Keoph," she said with a smile. "Miss Moffett said the office was yours. How can I help you?"

"I need your best searcher."

"Searcher?"

"There's one in every office. Someone who's able to find *anything* on the Internet. Do you have someone like that here? An Internet wizard?"

"That would be Winona Heath."

"Could you ask Miss Heath to come to the office, please?"

"Sure. And it's *Mrs.* Heath."

Keoph went back into Karen's office and seated himself at the desk. A couple minutes later, a short, plump woman with dark blond hair and a pleasant face came into the office.

"Hi, Winona, I'm Gavin. I have a job for you. I need you to find everything you possibly can about Victor Barna."

Winona took a pad and pen from her pocket and wrote down the name.

"I did a search online earlier this morning," Keoph said. "All I could find was gossip. I need personal information. I'm not that interested in his business, although I wouldn't mind having some idea just how big this guy is. Mostly, I'm interested in anything personal you can find. Anything besides gossip."

"How soon do you need this?"

"As soon as possible." He took a Post-It note from a pad on the desk, wrote his number on the back, and handed it to her. "That's my cell. Call when you're done, unless I'm here. And if you need help, pull a couple other people in and delegate. This comes straight from Karen Moffett, by the way."

"I'll start right away," Winona said. "Is that all?"

"That's all. Get to it."

She left the office.

Keoph drove to a coffee shop and had breakfast. When he was done, he didn't linger—he left the restaurant and headed into the Valley. He drove to North Hollywood and looked for the Royal Arms Hotel. It wasn't a very big town, and he found it on Newton Street. It was an old blocky grey building that stood five stories. He parked the car and crossed the street to the hotel. In the lobby, he took his wallet from his pocket as he approached the front desk.

"I'd like to get a room," he said to the skinny young man behind the counter.

"Sorry, but we're all booked up," the young man said.

"You're kidding, right?"

"No, not at all. We have a lot of residents here."

"Well. Okay." He put his wallet back in his pocket and turned to go. He took in as much as he could—

the run-down lobby was a bland room with beige walls and a hideous gold carpet, a couple sofas, a few chairs, none of which matched.

Outside, Keoph looked up at the building. All the windows were dark.

CHAPTER TWENTY-TWO

Karen felt numb. A man she had never met before was anally raping her, but she'd gotten past the pain and had become numb. He pulled her hair from behind as he slammed into her. She was on hands and knees on a couch in one of the rooms in the hotel—that's how she thought of the building she was in, as a hotel—but her arms weakened as she seemed to leave her body and float into a corner to watch.

The man behind her had shaggy dark hair and a muscular body. He grinned as he sodomized her and pulled her hair, and the cameraman moved around with the camera, going from one angle to another, then another. Suddenly, the man pulled out of her and hurried around to face her. He masturbated until he ejaculated all over her face.

Karen made a gagging sound and struggled not to vomit.

"Cut!" the director shouted. "Beautiful, beautiful. Looked like a real rape to me, and that's what we want." He turned to Karen and said, "You, uh, what's your name?"

"Her name is Candy Starr, with two 'r's," a woman said.

Karen was only vaguely aware of her surroundings. Her arms gave way and she lay forward on the couch, curled up into the fetal position. She looked at the woman through half-closed eyes.

She was beautiful, tall, with long black hair. She wore a smart black-and-red suit with a short skirt that displayed her long, black-stockinged legs. She had come into the room without anyone noticing. She walked over to the director.

"What's next on your schedule?" she said.

"A gang-bang."

"She should rest a bit."

"Oh, yeah, sure."

The woman went over to the couch and sat down on the edge beside Karen.

"Tell me now the names of those you've told about us, and you won't have to do that again. Otherwise, you've got a gang-bang coming up."

Karen wanted to cover herself, but had nothing to use. She lay on the couch and shivered, huddled up beside the woman.

After a couple unsuccessful tries, Karen finally spoke: "Who . . . are you?"

"I'm keeping an eye on you for Mr. Barna. What'll it be?"

"I didn't tell anyone," Karen said slowly. "Neither of us did."

"Yes, I understand that's what you said before."

"Because it's true. We told no one. It was a confidential investigation."

"You enjoy that gang-bang, Karen," the woman said as she stood.

Karen sobbed, "No, please, no more. Please."

"I have no choice, Karen. We need to know. This won't stop until you tell us."

Crying, Karen said, "Who *are* you?"

The woman smiled. "My name is Anya."

Back in the darkness of her room, Karen pulled the blanket back on the cot and got in.

"Karen?" Casey said.

Karen could not talk for awhile, she was sobbing too hard, in too much pain. She had been repeatedly beaten and sodomized by several men.

"They're trying to humiliate us, to mortify us, Karen," Casey said. "They're trying to tear us down." Her voice was weak and quavered when she spoke, as if she were shivering.

"They won't believe me," Karen said. "I've told them again and again that we didn't tell anyone about them, but they won't believe me."

"You've gotta hold on, Karen," Casey said. "You hear me?"

"Did they . . . do it to you, too?"

After a moment, Casey said, "Yes. They won't believe me, either. They're doing something . . . draining me of strength. I tried to fight them, but couldn't. Too weak. I haven't fed. I'm shaking all over."

Karen curled up on the cot and pulled the blanket up tight to her chin, trying to get warm. "They've got to find us," she said. "They've got to."

"I've got a feeling, Karen, that if we're going to get

out of here, we're going to have to do it ourselves. Davey and Gavin have no clue where we are, and even if they did, how could they get in here?"

"Are you *always* so fucking positive about everything?"

"I'm sorry, I'm just telling you how I see it."

The lights came on and the sirens sounded. Karen put her hands over her ears. It happened regularly, but it never failed to make her jump. It kept them from sleeping, made them edgy.

"They've *got* to find us," Karen whispered when it stopped. "They've got to."

The door opened and light from the hall fell into the room. Anya came in and closed the door behind her.

Karen felt the cot sink a little when Anya sat on the edge.

"Have you thought about it, Karen?" Anya said.

"Thought about . . . what?"

"Are you going to tell me who you've told, or not?"

"I'm telling you the *truth*, Anya, *please* believe me. We talked to *no one*. We only worked the investigation for two days, then it was called off."

"If you insist," Anya said, but her voice made Karen jump because it was next to her left ear now.

A hand gently rested on Karen's chest and Karen experienced a rushing feeling, as if her very life were being drawn out of her. It was a horrifying feeling, made only worse by the fact that it was so erotic, as if she were being touched everywhere. She could not move or speak.

She barely felt Anya's needle-fangs sink into her neck.

The rushing feeling grew more intense and Karen's

heart rate and breathing increased. She felt an orgasm rolling toward her inside. It was an undulating feeling, passionate and hot. Through the sound of her beating heart in her ears, she could only barely hear the sucking sounds. A bead of sweat trickled over her temple as she came, crying out.

Then it stopped.

"Thank you," Anya whispered before taking her hand from Karen's chest. She got up and went to the door, opened it, and left.

Karen curled up again and stared into the darkness.

"You okay?" Casey said.

Karen said nothing. She felt the cot move when Casey sat down beside her. She put a shaking hand on Karen's shoulder and squeezed, then took her hand.

"Karen? Talk to me."

Several long seconds passed before Karen said, "This isn't going to stop, is it? They'll keep doing this until they kill us."

Casey said, "You've got to hang on, Karen. Listen, did I hear you correctly? Was that woman's name . . . Anya?"

"Yeah."

After fifteen seconds of silence, Casey whispered, "Anya."

CHAPTER TWENTY-THREE

I don't think you'll get anything out of her," Anya said later that day in Victor Barna's office in Los Angeles. She had used Barna's private elevator and had entered his office through a back door that only he used. She had been seen by no one in the building.

"Why not?" he said.

"Because I believe her. She says they didn't tell anyone. I don't think they did."

"You're sure she doesn't need more persuasion?"

"Castlebeck used them both today," she said. "Karen did a rape video with rough anal sex and a gang-bang with thirteen men. I thought she was going to lose consciousness during the gang-bang."

"You think she would've talked if she knew anything?"

"I'm sure of it."

Barna thought about it a moment. "All right. I trust you."

"What are you going to do with her?"

"I'm not sure yet."

"Give her to me."

"Really?"

"Please."

"I was planning to ask you to go hunting with me this weekend. You wouldn't want me to get jealous, would you?"

She smiled. "Don't worry. She won't cut into my time with you. Think of her as a . . . well, a playmate for me."

He smiled. "Fine. What about this weekend?"

She smiled. "I'm available."

"Saturday night at ten?"

"Sounds good. What are you going to do with the vampire, Casey Thorne?"

Barna frowned. "I'm not sure. Actually, her name is Casey Owen."

Anya turned her head to one side. "Really? She married Davey Owen."

"Who?"

"He was the one who brought down Live Girls in New York."

"Is that so?"

"Yes. I turned him. I had great plans for Davey. He had . . . other ideas. He killed a lot of vampires and came very close to exposing us. He nearly killed me, but I managed to get out."

"The reporter who wrote that article in the *Post* in 'eighty-seven has been killed, you know."

She nodded. "Yes, Benedek. I heard. That's good. Now we need to do something about Casey and

Davey. If Davey knows about us . . . well, if I know him, he's likely to try something stupid."

"Maybe we should use Casey to show him what a mistake that would be."

Anya smiled. "Yes, I think that would be a good idea. A very good idea."

"We also have the wife of the writer who's been investigating us," Barna said.

"I didn't know that. What do you want to do with her?"

"She's been shooting movies since she got here. Gang-bangs. I want to tear her down completely, and quickly. Then I want to send her back to him."

"That should make your point. Well, I have things to do. I'm going back to the hotel."

They leaned toward each other over the desk and kissed.

CHAPTER TWENTY-FOUR

Back at Karen's office, Keoph met with Winona.

"There's not much to be found about Mr. Barna," she said, looking at her writing on a yellow legal pad. "He's single, he lives in the penthouse of the Barna Tower in downtown Los Angeles. He has several other homes, in and out of the country. He owns a number of hotels and resorts, and he has more money than he'll probably ever need. He's sort of like Donald Trump, but without the flash. He keeps a very low profile. The press would love nothing more than to learn more about him, but they can't. He's a bit of an enigma. There is one beautiful woman who's been seen with him on more than one occasion, but I haven't been able to identify her or figure out what kind of relationship they have. Would you like me to keep trying?"

Keoph said, "Yes, please, by all means keep trying, Winona. Is that it?"

"Like I said, he keeps a very low profile. I did the best I could. There's just not much information to be found."

"I kind of suspected that. Thank you, Winona, thank you very much."

After Winona left, Keoph sat back in Karen's comfortable chair and intertwined his fingers behind his head, elbows out at each side. He thought of the Royal Arms Hotel. Karen and Casey Owen were somewhere in there, enduring God only knew what. Burgess's wife Denise was probably in there, too. He felt helpless, hands and feet tied, mouth gagged. Then he got an idea.

Keoph got up and went out to Libby's office, where she was typing on a keyboard.

"Libby, Karen and I are going to need the floor plans for the Royal Arms Hotel on Newton Street in North Hollywood. Could you have someone get that for me?"

"Sure, Mr. Keoph. I'll get right on it." She picked up the phone and punched two buttons. As she talked, Keoph went back into Karen's office. He sat down at the desk again, still feeling helpless.

No one in the office had asked where Karen was yet. He did not know what he was going to tell them when they did. He needed to come up with a story.

He hoped she was all right.

Davey slept fitfully. He kept waking up from vivid, smothering nightmares. They were mostly nightmares he hadn't had in years—about what had happened in

Times Square in 1987, about Anya, the beautiful vampire who had seduced and turned him, about the hideous things living in the basement of Live Girls. Each time he woke up, always in a sweat, his first thought was Casey.

Hardly a day went by that Davey didn't think about Anya. In a sense, this was all her fault—had she never turned him, none of this would have happened. His biggest regret about blowing up Live Girls had been that the explosion had killed Anya—he'd wanted to do that himself, up close and personal. He had been more weak and vulnerable when she'd seduced and turned him than he'd ever been in his whole life. He'd been foolish, too, he could not deny that. Foolish and stupid and filled with self-pity. He could not think about Anya for very long—it made him too angry and could ruin his whole day—but she crossed his mind every day.

The bed felt so huge without Casey, the house so empty. He could smell her in the bedroom, as if she were there with him. He did not want to imagine what she was going through, but his mind kept returning to the possibilities, and they made his stomach turn.

Finally, he got up and paced in the living room, a sheen of sweat on his naked body. He felt impotent, useless. He hoped Keoph was accomplishing something.

Burgess sat on his couch watching television and drinking. He was drunk, but he didn't stop. He wanted to pass out.

They had told him not to go to the police, that he could endanger Denise further by notifying them.

So he numbed himself. He was unable to think of anything but Denise.

He took another drink of vodka and sat back on the couch.

He felt responsible. If he'd never started the investigation, this wouldn't have happened. He numbed himself to his own guilt, as well as Denise's capture.

He took still another drink.

Karen was torn from sleep when the lights came on and the sirens blared again. She sat up suddenly, and winced with pain. Her whole body hurt, but most of her pain was between her legs. Her torn anus throbbed as it continued to bleed. She was bruised all over. She felt covered in filth and wanted so much to take a long shower. She felt sticky and smelled of sex, and started to cry.

In the other bed, Casey sat up, too. Her face was drawn and bruised and lumpy from swelling, as were her arms and legs. She looked half-awake and trembled all over. "It's all right," she said, her voice barely audible. "It's just that noise."

The sirens stopped, but the light remained on.

The door opened and Anya walked in. She walked over to Casey's bed. "Come with me," she said.

"Where?"

"Never mind that, just come," Anya said.

"Please don't take her away, Anya," Karen said. "I don't want to be alone." She sniffled and forced herself to stop crying. "Please. Don't."

"Come with me, Casey," Anya said.

Casey sat on the edge of the cot, staring at Anya. "You're . . . Anya?"

Anya smiled. "That's right. The name's familiar?"

"Yeah. Familiar."

"Come on, get moving," Anya said.

Casey left the cot and walked unsteadily to the door with Anya. She turned back to Karen and said, "Don't worry, I'll be back."

Anya let Casey go out first, then turned to Karen and smiled. "Don't count on it," she said before leaving and closing the door.

Seconds later, the lights went out again, leaving Karen alone in the dark.

Denise Burgess lay in the dark, her body in agony. She had been brutally raped by numerous men, and beaten by some of them, all in front of cameras. She could find no part of her body that did not ache. Her face was swollen, one eye all the way shut.

Light poured into the room when the door opened. A woman said, "Come on, it's time to go."

Denise tried to move, but only groaned in pain.

The woman in the doorway sighed and left, closed the door. She returned a little later with a large, brawny man.

"Take her," the woman said.

The man went to Denise and picked her up in his arms. She grunted and groaned as he carried her out of the room.

The woman closed the door as she left.

CHAPTER TWENTY-FIVE

The sun set on Los Angeles in a smear of purple and pink with black sillhouettes of palm trees standing against it.

Burgess missed the sunset. He lay sprawled on his couch, snoring. The television was tuned to TV Land, and a studio audience laughed every few seconds. His gray cat Angie was curled up and sleeping on the top of one of the couch's back cushions.

His dog Hubert, an enormous Rottweiler, strolled into the living room, went to the end of the couch, and licked Burgess's face with his big pink tongue.

Burgess sputtered and turned his head away. He pushed the dog back and said, "Stop it, Hubert, dammit, just stop it."

When he heard the doorbell, he thought the sound had come from the television—another Domino's commercial, or something. It sounded again during a commercial for Sara Lee cheesecake, and Burgess sat up on the couch.

"Who is it?" he shouted.

No one responded from the other side of the front door, and the bell did not ring again. Burgess wondered if he was hearing things.

Something scratched on the front door.

Burgess slowly got to his feet and turned to the door, frowning. He went to it, though he couldn't walk in a straight line, and looked out the peep-hole. His vision blurred, but he could tell there was no one standing there. He unlocked the door and opened it. Movement below, on the concrete porch, drew his eyes downward.

He stared down at the battered, naked woman on the porch for a long time.

Her right arm moved. She had been scratching on the door to get his attention.

Burgess stared down at the woman on the porch for a long time before it registered that he was looking at Denise.

Her hair was matted and dirty, her face lumpy and bruised, her right eye swollen shut. She bled from wounds to her neck. Bruises were developing all over her body.

Burgess heard himself babbling in a panic as he knelt down beside her.

"Oh my God Jesus Denise Denise what did they do Denise oh Jesus oh my God . . ."

Sobriety struck him like a slap in the face. He slid his arms beneath her and very carefully picked her up. He took her into the house and put her down on the couch. He realized he was crying—tears wet his cheeks.

"Mar . . . ty?" Denise said. Her lips were swollen and bloody.

"I'm right here, honey, right here," he said as he hovered over her on the couch.

"Vam . . . pircs."

"Yes, honey, yes, I know." Instead of looking for the phone, he took his cell phone from his pocket and punched in 911.

Keoph was in the dining room with the plans of the Royal Arms Hotel spread out on the table before him when Davey came out of his bedroom. He wore a shortsleeve plaid shirt and jeans, and he walked slowly, shoulders slumped. He had dark crescents beneath his eyes. From the looks of him, Davey had not slept well.

"You okay?" Keoph said.

"Yeah, I'll be fine. Soon as I wake up. What's that?" Keoph told him.

"That was a good idea, Gavin."

"You think so?" Keoph rubbed the back of his neck. "I don't know what good it'll do us, to tell you the truth. Might just be a waste of time."

"We may have to go in."

"Wait. You're not serious."

"I am. We may have no choice. Well, *I* may have no choice. I wouldn't expect you to come."

"What good would you be to Casey if you were dead?"

Davey smiled, bared his fangs for a moment. "Don't forget, I don't die that easily."

"Even so—" Keoph's cell phone played its little fanfare and he took it from his pocket. "Keoph."

A man began to babble at the other end of the line.

"Whoa, hold on, I can't understand you," Keoph said. "Who is this?"

"Martin Burgess."

"Mr. Burgess, what's wrong?"

"They dumped her at my door, naked and beaten," Burgess said. "I'm at the hospital. Denise has been raped repeatedly, bitten and beaten and, and, and she's in the Emergency Room right now."

"What hospital?"

"Cedars-Sinai."

"How's she doing?"

"I don't know, dammit, but she looked bad, Mr. Keoph, she looked so bad." A moment of silence on the line was followed by a sob from Burgess.

"I'll be right there, Mr. Burgess."

"Will you? Thank you. Thank you, Mr. Keoph."

Keoph put the phone back in his pocket. "I've got to go."

"What's wrong?"

"Denise Burgess was—I mean, my client's wife was returned to him in pretty bad shape."

"Hold it," Davey said. He hurried into the kitchen and came back a moment later with a bottle of blood in hand. "I'm going with you."

In the car, on the way to the hospital, Keoph said, "What do you think it means?"

"What do I think what means?" Davey said. He unscrewed the cap and drank a few gulps from the bottle.

"They dumped Mrs. Burgess on the porch, naked and bleeding, and Burgess says she was raped multiple times." Keoph realized he'd just blown his client's anonymity, but found he could not care too much about that at this point. He seriously doubted that Burgess would mind—he had more urgent matters to think about.

"Oh, my God," Davey said in a low voice.

"What do you think it means, Davey?"

"They're just giving him a warning," Davey said. He looked ahead as he spoke, eyes beyond the windshield. "It's their way of saying, 'Stay away from us.'"

"I imagine the police have become involved," Keoph said. "I wonder what he's told them." He glanced at Davey. "This could lead to exposure. Are you sure you want to be involved?"

Davey thought about that a moment as he kept his eyes on the road. Finally, he turned to Keoph and said, "Well, if it'll help get Casey back, exposure's fine with me."

Davey said nothing as Keoph found a parking space in the ER lot. He finished his drink and put the bottle on the floorboard in front of his seat. They got out and crossed the lot to the entrance. Keoph was saying something, but Davey barely heard it. He was busy with his own thoughts.

Exposure. He let the word fill his mind. It frightened him because he had no idea what to expect from it. He liked to pose theories to himself, but none of them ever made any sense—they were more fantasies than theories. He once tried to convince himself that mortals and vampires could live together peacefully. That was a fantasy.

He could not honestly take seriously any scenario that did not involve Davey and Casey and others like them being in constant grave danger. He was not sure exactly how, but he had no doubt of it. Exposure could mean death.

But Casey was trapped in the Royal Arms Hotel with a bunch of savage vampires. Davey thought of what had been done to the woman Keoph called Denise Burgess. He shuddered and tried not to think about what was being done to Casey.

In the ER waiting room, Keoph approached Burgess. He sat with his elbows on his thighs and his head in his hands, the only person in the room besides an elderly man seated over by the window.

"Mr. Burgess?" Keoph said.

The man lifted his head. His eyes were puffy, cheeks red, his mouth a tense line. "Hello," he said as he stood.

Davey recognized the writer.

Keoph said, "I didn't properly introduce you two earlier, so Mr. Burgess, I'd like you to meet Davey Owen. Davey Owen, Martin Burgess."

As Burgess stared at Davey, his mouth slowly opened and he reached out a hand to shake. "We talked on the phone."

"Yes, I remember," Davey said as he shook his hand.

"You . . . you're a . . . a . . ."

"Yes, I am," Davey said with a nod.

"How is your wife?" Keoph said.

Burgess shook his head. "She's badly beaten. I'm just waiting out here while they treat her. As soon as they're done, I'm going back in with her. The police are here. The cop was asking Denise questions awhile ago. He may be trying again now, I don't know."

"What has she said?" Keoph asked.

"Nothing. Well, she speaks sometimes, but only to say, 'Vampires. Vampires.' She's . . . not herself. What . . . what am I going to tell the police? They're going to want to know why I didn't call them as soon as she disappeared."

Davey stepped forward and said, "Tell them the truth, Mr. Burgess. Any vampires on the force would have a hard time covering this up. It's a matter of hospital record. Just tell them the truth. I'll back you up."

Keoph gave him a questioning look. "Are you serious?"

"Dead serious."

"What do you think Casey would say?" Keoph said quietly.

Casey would be against it. But if she were by his side instead of in that hotel, there would be no problem. "It's time this got out. And it might help me get Casey out of that hotel before they kill her."

A uniformed police officer came through the swinging double doors that led back to the ER. He was a stout man with a ring of greying dark hair that went from ear to ear around his bald crown. He had a bulldog look to him—he even had an underbite. He approached Burgess. His nameplate read Offcr. N. Keaton.

"I've been trying to talk to your wife, Mr. Burgess," the officer said. "But all she says is, 'Vampires,' over and over again. Do you have any idea what that might mean?"

Burgess looked at Keoph for a moment, then at Davey. He turned to the officer and said, "Officer Keaton, my wife is saying, 'Vampires,' over and over again because . . . well, that's who kidnapped her."

Keaton's eyebrows rose. "I'm sorry?"

"She was kidnapped by . . . vampires. They held her—" He turned to Keoph and Davey. "—where was it again?"

Keoph said, "We're pretty sure it's the Royal Arms Hotel in North Hollywood."

Keaton turned to Keoph and said, "Who're you?"

Keoph introduced himself.

"What's your involvement in this?" Keaton asked.

"Well, it's, uh . . . I'm a private investigator. Mr. Burgess hired me, and his wife's kidnapping was related to my investigation."

Frowning now, Keaton took a pad and pen from his pocket and wrote on it. "Keeph?"

"No, *Kee*-off." He spelled the name.

"You have an office here in Los Angeles?" Keaton said. Keoph said, "No, I'm from San Francisco."

"What did Mr. Burgess hire you to investigate?"

Keoph looked at Davey for a moment, then said, "He hired me and my partner, Karen Moffett, to investigate . . . vampires."

Keaton used the pen to scratch his bald head. "Look. I have to write a report about this, okay? I've got to write all this information up. And you're telling me that Mrs. Burgess was kidnapped and brutalized by vampires?"

Davey said, "You saw the bite wounds on her neck, didn't you?"

"Who're you?" Keaton said.

"Davey Owen. Their investigation led them to me. Along with Mrs. Burgess, they kidnapped my wife and Mr. Keoph's partner Karen Moffett. They're being held in the Royal Arms Hotel right now."

"When did this happen?" Keaton said. "Didn't you call the police?"

"There are those in the police department who cover for them," Davey said.

Keaton laughed. "Okay, I've had enough of this. Mr. Burgess—"

"But it's true," Burgess said. "What they say is true. I hired them to investigate vampires and . . . they *found* some."

"Yeah," Keaton said. "Listen, I need to know—"

Davey stepped up close to Keaton, and in that moment, his face changed—it grew hair, his brow became more pronounced, his eyes became bloodred except for a pinpoint of black in the center of each, his ears sprouted hair and became pointed, and his nose flattened and turned black on top of a snout filled with fangs.

Keaton dropped his pad and pen and immediately went for his gun as he stumbled backward and said, "Holy fucking shit!" He unholstered his weapon, then dropped it on the floor. By the time he picked it up, Davey looked himself again.

Davey slowly opened his mouth and showed his fangs. "You going to tell me I don't exist?"

Keaton returned his gun to its holster and frowned at Davey.

"I'm a vampire, Officer Keaton," Davey said. "The city is full of people like me. I'm harmless, and so is my wife—we don't want to hurt anybody. But there are a lot of vampires out there who aren't so harmless. Some of them have kidnapped my wife and Karen Moffett, and they're the same people who kidnapped Mrs. Burgess. They were unhappy about the investigation and wanted to persuade Mr. Burgess to call it off. The only problem is, that's not enough for these vampires, Officer Keaton, because they're bloodthirsty, and God only knows what they're doing to my wife and Karen Moffett."

Keaton slowly bent down and picked up his pad and pen. He took a deep breath and let it out slowly.

"Who are these . . . vampires?" Keaton said.

"They're working for Victor Barna," Davey said.

"Victor . . ." Keaton laughed. "Okay, okay, you almost had me convinced for a minute, there, but then you went over the line. You know, I hear Donald Trump heads up a little group of werewolves, maybe he and Victor Barna should get together, you think? Look, Mr. Owen, I have no idea how you did that, but keep in mind, this is Hollywood, where giant gorillas climb skyscrapers and tidal waves destroy New York, so we aren't that easily impressed here. Mr. Keoph, I'm not interested in talking to you right now, I'm talking to Mr. Burgess." He turned to Burgess. "I'll be back later to see how your wife is doing and see if she's talking. They're doing a rape kit right now, but I'm sure they'll let you in to see her soon. Look, Mr. Burgess, if you want to know my opinion, you should leave the stuff you write in the books. It doesn't work well in real life, and I really don't appreciate being fed a line like that in an investigation, okay? You'll be hearing from me soon." He looked at Keoph and Davey again. "It's been very strange meeting you, gentlemen."

Keaton turned and left the waiting room through the main entrance, out into the night.

"Didn't take him long to convince himself he didn't really see that," Davey said.

"If it's any consolation," Keoph said, "you scared the shit out of me."

CHAPTER TWENTY-SIX

Denise has a psychic," Burgess said. They sat in a booth in the diner end of a diner/cocktail lounge called Sneaky Pete's.

Davey and Burgess had cocktails in front of them while Keoph drank a diet cola, because he was driving. They had just finished a delicious steak dinner. Davey's rib-eye had been seared on the outside, but it was raw all the way through, and blood pooled on his plate, which he'd dabbed up with a dinner roll. They were awaiting their slivers of cheesecake.

"I figured, she has a psychic," Burgess said, "I can have my little investigations. I mean, she actually *listens* to this psychic and takes advice from her. But when I told her some time ago, rather vaguely, what *I* wanted to do she blew her top. She thought it was a terrible idea and would most likely be an expensive one. But I had some money put aside for . . . playing around. I was determined to go ahead with my little investigation, I just didn't tell her about it. Now this. It's my fault."

Davey said, "My guess is, they've been following you for awhile. You managed to accomplish what they apparently couldn't—you found Walter Benedek."

"And now he's dead," Burgess whispered, shaking his head. "Because of me."

"If you want to know the truth, Mr. Burgess," Davey said, "I'm amazed Walter lived as long as he did. I expected them to get to him years ago. You shouldn't be too hard on yourself. Walter was living on borrowed time, and he knew it. The story he wrote for the *Post* will not soon be forgotten. It brought them very close to exposure for a short time, and it scared them. I'm sure they've been watching Casey and me ever since my brush with them. I often wonder when my time will come. If they couldn't forgive Walter for writing that story, how must they feel about me? I blew up Live Girls. I killed a lot of them and put them closer to exposure than they've ever been. Yeah, I often wonder what they have planned for me. And when."

To Burgess, Keoph said, "Your wife is badly beaten, but she's going to get better."

"She's very fortunate," Davey said. "It's not like them to let someone go. They were sending you a message."

"I already *had* the message, before they took her," Burgess said.

"They just want to make sure you *got* the message," Davey said. "What they did to your wife—it's their way of saying, 'Is that perfectly clear?' "

Burgess scrubbed his face with both hands. "I've been doing this for eighteen years—collecting these articles, talking to people, making calls. How long have they been watching me? Is this something I'm going to have to worry about the rest of my life?"

"I think they're giving you an opportunity to back off now," Davey said. "You'll probably never know if they keep on watching you or not, so there's no point in dwelling on it. Drop your investigation. No more clippings, no more phone calls, no more interviews. Don't research anything remotely related to vampires for a good long time. But don't ever assume they've gone away."

"That's—" Burgess sighed, then shook his head. "—not very encouraging."

"I'm sorry," Davey said, "I don't mean to be discouraging. I'm just explaining to you how it will be. They're letting you go. Take advantage of it. Stay out of their way, and don't worry about them."

"But Denise," Burgess said. "What's been done to her will leave scars."

"She's going to need you," Keoph said.

"Yes," Burgess said. He sat back and thought about that for a moment. Finally, he nodded and said, "Yes, maybe she will."

After dinner, Keoph drove Burgess back to the hospital and dropped him off with the assurance that he would call them with any updates about Denise.

"Have you read his work?" Davey asked as Keoph drove them back to Davey's house.

"No, I haven't. Karen has. Have you?"

"Yes, I've read a few of his books. Some of it's genuinely spooky stuff."

Keoph shook his head and smiled. "I think he's crazier than a shithouse rat."

"Seriously?"

"I don't think you write that kind of stuff unless you're . . . well, different."

Davey chuckled. "Yeah, well, he's different all the way to the bank."

"You don't do so bad with your screenplays, do you?" Keoph said.

"They've given us a good life." Davey's face fell, and for a moment, he looked as if he were going to cry. "I'm very scared, Gavin. For my wife, I mean. Very scared."

Davey had left the porch light on when he left, so he saw the package on the porch before Keoph had even stopped the car in the driveway.

"I don't suppose you're expecting a package?" Keoph said.

Davey shook his head. "Afraid not." He got out of the car and went up the steps to the porch, with Keoph right behind him. He picked up the package and found it wasn't very heavy—a few pounds at most, securely taped up. There was nothing written on the box, no name or address, nothing at all.

He unlocked the front door and led Keoph inside. He closed and locked the door behind them. Davey took the package to the kitchen, turning on lights along the way. He put the box on the counter and took a knife from a drawer.

"Are you sure that's a good idea?" Keoph said.

"You don't have to stand in here if you don't want to," Davey said. "Go out in the living room. If it explodes, you'll be safe."

"No, wait, let me take a look at it." Keoph approached him and held out his arms for the box. Davey handed it over.

Keoph considered the weight, put his ear to the box, then moved it gently back and forth and made the object inside shift. He stood up straight and said, "I hear Styrofoam popcorn."

"I'm serious, Gavin. Go."

Keoph reluctantly left the kitchen.

Davey sliced the knife along the tape on the box. He opened the four flaps and found that it was indeed filled with the white bits of Styrofoam. He reached into the popcorn and almost instantly jerked his hand back. He had touched something that felt like cold skin.

He carefully began to sweep the popcorn out of the box using both hands.

He found a nose.

"No!" he shouted.

A clenching pain moved through his entire being as he moved his hands faster and sent the chunks of Styrofoam flying in all directions, until he could see it.

Casey's sad, dead, decayed face peered up at him, eyes and mouth open, in a pool of lustrous reddish hair.

Davey heard a strange sound, and quickly realized it was coming from him, a sound deep in his throat, which grew louder, until he was growling, and louder, until he was shouting. He did not form words, he simply cried out in a broken voice as he dropped to his knees.

Then Davey lost control.

Keoph paced in the living room until he heard Davey cry out. He turned and hurried back to the kitchen, where he jerked to a halt in the doorway.

Davey put his right hand on the back edge of a

hutch filled with china and silverware and pulled it away from the wall, knocked it over. Dishes shattered and silverware clanged.

Keoph took a step back because Davey had changed. His face was dark with hair and he bared his fangs in his snout, nose flat against the top of it, ears hairy and pointed and pink on the inside. His eyes were deepset beneath a suddenly pronounced ridge of brow. As he continued to cry out, he tore at his shirt until it was off and he threw it to the floor in tatters. There was hair on the back of his right hand, while his left remained twisted in its black glove. He grew dark hair on his chest, shoulders, arms, and back as Keoph watched.

Keoph backed out into the hall. He wondered what was in the box. He assumed the box contained a part of Casey, a part that left no doubt in Davey's mind that she was gone—only death could get that kind of reaction.

He could hear Davey breathing heavily in the kitchen, but he had stopped growling and shouting. He stepped toward the doorway and peered around the doorjamb. Davey looked like himself again. He stood with his hips leaning against the edge of the counter, bent forward at the waist with his hands on his knees, elbows locked.

"They . . . killed . . . Casey," Davey said, hoarse and breathless. "Those . . . fucking bastards . . . killed her."

Keoph stepped back into the doorway as Davey paced the length of the kitchen, rubbing his face with his right hand.

"What am I going to do?" Davey said. "What . . . what am I going to *do?*" He went to the kitchen table, sat down, and began to sob.

Keoph went over to him and put a hand on his shoulder. "Is there anything I can do, Davey?"

Davey shook his head slightly, face down.

"Would you rather I leave you alone?"

A faint nod.

Keoph left the kitchen and went to the living room. He sat down on the couch and took the television remote from the coffee table and turned it on. He channel-surfed, seeing nothing on the screen—his thoughts were too demanding.

What hope did Karen have of surviving? Keoph knew there was a chance she was already dead. But he was determined to remain positive about it and assumed she was still alive. Davey wanted to go into the Royal Arms. The thought of it made the skin shrink across the back of Keoph's neck, but he agreed that it might be necessary. If Karen had been able to get away from them on her own, she would've shown up by now. The idea of going in there terrified him, but he was not going to abandon Karen. But if he was going to do it, he wanted to be armed. He tried to think of someone he knew of in Los Angeles who might be able to provide them with weapons. No names came to mind.

Keoph stopped channel-surfing on a competition between battling robots in a caged arena. As he watched the show, he slowly drifted off to sleep.

CHAPTER TWENTY-SEVEN

Davey went upstairs and out on the deck outside his bedroom and took off all his clothes. He became airborne and flew through the night. It was a hot, humid night that would be ending in a few hours. Fat dark clouds rolled in from the north.

He could not conceive of never doing that with Casey again—taking flight just for the sake of it, to be free with her in the sky again. His marriage to Casey was the only thing in his life from which he had derived true pleasure. It had been a quiet, comfortable marriage. Davey remembered how good it had made him feel when, while sitting in his favorite chair reading a book, he had looked up to see her sitting in her favorite chair reading a book, and she had looked up at the same instant, and they had smiled. That had happened too many times to count. It had been a passionate marriage, too, and it caused Davey great physical pain, deep in his gut, to know they would never touch again.

As he flew, Davey lifted his head, opened his snout and howled. He howled at the fat, waning moon. It was a howl made up of all his pain, and the sound cut through the night like shards of glass.

His pain was dark against the white hot glow of his anger.

They had to pay for this. There was no way Davey was going to let this slide by without some kind of retaliation. He'd gone up against them before—he'd been afraid then, too, but had plowed forward and done what he'd set out to do in spite of himself.

The only difference was that this time, he had nothing to live for, so it didn't really matter to him if he lived or died.

But he couldn't do it alone. He would need help. For one thing, he would need guns.

He circled back around and returned to the deck. He stood there naked for awhile, leaning on the rail. He waited for the sobs to pass, gave them time to work themselves out. Then he slowly put his clothes on and went back inside.

Davey taped the box up and carried it out to the side of the house and dropped it into the green trash bin. The garbage man would come tomorrow and take it away.

Back in the house, Davey went to Keoph, who sat slumped on the couch watching TV. "Come on, let's go. We have to go see Mrs. Dupassie again."

They went outside, and got back into the Mercedes.

"Listen to me, Gavin," Davey said. "I'm going into that hotel, and I'm going to get Karen out. You are not obligated to go with me. It's going to be very dangerous, and I don't plan to go in alone, but I plan to take other vampires with me. You don't have to go."

"I want to go," Keoph said.

"Are you serious?"

"Getting Karen out of there is now my job," Keoph said. "I'm not going to walk away from it."

Davey sighed and unconsciously tugged at his beard.

Keoph said, "I'm serious, just tell me what to do. How do we kill them? What do you want me to do?"

"We're going to need weapons. Fully automatic weapons. Without the right weapons, there's no point going in."

"What do you want me to do?" Keoph asked again.

Davey said, "We heal fast, so if you shoot one of us with a single bullet, the bullet is just rejected by the body and the hole heals up, all within seconds. You have to keep those bullets coming, fast. That's why we need machine guns. Destroy the head if possible. If not, just keep shooting until you cut him in half. The more damage you do and the faster you do it, the better. You can't give him time to heal up, just keep firing. Pretty soon, his body won't be able to keep up with all the healing that needs to be done, and he'll die."

"I can handle that," Keoph said. "Where you going to get the guns?"

"I have no idea yet. But Mrs. Dupassie is a good place to start."

Keoph sat at the dining table with Mrs. Dupassie as Davey paced the kitchen.

"They sent me her head, Mrs. Dupassie," he said with a broken voice. "They put it in a box and sent it to me. I can't take it lying down, Mrs. Dupassie. I'm sure you understand that I have to strike back." He stopped pacing and turned to face her. "Do you understand?"

"Of course I understand, Davey," she said with a nod. "But it's so dangerous."

"I intend to get a few others together," Davey said, "and I plan to be armed to the teeth. That's why I've come to you, Mrs. Dupassie. I need some very serious guns. Do you have any idea where I can get some?"

Mrs. Dupassie put her right elbow up on the table and rested her head in the palm of her hand. "I used to know someone, Davey, but that was a long time ago, and he only dealt in handguns, nothing bigger. I'm sorry, but I'm afraid I don't know anyone right now."

Davey closed his eyes a moment as he nodded. "All right. I have one more thing to ask. There's no way I'll do this unless I can get Norman to join me."

A frown creased Mrs. Dupassie's brow. "Norman? Involved in something like that? But . . . it's very dangerous."

"With all due respect, Mrs. Dupassie, I think Norman can take care of himself, I really do," Davey said. "And you said he hates brutals. When he finds out they killed Casey, he's going to *want* to do something."

"That's true. I know him well enough to know that. But to go into that hotel . . ."

"Mrs. Dupassie, I suspect that a lot of them will look at Norman and turn tail and run."

"That could be." She turned to Keoph. "What do you think of all this?"

"I think we should go in and get Karen, and kill as many of those damned things as we can doing it," Keoph said.

Mrs. Dupassie said, "I can tell by the very way you

say that, Gavin—you have no idea what you're getting yourself into."

"I feel responsible for Karen's situation," he said. "If there's going to be a group going into that place, I want to be part of it."

"If you say so." Mrs. Dupassie went to the short bar and took another cigar from the box on the bar and lit up. Then she took the receiver from its hook and dialed a number. She waited a moment, then smiled and said, "Hello, Norman, honey. Whyn't you do me a favor and come on over here. Somebody wants to ask you something." When she was done, she hung up the phone and returned to the table.

Davey continued to pace the length of the kitchen. He seemed unaware of Keoph and Mrs. Dupassie. Finally, he stopped and turned to the old woman.

"Mrs. Dupassie," he whispered, "what am I going to do? How am I going to live without her?"

Mrs. Dupassie reached over and took his right hand between both of hers. "You're gonna do what we all do when death touches us, Davey. You're going to mourn for awhile and it'll seem like the pain will never go away. But time passes, and the pain slowly eases, until you can look at her picture without falling apart. Don't worry, Davey, it'll happen the same with you as it does with everyone else. Of course . . ." She thought about her next words carefully before saying, "If you go into that hotel, Davey, there's a chance your pain will be brought to a halt for you, if you know what I mean."

"I realize how dangerous it is, Mrs. Dupassie," Davey said. "But I don't care."

"No," she said, "I don't imagine you do."

There was a knock at the door and Mrs. Dupassie got up and went to it.

Norman ducked through the door, crossed the living room, and came to the table.

"Pull up and a chair and sit down, Norman," Mrs. Dupassie said.

The enormous young man pulled a chair away from the table and sat down, facing the others.

"Norman, I have some very bad news," Mrs. Dupassie said. "It's about Casey."

"Where's Casey tonight?" Norman said, turning to Davey. Davey bowed his head.

"Norman, some brutals killed Casey," Mrs. Dupassie said quietly.

Norman's face slowly changed—he frowned, his chin came out, his face turned red. In his lap, he clenched both hands into fists.

Mrs. Dupassie said, "They cut off her head and sent it to Davey."

He worked his jaw back and forth slowly.

"They still have Gavin's partner, Karen. Remember her?"

He nodded once.

"Well, they have her, and they're doing things to her, very bad things. Davey wants to go in and get her. He's going to get guns. He needs help."

"I'll help," Norman said. He smiled, but it was a smile of angry anticipation, with his chin jutting, and a slight sneer on the right side of his mouth. "I can help at that real good."

"I'd really appreciate your help, Norman," Davey said. "You're stronger than any of us. We really need you."

"Yeah, yeah, I'll help," Norman said. "I got some friends who'll help, too."

"Really?" Davey said.

"Yeah, three guys I know who hate the brutals as much as I do. You know them, Mrs. Dupassie—Steve and Neil and Darin. I know they'd help."

"Are you sure?" Davey said. "This is going to be dangerous."

Norman smiled. "Those guys will like it *because* it's dangerous. They're bodybuilders like me. They're . . . tough, yeah, they're real tough."

"Then by all means call them," Davey said. "See if they'd be interested in going in there with us and getting Karen out."

"Yeah, sure," Norman said. "Can I use your phone, Mrs. Dupassie?"

"Of course, Norman, honey."

As Norman talked on the phone, Keoph thought of the dark, gloomy Royal Arms Hotel in North Hollywood. He thought of storming the place armed to the teeth and looking for Karen. It wasn't something he *wanted* to do—he felt it was something he *had* to do.

Vampires. He had trouble *thinking* the word, never mind saying it aloud.

Keoph shook his head and said, "I'm still having a hard time wrapping my brain around . . . well, *vampires.* I've lived my whole life without a doubt in my mind that they were nothing more than fiction."

"We're real, all right," Mrs. Dupassie said. "And when you come face to face with one of those brutals, trust me, he'll be real enough for you, too."

Chapter Twenty-eight

The next day, Saturday, was gloomy beneath the coverage of fat dark clouds, and the air was damp, but it was still hot.

Keoph had gone back to his hotel room after leaving Mrs. Dupassie's in the early morning hours. He'd gotten a few hours of sleep, and had showered and shaved. In fresh new clothes, he felt human again as he went to a small café for breakfast. On his way back to Davey's house, it began to rain. It was a hot, sticky rain, not at all pleasant.

Davey came to the door in blue sweatpants and a white T-shirt.

"Sorry to wake you," Keoph said.

"You didn't. I wasn't sleeping, only wishing I could. I'm glad you're here. We've got work to do."

"What kind of work?"

"We need to find Isaac again. I want to ask him if

he can get us some guns. Or maybe he knows some-one who can. Let me take a quick shower and put on some sunblock and clothes, then we'll take off."

While he waited, Keoph went to the fireplace and looked at the pictures on the mantel. Almost all of them were of Davey and Casey together. They'd been a good-looking couple, and they appeared to be very much in love in the pictures.

Keoph wondered how Davey managed to hold up so well. He imagined that he, himself, would be too crushed to function. But there was an anger about Davey now—it was in his eyes and the set of his jaw, in the movements of his body. Keoph suspected that anger was what continued to propel him.

Half an hour later, Keoph was seated in Davey's Mercedes. Davey wore wraparound sunglasses as he drove them to the Corner Pocket in Sherman Oaks, where they had met with Isaac Krieger the night before.

Davey went to the bar and said to the bartender, "Has Isaac been in today?"

The bartender chuckled. "I doubt Isaac's even out of bed yet," he said.

"Does he still live in that trailer park?" Davey said.

The bartender nodded. "Far as I know."

Davey took Keoph's elbow and turned him around. "Off we go again. We'll go to his house. Or rather, his trailer."

The Twin Oaks trailer park in Encino was, as trailer parks go, pretty shabby. There were a lot of trees throughout the park—silk trees, fruitless mulberries, a couple oaks—but the shade they provided only gave the park of a gloomy look. Almost all the trailers looked like they had seen better days, and some of them were so tiny, they almost looked like toys. In front of some of the trailers, cars were up on blocks. Attempts had been made to dress up some of the spaces, like pink flamingos or sunflower pinwheels stuck in wooden boxes of brightly colored flowers.

The road through Twin Oaks was labyrinthine, sometimes turning back on itself, with dead-end side streets.

"I haven't been here in a long time," Davey said, "but I think it's up here on the right."

Davey stopped the car in front of a battered old Airstream.

"He's probably still in bed," Davey said.

They got out of the car. Davey climbed the three steps to the small porch outside the trailer's door. Keoph waited at the foot of the steps. Davey knocked on the door hard. He waited several seconds, then knocked again and said, "Isaac? It's Davey Owen."

It took awhile, but they finally heard the creak of the floor inside as someone came to the door.

"*Who* is it?" Krieger said inside.

"Davey Owen."

Krieger opened the door and stuck his head out. He squinted his eyes so much, they were almost closed. "Yeah?" he said.

"I'm sorry to wake you, Isaac," Davey said, "but I need help. It's an emergency."

"Well. Yeah. Well. Sure. Okay. Well. C'mon in."

Davey went in and Keoph followed him.

Krieger wore a pair of khaki shorts and no shirt. His upper body was tautly muscled. He had a curved scar on the right side of his chest, and a long jagged scar, several inches in length, down the left side of his back.

The trailer was a mess. Clothes and newspapers

and magazines were everywhere. The small couch was covered with blankets. The recliner was losing its stuffing from a number of holes in the brown vinyl upholstery. The place smelled of cigarette smoke and cooked grease.

"You guys sit down," Krieger said. "Just move shit outta your way. My head's fuckin' killin' me. I gotta have some hair of the dog." He went to the small kitchen area and poured some vodka into a glass, then some V-8 Juice from a can, and stirred with a spoon. He got an egg from the refrigerator and cracked it over the glass, dropped the shells on the counter. He gulped down the raw egg in the first swallow, but took a couple more gulps after that.

Krieger took one of the two chairs from the small table in the kitchen and pulled it into the living room area. He sat on the chair backwards, facing Davey and Keoph, who sat on the low couch, their knees up.

Krieger took another drink, smacked his lips, and said, "What can I do for you?"

Davey said, "Isaac, I need guns. I need machine guns."

Krieger frowned. "What're you talkin', like Uzis?"

"Exactly."

Krieger cocked his head to one side. "Davey, what've you gone and done that you need Uzis?"

"Vampires, Isaac," Davey said, barely above a whisper. "They killed my wife."

"*What* vampires killed your wife?" He drank some more of his drink.

Davey said, "We're dealing with some vampires who run a hotel in North Hollywood, the Royal Arms."

Krieger's eyes widened and his back straightened.

"The Royal Arms vampires? Fuck, man, don't tell me you got yourself in trouble with the Royal Arms vampires."

"No, Isaac, they killed my wife—they got themselves in trouble with *me*."

"You sure you know what you're doing, Davey?"

"Don't worry about me, Isaac, I'm fine. But I need guns. Can you help me?"

Krieger shrugged. "Well, *I* can't help you. But I know of somebody who can. As long as you don't mind doing business with a guy who's a little strange."

"Is he a vampire?" Davey said.

"No."

"Then I don't care how strange he is. How soon can we see him?"

Krieger frowned a little. "Well, he doesn't get up till about one or two in the afternoon. And I'll have to call him first. He's a little nervous about total strangers coming over. But I'll tell him I know and trust you guys. I should go over there with you, just to make him a little more comfortable with the whole thing."

"What's his name?" Keoph said.

"His name is Donald Melonakos. But he likes to be called Vicki."

CHAPTER TWENTY-NINE

Frank Castlebeck hated sitting in that drab, filthy lobby. It was meant to turn people away. Once in awhile, someone came in asking for a room. If the lobby alone didn't make them turn around and leave, they were told there were no vacancies. And that wasn't a lie—at the moment, there were none.

He was waiting for Anya to arrive. She was always cranky during the day—most of the vampires were—but he was hoping that the cloudy, rainy day had eased her mood a little. If so, it might work in his favor.

It was one minute to three in the afternoon, and Anya usually arrived about three or so. Castlebeck wanted to catch her before she disappeared. She was never around when she was needed, but she always seemed to be around when Castlebeck made disparaging remarks about his superiors. He had to be careful around Anya—he knew she was Barna's squeeze.

Anya was one of the vampires who gave Castlebeck an especially large case of the creeps. She was tall, with long black hair that fell to her waist. She was stunningly beautiful, but there was something about her, something Castlebeck couldn't pin down. Whatever it was, it frightened him. Castlebeck had decided long ago that if he were ever to have the opportunity to have sex with Anya—something he knew would never happen—he probably wouldn't be able to get an erection. His penis would probably shrink up and hide like a turtle. Talking to her made his testicles ascend. Maybe it was her eyes—as beautiful as they were, they were icy, with no compassion or warmth in them, and they bordered on menacing. But he had to talk to her today.

He'd just seen some footage that had taken the top of his head off. It was a clip from a rape video that was being edited. It had just been shot a couple days ago, and the girl in the video was new. It was the mortal who had come in with that vampire. She was in her late thirties, but the camera loved her and she was a natural under the lights. She looked great, and he wanted to use her again. Her name was Karen Somethingorother, but the name on her chart was Candy Starr. Whoever she was, Castlebeck knew his customers would want more of her, because she'd been incredible in the clip he'd seen. He'd like to use her in something a little more mainstream than a rape video.

As soon as Anya walked in—an umbrella in hand, sunglasses on, skin a bit shiny with sunblock, and a grocery bag held in one arm—Castlebeck stood and hurried over to her before she got to the elevator.

"Excuse me, Anya, I was wondering if I could have a moment with you," he said quickly.

She stopped walking and turned to him. "What is it, Castlebeck?"

"I'm looking for Candy Starr," he said, "but she's no longer in her room. Matthews told me you'd taken her someplace."

"That's right. Karen Moffett is no longer available to you, Castlebeck."

"I . . . I'm sorry? I don't understand."

"The beauty of it is that you don't have to. All you need to know is that she is no longer available to you, and she will no longer be living in her room. Do you understand?"

"Well, yes, I understand, but if I could be allowed one more—"

"Was there something *else* you wanted to talk to me about, Castlebeck?"

He knew the conversation was over, so he did not even try to say anything else. "No, there wasn't."

"Then I'm going upstairs to my office." She turned away and went to the elevator.

Dammit, Castlebeck thought. He wondered what had become of Karen Moffett. It was impossible to tell with vampires involved. For all he knew, she could be dead. In fact, that seemed more likely to him than anything else. Someone had drunk every last drop of her blood, or she'd died while being tortured, or something.

Castlebeck shook his head as he thought about what a shame it was, what a waste. She had looked so good in that clip, he'd immediately wanted to direct her himself, something he hadn't done in years.

As beautiful as she was, she was probably better off dead. Castlebeck knew if he had to choose between being in the hands of those vampires and dying, he'd want to check out, too.

Karen felt much better. It helped that she was now in a room with light, with a nice bed, and she was wearing a burgundy silk nightgown. There was a bathroom with a shower, which she'd used shortly after waking up in the big bed. She'd taken a long, hot shower and put the nightgown on, but her body still ached all over, and she still felt dirty. She pushed from her mind the images of what she'd endured from those thirteen men all at once, of all of them ejaculating on her. It would take a long time to wash all that away—she feared it may never go away.

There was one door in the room, but it was locked. The doorknob turned, but there was a deadbolt above it with the latch on the other side.

The room was equipped with a television and a stereo system, a couch, a chair, a small coffee table, everything in creams and earth tones. There was a colorful abstract painting on the wall above the couch.

As comfortable as her surroundings were, Karen was still afraid. She did not feel groggy anymore and was getting her strength back, but she was afraid of what would come next. Her body ached everywhere. The hot shower had helped some, but she still felt as if she'd taken a beating. She reminded herself that she had.

Karen was on the couch watching television when she heard movement outside the door. She quickly grabbed the remote and turned off the TV, and curled her legs under her.

The door swung open and Anya came in carrying a tray with a bottle of champagne and two glasses on it, and something else.

Instead of staring at the tray, Karen quickly looked beyond Anya through the open door. All she saw was part of a wall before Anya kicked the door closed.

"I hope you like champagne and caviar," Anya said as she put the tray on the coffee table. The tray also held a mound of caviar in the center of a plate, surrounded by crackers.

"I love caviar," Karen said, her voice hoarse.

"Good. Help yourself, and don't be shy."

Karen put her feet on the floor and bent forward, took a cracker, and scooped up some caviar on a corner. She was starving. While she did that, Anya popped the cork from the champagne bottle and poured it into the two fluted crystal glasses. She handed a glass to Karen, lifted hers, and said, "To you and me."

Karen did not return the gesture before sipping the champagne. "What's the occasion?" she said.

"I thought you knew. You've been brought here to my apartment in the building. I never use it, so I've moved you in here. You have clothes, a television, music if you want. I thought you would at least be grateful."

"I am grateful. Very grateful. But how long will I be here? When will you let me go?"

"Who knows, Karen," Anya said with a smile as she sat on the couch, "maybe with enough champagne and caviar, you won't *want* to go."

"That doesn't answer my question."

Anya sighed, then sipped her champagne. "Your friends have been told you will not be coming back. That you are the price of investigating us."

"What about Casey? Where is she?"

"You're full of questions, aren't you?"

Karen said nothing. She scooped up more caviar on a cracker and ate it. She wondered if Anya could hear her stomach growling.

"You and I are going to be together for awhile, Karen," Anya said. "We're going to have a relationship, and I think it should be an honest one, don't you? So I will tell you where Casey is. She's dead. Her head was cut off and sent to Davey Owen. That's *his* price for blowing up Live Girls back in 1987, killing a lot of vampires, and nearly exposing us. You, on the other hand, are in this comfortable apartment, drinking champagne and eating caviar. Do you understand? I'm trying to tell you that if I wanted you dead, you'd be dead already. So you can relax. You're afraid of me, and I don't want you to be."

Karen sat back and looked down at her lap for a long moment. She thought of Casey, of Davey, and her throat burned with tears. But she held them back. She was determined not to cry in front of this woman.

"Are you . . . will you ever let me go?" Karen said without looking up.

"Worry about that later, Karen," Anya said. She bent forward and poured more champagne into their glasses on the coffee table. She scooted closer to Karen on the couch and put her left arm across her shoulders. "Let's try that toast again," she said as she lifted her glass. "To us."

After a moment, Karen lifted her glass and touched

it to Anya's with a musical *ting*. "To us," she said. She sipped the champagne. It made her head feel a touch fizzy, and she began to feel groggy again. She said, "I'm not . . . I haven't . . ." She took a deep breath and let it out in a big puff. "I'm straight."

Anya smiled as she moved in and said, "I don't mind."

Karen wanted to move her head, but she could not, and Anya's lips pressed to hers. Anya opened her mouth and lightly traced her tongue around Karen's lips. Karen wanted to protest, to push her away, but a wave of physical weakness passed through her and she slowly slid over on her side, with Anya on top of her, still kissing her.

Anya sat up and put their champagne glasses on an end table. She kept her eyes open and looked directly into Karen's. As Anya kissed her again, strength drained from Karen's body like blood from a wound. The room darkened until she could see nothing but Anya's eyes. She felt Anya's hands moving over her body and they seemed to deliver an electrical current that made Karen tremble.

Anya pulled the nightgown up and up, and Karen sat up so Anya could pull it off over her head. She lay back on the couch naked as Anya slowly, lightly ran her fingertips all over Karen's body. Her eyes slowly closed as she became immersed in the sensation. It was like butterflies fluttering their wings against her, all over her body.

Karen's heart beat faster, her breaths became tremulous. Her hands bunched into fists at her sides as electricity coursed through her body, and she became wet. She could no longer feel the couch beneath her there was nothing in the world but the sensation of Anya's fingertips running all over her body. Karen lost all track of time and it seemed to go on forever, until the only sound she could hear was that of her heart pounding in her ears.

When Anya kissed her again, Karen surrendered and opened her mouth. Their tongues met and writhed together. Anya kissed her throat then, kissed her shoulder, her chest, then put her mouth over Karen's left breast. She nibbled on Karen's nipple until it became hard as a pebble, then she moved to the other breast, and all the while, her fingertips continued to pass up and down over Karen's body.

Anya kissed her way down to the triangle of auburn hair between Karen's legs. With the fingers of her right hand, she separated Karen's labia and ran her tongue up and down between them slowly, kissed her, sucked and nibbled.

Karen cried out as Anya put her mouth over her erect clitoris, sucked it in hard, and rapidly flicked her tongue over it, then slipped a finger inside her, then another finger. Karen clawed at the couch and clenched her teeth as she thrust her hips forward, pressing herself against Anya's mouth.

She felt a sharp sting in her groin, but barely noticed it because Anya was fucking her with her fingers. She did not hear the sucking sounds because of the thundering of her heart.

Karen felt herself melt into a liquid mass, a puddle on the couch. She heard her own cries of release as if from a great distance as she exploded with one orgasm after another. They came in great waves that splashed over her and made her dissolve.

There was a moment when everything, even the sensations, blacked out and she floated in utterly silent darkness, everything forgotten. Then the feelings rushed in again in wave after wave.

Even after Anya stopped touching her, Karen's body continued to shudder with pleasure as she slowly came down, gasping for breath.

Karen opened her eyes and saw Anya smiling down at her. Something dark was smeared by the right corner of Anya's mouth, and she licked it away.

"Now, aren't you glad you came here?" Anya whispered. "You rest. I'll be back later for something a little more . . . mutual. I'll bring some more food, too. Is there anything in particular you'd like?"

Karen opened her mouth but could not speak. She still had no voice.

"Don't worry," Anya said, "I'll bring something good."

Karen closed her eyes for a moment, and when she opened them again, Anya was gone. She'd heard the door open and close.

She tried to sit up but could not. She was completely drained of energy, empty and limp. She lay there naked on the couch and drifted off to sleep.

Chapter Thirty

Vicki LaRue lived in an expensive neighborhood in Toluca Lake, in a development called Vistawood. The homes were a good distance apart in hilly country. Davey stopped at the gate as a camera watched them. In the backseat, Isaac rolled down his window and said, "Hey, Vick, it's me!"

Keoph wondered what they were getting into. "Look," he said to Davey, "I think we should make this visit as short as possible, okay?"

Davey shrugged. "If you want. Why?"

"A place where illegal guns are being sold is not a safe place to hang out, okay?" he said.

"Oh, yeah," Davey said, nodding, "that makes sense. Okay, we'll try to keep it short."

Vicki had a sprawling estate at the end of a long driveway through a patch of enormous oak trees. Davey parked the Mercedes in the circular drive in front of the house. As Isaac led them up the front steps, the double doors opened and in the doorway stood a handsome, olive-skinned man wearing a pewter-colored negligee and black mules with heels.

"Hello, Isaac," the man said, making no effort to disguise his deep voice. "How are you?"

Vicki wasn't very effeminate, and he appeared to be a little shaky on those heels.

"Vicki, this is Davey Owen and Gavin Keoph. Guys, this is Vicki LaRue."

"Gentlemen, a pleasure," Vicki said, shaking their hands. He had a strong grip. "Why don't we go inside." He stood back and welcomed them with a flourish of his arm. Vicki closed the doors behind them, then led them to a room in the back of the house. "This is the library, although I haven't read very many of the books in here. I stick to Jackie Collins and that ilk, myself. Maybe a little Mary Higgins Clark now and then, but not often, because her books keep me up nights."

Vicki went to one of the enormous bookshelves and pulled it easily away from the wall. There was a door behind it, which Vicki opened.

"In here, gentlemen," he said. He turned to lead them through the door, then stopped and turned back to them. "You know, I'm usually a good judge of people, and you don't look to me like the type of guys who need guns. You know what I mean?"

Keoph said, "We'd rather not answer any questions, if you don't mind."

"Oh, I'm not asking questions, I know better than to do that in my business. Just making an observation. You'll have to forgive me, I talk too much. At least, that's what my wife is always telling me. Especially when we go shopping together. People just open up to me once we start talking, I make friends very easy. In fact, in the shop where I bought this negligee, I started talking to the girl who waited on me, and by the time we were done, she'd told me she was from Texas, had just broken up with her boyfriend, and had had two abortions before she turned twenty. It drove my wife crazy. She didn't want to hear all that, so I—oh, look at me. I'm doing it again. I'm sorry. This way, gentlemen."

Keoph and the others followed Vicki through the door into a large room that was full of guns. There were guns everywhere—on the walls, on shelves, in cabinets—*everywhere*.

Vicki turned to them and folded his arms across his chest. "All right, gentlemen, what are you looking for?"

Davey said, "We're looking for some kind of machine gun, something light and . . . convenient."

"Well, I have a wide variety to choose from. What do you say we try a few out?"

Vicki gathered up a number of guns and took them down some stairs from his secret room to his basement, where he had a shooting range. He gave them headphonelike protectors to put over their ears for protection from the loud noise of the guns. Keoph tried different machine guns and machine pistols, and decided he preferred the HK MP5 submachine gun. Isaac tried a couple, too, for the fun of it, but mostly he just stayed out of the way.

Davey's useless hand created a problem. He could not shoot a submachine gun with just one arm, but he couldn't clutch the hand guard with his left hand.

"I think I have something that might work for you," Vicki said. "I'll be back in a few minutes, don't go away."

While Vicki was gone, Keoph fired the MP5 some more.

Vicki returned with a rather short, black shotgun. Its barrel and the magazine tube beneath it were a little over a foot long. It was semi-automatic, with a synthetic stock and sights like a rifle, rather than the small gold bead on the end of the barrel. In his other hand, he held some kind of strap.

"Not too long ago," Vicki said, "I had a client who'd lost his left arm. We devised this contraption to allow him to shoot with just one arm. I had three made, but he only bought two, so I've got this one left over." He unfolded the long, wide slingstrap, which he attached to the stock, and to the slingswivel on the magazine tube. He hoisted the sling over Davey's head and onto his left shoulder. The shotgun hung at his right side, parallel to the floor. Along the sling were stitched a couple dozen loops filled with fat black 12-gauge cartridges. "Now," Vicki said, "slide your left hand through this loop." Davey slipped his gloved hand through a wide, padded, nylon loop attached to the same forward clip as the sling. Vicki cinched down a Velcro strap on his arm. "All you need now," Vicki said, "is a bag to carry more cartridges. Isn't this nice?"

"It's perfect," Davey said. He raised and lowered his left arm and guided the shotgun's muzzle up and down, then left and right. With his right hand, he took a cartridge from the loop on the strap and fed it into the magazine. He put in one cartridge after another, until the magazine was full. He reached up and pulled the bolt back and released it, allowing it to slam forward and chamber the first round.

"You've got the hang of it already," Vicki said.

"Thank you, Vicki," Davey said.

"You can try the gun out in a minute. But first, I brought something else down that you might be interested in," Vicki said. He went out the door, and came back a moment later with a box. He removed something from the box and handed it to Kcoph, a black cannister that fit niccly in his hand.

"A hand grenade?" Davey said.

"This is an XM84 stun grenade," Vicki said. "Set this off in a room full of people and nobody gets hurt, but it stuns them for awhile. Would you have any use for them?"

Davey said, "Yes," and Keoph said, "Absolutely," at the same time.

Vicki smiled. "Very good. What do you say we try a couple out, just so you'll know what to expect?"

Davey's cell phone chirped and he took it from his pocket, flipped it open. "Hello?" As he listened, he turned to Keoph. "Yes, Mrs. Dupassie, I'm very interested, but I'm kind of busy at the moment. Would you mind if we came over to your place in the next hour? . . . Great, that's what we'll do then. Thank you." He folded the phone up and put it back in his pocket. "That was Mrs. Dupassie," he said to Kcoph. "She's picked something up about Karen and wants to talk to us. We'll go over there as soon as we're done here."

Vicki clapped his hands and rubbed them together as he smiled and said, "Well, shall we set off a couple grenades?"

* * *

After Davey made a trip to the bank for a lot of cash, they left Vicki LaRue's house with five HK MP5 sub-machine guns, sixty magazines capable of holding thirty rounds each, three cases of 9mm ammunition, the shotgun and strap device and lots of ammunition, and eight XM84 stun grenades in a box in the trunk.

Before leaving, Davey asked Vicki if it would be possible to use his shooting range later that night.

"We've got some guys who've never used these guns before and need a chance to get familiar with them," Davey said, "but we have nowhere to go. If we could use your range awhile tonight, I'd sure appreciate it."

"Nothing makes me happier than the sound of gun-fire in my shooting range," Vicki said with a smile. "Does nine o'clock sound okay?"

"Perfect," Davey said.

"I'll be expecting you."

It was still raining outside, still hot and sticky.

Davey drove Isaac to his trailer and dropped him off, then drove to Mrs. Dupassie's apartment. The shades were all pulled down to keep out the sunlight, and the apartment was dark.

The old woman looked tired.

"It woke me up from a sound sleep," she said after letting them in. They went to the small dining table and sat down. "See, if I'm looking to pick something up on someone, I'll sometimes handle the personal item for awhile before going to bed, and sometimes I get something in my sleep. It's something more than a dream—more vivid, more . . . immediate. More of a vision. So this morning, before going to bed, I held

Karen's purse for awhile. I picked something up in my sleep."

She got up and went to the refrigerator, where she got a bottle of blood.

"Anything to drink for either of you?" she said.

"I could use some of that," Davey said.

"Nothing for me," Keoph said.

She got another bottle of blood and handed it to Davey as she sat down. "For awhile, all I got was darkness. But that's changed. Karen is now in a nice room with a nice bed, clothes, light, a television. She's been moved."

"From the hotel?" Keoph said.

"No, I don't think she's been taken out of the building, but she's been moved to a different place, another room, something like that."

"Anything else?" Davey said

"I get the sense that she's up off the ground, up high," Mrs. Dupassie said.

"Like on an upper floor?" Keoph said.

She nodded. "Yes. She's definitely not on the ground floor."

"That's helpful," Davey said.

Keoph said, "It's still not going to be easy to find her in there. I'm sure she's locked up."

"No, it won't be easy," Davey said.

"But I don't like the alternative," Keoph said.

"Is there anything else, Mrs. Dupassie?"

Mrs. Dupassie said, "I don't know what's been done to her, but she's been hurt in some way, and she feels . . . filthy. She feels defiled, contaminated. But most of all, she's terrified."

* * *

Davey drove them back to his place in Laurel Canyon.

"When are we going to do this?" Keoph said once they were inside.

"We can't do it today," Davey said. "It's late in the afternoon. I want to do it late morning, or noon, thereabouts. We'll have to wait till tomorrow. They'll be at their weakest then. I still expect a fight, but midday is the most vulnerable time for us, we're weak and not thinking as clearly as usual. That's why we sleep during the day. Of course, that means that I and Norman and his friends will be weak, too. So, in the meantime, I'm going to get some sleep. I suggest you do the same. You can stay here if you want, we've got three guest rooms."

"I think I'll do that," Keoph said. "To tell you the truth, I don't feel all that safe wandering around out there."

"That's wise. Let's take a look at the hotel's plans."

Keoph got the plans and rolled the sheet out on the dining table. They took the two candlesticks from the center of the table and put them on each curled end of the sheet. They studied the plans silently for awhile.

"We could always go in the front door, guns blazing," Davey said.

"That might draw a lot of attention to us," Keoph said.

"Yeah, we don't want that."

After thinking for awhile, Keoph said, "Look, there's a sub-basement connected to the storm drain. Providing we can remove one of those damned manhole covers, we can go down the manhole, go to the hotel's sub-basement, go up through the basement and into the hotel."

"Excellent plan," Davey said. "As for the manhole cover—we'll take a crowbar. Hell, maybe Norman could lift it off."

"I think Norman could lift most things," Keoph said.

"There's no way I'll be able to get down a manhole with that shotgun contraption on me. I'll have to put it on once we're down there."

They both yawned as they rolled the plans up.

Davey called Norman and told him to get his friends together and meet him and Keoph at Mrs. Dupassie's at eight-thirty that evening. From there, they would go to Vicki's and get familiar with their guns.

"I'm going to bed," Davey said after hanging up the phone.

"Yeah, me, too," Keoph said.

"I'll set an alarm and come wake you up."

"Sounds good."

Davey showed Keoph his room. Keoph closed the door, kicked his shoes off, and flopped onto the bed. He was asleep in less than a minute.

CHAPTER THIRTY-ONE

After taking a second shower, Karen put the nightgown back on, limped to the bed, and stretched out.

She couldn't make herself clean enough. She feared she never would.

She was having difficulty with her experience with Anya. She had never been with a woman before and found the idea mildly repulsive. But she had never experienced sex so intense, so completely immersing—Anya had made her feel pleasure she had not known possible. Afterward, though—after Anya had left and Karen had slept for awhile—it bothered her. It made her feel even dirtier. It made her feel something she hadn't felt since she was a child—shame.

There were no clocks anywhere in the room and her watch had been taken from her, so she did not know how much time passed until Anya came back into the room.

"I hope you like Chinese," Anya said. She carried a brown paper bag and put it on the coffee table. From the bag, she removed four cartons of Chinese take-out.

Karen was famished. She'd finished off the caviar and crackers earlier, but that seemed so long ago, and had not been very satisfying. She unwrapped the chopsticks, pulled them apart, and opened the cartons. It all smelled so good, she started eating even before she knew exactly what it was she was putting into her mouth.

"How would you like some music?" Anya said. "You like Norah Jones?"

Karen did not respond—she was too busy eating. She did not look at Anya, did not make eye contact with her. She kept her head down as she ate.

Norah Jones began to sing over the stereo speakers, the volume low.

"I like Norah Jones," Anya said. She sat down on the couch beside Karen, reached over and touched her earlobe.

Karen jerked away, startled.

"You're still afraid of me, Karen," Anya said. "I don't want you to be afraid of me."

"Then leave me alone," Karen whispered after swallowing some food. "Then let me go, if you don't want me to be afraid of you."

"I could do that. But I don't want to. Do you know that your eyes are among the most beautiful I've ever seen? And I've been around a long time, Karen, a very long time. I've seen a lot of eyes. I've watched the life drain from a lot of them. Others, I have just . . . loved. You're a beautiful woman, Karen. I enjoy giving you pleasure. This evening, we're going to give each other pleasure."

Karen continued to eat.

"I can make you, you know," Anya said. "I can and I will. That's the only reason you're here, Karen. As soon as I saw you, I wanted you. I get what I want. Always. I take it, because I never expect anyone to give it to me. And because I can."

Karen said nothing as she chewed her food.

"You don't believe me?" Anya said.

No response from Karen. She went on eating, until she felt a dull ache in her head. It quickly grew worse and she stopped chewing, closed her eyes, and put a hand to her temple.

"You're getting a nasty headache, aren't you, Karen?"

Karen put down the chopsticks and pressed the fingertips of both hands to her temples as the pain grew worse.

"It feels like someone is stabbing a hot poker through the center of your skull, doesn't it?" Anya said.

The pain became steadily, rapidly worse, until she was pressing both palms to the side of her head, eyes tightly closed. Through clenched teeth, she said, "Please . . . stop."

The pain was gone instantly, but not before tears spilled down Karen's cheeks.

"See?" Anya said. "The pain's gone, that quickly. Like I said, I can make you if you refuse. I can make you do anything." She reached over and slowly ran her hand through Karen's hair. "If I wanted, I could give you eternal life. Did you know that? You would never age a day afterward. I *could*. If I wanted to. But I've learned to be very careful about whom I turn. It'll all depend on how cooperative you are this evening. But you go ahead and eat now. I know you're hungry."

She lightly touched the back of Karen's neck, then came around and stroked her throat with a knuckle. "You have such beautiful skin. You must take good care of yourself. Do you moisturize?"

Karen said nothing. Instead, she fought the urge to shrink away from Anya's touch. She picked up a carton of Peking beef and continued eating.

"You eat until you're full," Anya said. "I have some wine, too, if you'd like."

No response.

"Okay," Anya said. "You eat and I'll be back in a little while."

As soon as Anya left, Karen looked around the small apartment again. No windows, and only one locked door. The room seemed smaller now than it had earlier. She felt claustrophobic. She paid no attention to it and went on eating. She ate until she felt like she would explode. It felt good to be full, sated. She lay back on the couch with a hand on her belly and fell asleep.

She awoke to a kiss from Anya. When she opened her eyes, Anya's face filled her field of vision, smiling.

Anya took Karen's hand and lifted her to a sitting position. "Come with me," she whispered.

Karen got up and allowed Anya to lead her to the bed. She suddenly felt sick to her stomach. She did not want to do what was about to be done.

"Take off the nightgown," Anya said.

Slowly, Karen removed the gown. She trembled, afraid she was about to throw up. Naked, Karen lay on the bed.

Anya began to remove the forest green suit she wore, a suit that made her look like a savvy businesswoman, a mover and shaker. In that suit, she looked like she should be carrying a briefcase. "We can do this the easy way," Anya said as she undressed, "or I can make you. It's up to you, Karen." Clothes off, Anya got onto the bed with her. "What'll it be."

Karen's lips pressed together so hard, they turned white. She said, "You'll . . . have to make me."

"All right, then. But it's much more fun when you play along."

Karen said nothing more.

Anya lay down on her back beside Karen.

Karen lay there for awhile and did nothing. Then she felt herself sitting up and rolling toward Anya. Against her will, Karen kissed her. She passed her hand over Anya's ample breasts and slowly moved it down, down, until it was between her thighs. Karen could not fight it. She could not even *try* to fight it. Her actions were completely out of her control. She tried to make her body go limp, but nothing happened—she continued to kiss Anya's body and stroke her middle finger up and down between her labia as she grew moist. She felt like a big marionette, as if she were being manipulated by some great puppeteer.

She closed her eyes as she kissed her way slowly down Anya's body, until her mouth touched the strip of hair that went down the center of Anya's trimmed pudenda. She smelled Anya's musky odor. Her eyes remained closed as she buried her face between Anya's legs and tasted her moisture. She slipped her tongue inside Anya, completely against her will. She tried to groan, to make some sound of protest, but she had no voice. She was allowed to lift her head for a breath, but went right back to what she was doing.

Anya squirmed and moaned and clutched at the blankets as Karen licked her, sucked on her clitoris, and finally slipped a finger inside her.

Karen was doing to Anya exactly what Anya had done to her.

She loathed every second of it.

As she made love to Anya unwillingly, she wondered where Keoph was. Was he looking for her? What had become of Davey after Casey's death? It seemed she had been locked away for a long time—weeks, perhaps even months.

Anya cried out as she reached orgasm. She reached down and put both hands on Karen's head and pressed Karen's face to her hand.

When it was over, Karen found she was once again in control of her own body. She rolled off Anya and gasped for breath, Anya's fluids glistening on her face.

They lay there in silence for a long time, both naked and breathing hard.

Finally, once her breathing calmed down, Anya sat up and got off the bed. She started to put her clothes back on.

"I have work to do," she said. "But I'll be back. I'll spend tomorrow here with you. We can sleep together." She grinned. "And play together."

After Anya left, Karen got up, went to the bathroom, and vomited into the toilet. She took another shower, a long one. Long and hot. She scrubbed her body furiously, but she could not remove the filth.

CHAPTER THIRTY-TWO

As I said before," Vicki said as they went back upstairs from the basement, "nothing makes me happier than the sound of gunfire in my shooting range. I have friends who come over and use it frequently. I'm so glad you gentlemen got some use out of it tonight. Is everyone comfortable with their guns now?" Vicki was in full makeup and wore a dark-blue pantsuit and a pair of black pumps.

They had spent two hours familiarizing themselves with their guns—Keoph, Davey, Norman, and Norman's three friends, Darin and Steve and Neil.

"I think it helped a lot, Vicki, thank you," Davey said.

Keoph was impressed with Norman's three friends. They were not as big as Norman, but they were quite sizeable with what appeared to be muscles on muscles. Unlike Norman, their bellies were flat, and their tight T-shirts displayed their six-pack abs. But Norman, who had been very quiet all evening, towered above them and looked more menacing.

Darin was of average height with buzz-cut blond hair; Steve was shorter and had completely shaved his head; Neil was the tallest of three and heavily tattooed, with long black hair in a ponytail, and large intense eyes. They all looked young, no older than their early twenties.

Vicki had instructed them on the use of the HK MP5 submachine guns, and had set off another couple of the XM84 stun grenades so they would know what to expect when they used them.

"Could I interest you gentlemen in a drink?" Vicki said as they headed down a hall to the front of the house.

"I could sure use one," Keoph said.

Vicki took them into the den, where there was a full bar. "What's your poison, Gavin?" he said.

"Scotch, please. Neat."

"One scotch coming up," Vicki said as he went behind the bar. "Anyone else?"

"Nothing for me," Davey said.

Norman and his friends just shook their heads. They'd hardly said a word all evening. Keoph had noticed their failed attempts not to stare at Vicki when he wasn't looking.

A lovely blond woman in a long robe came in with a wineglass in hand.

"Gentlemen," Vicki said, "this is my wife Lynn." He introduced all of them to her and Keoph and Davey said hello.

"I came for a little more wine," Lynn said with a smile.

"Allow me," Vicki said. There was a half-full bottle

of red wine on the bar. Vicki uncorked it and poured some into Lynn's glass.

"I'll leave you boys and go back to the old movie I'm watching," she said, then left the den.

"She's great," Vicki said after she left. With a laugh, he added, "We do all our clothes shopping together."

Vicki poured Keoph's drink and handed it to him. "I'm not asking, so don't think I'm being nosy, but I'd sure love to know what you boys are up to with these guns and grenades. Am I going to read about you in the paper?"

Davey smiled and said, "We're hunting vampires."

Vicki tilted his head back and laughed. "All right, I get it, no more questions." He poured himself some wine and lifted his glass. "To good luck in whatever you're doing," he said.

Keoph raised his glass and nodded before taking a sip.

They were going to need all the luck they could get.

In the car, as Davey drove them away from Vicki's house, he said to Keoph, "I thought you wanted to get out of there fast."

Keoph shrugged. "I really needed that drink. Firing those guns suddenly made it . . . I don't know . . . *real*. Know what I mean?"

"Oh, yeah."

Keoph turned in his seat and looked at the four muscular boys cramped together in back. "You guys know the schedule, now?" he said.

They all nodded.

"We meet at Mrs. Dupassie's tomorrow at eleven," Keoph said. "From there, we go to the hotel. Davey and I are going to go over there tonight and look for manholes. We'll try to find one that's nearby but not too out in the open because we'll be climbing down there in broad daylight with guns and grenades, so we can't afford to be seen."

"What if we *are* seen?" Norman said.

Keoph looked at Davey. "That's a good question."

Davey said, "We just have to look like we've got every right in the world to do what we're doing, and we've got to do it fast."

"Maybe we should put the guns in something," Keoph said.

"That's not a bad idea."

They dropped Norman and his friends off outside Norman's house in Sherman Oaks. Then Davey drove to a nearby all-night Walgreens drugstore. He and Keoph went into the store and found some grey canvas satchels with shoulder straps. Each was just big enough to carry one of the guns, extra magazines, and a couple grenades. Davey's shotgun wouldn't quite fit in the satchel, so he would have to be as inconspicuous as he could on the way from the car to the manhole. Davey bought five of the satchels, and a simple black cloth purse with a long shoulder strap.

Back in the car, Keoph said, "What's the purse for?"

"Something for me to carry more cartridges in."

"Mrs. Dupassie says Karen's not on the first floor, so as soon as we get in there, we should go upstairs."

"The elevator goes down to the basement," Davey said. "We can use that."

Keoph's neck and shoulders were tight and achy. There was tension in his voice—in Davey's, too.

We're really going to do this, Keoph thought. He felt a tingle move down his back. Davey and Norman and Norman's friends had an advantage—they were vampires. Keoph was far more vulnerable than they.

Davey drove them to North Hollywood, to the Royal Arms Hotel. He drove by slowly.

The hotel was on the corner of Newton and a narrow side street called Halley. On the opposite corner was a strip mall with only one store, a nail salon—the other windows had FOR LEASE signs in them. Davey pulled into a gas station down the street and turned around, went back by the hotel, and turned down Halley. Behind the strip mall was a deserted lot, and beyond that, an apartment complex. Davey made a U-turn in front of the apartments, went back up Halley, pulled into the strip mall, and parked.

"Come on," Davey said. "Let's see if we can find any manholes."

They got out of the Mercedes and walked away from the strip mall to Halley.

"There," Keoph said when he spotted one in the glow of a streetlight.

Davey went back to the Mercedes and opened the trunk. He came back with a crowbar and they went to the mahole. Davey shone his light on the cover.

There was a hole near the edge of the manhole cover. Davey wedged the end of the crowbar in the hole and lifted. It was heavy, but the cover came up. He let it drop again, and said, "Come on."

Davey put the crowbar behind his seat as he got into the car.

As Davey pulled out of the strip mall parking lot, Keoph said, "It worked."

"Yep, that's all I wanted to know. Now, I suggest we go back to my place and you get a good night's sleep," Davey said. "If you can't get to sleep, I've got some sleeping pills in the medicine cabinet, I think. You need to rest up and be ready for tomorrow. I'll go to bed early in the morning and sleep awhile before we go. They'll be sluggish in the middle of the day—the only problem is, so will we. Our advantages will be surprise and those guns. Since all the victims are probably locked up, I think it'll be safe to shoot anything that moves, and keep shooting until it goes down and stays down." He looked at Keoph a couple times and said, "You ever shoot anybody before?"

"Once," Keoph said. "Early in my career. This woman hired me to find her husband, who had disappeared a week or so earlier. She knew he'd run out on her, but she wanted me to find him so she could get a divorce and hit him up for child support. I traced him to Las Vegas. He caught me following him and didn't like it. He took a shot at me. I took a shot at him. He missed, but I caught him in the thigh."

"What happened to the guy?"

"His gun was stolen. He was arrested in the hospital emergency room. I'm assuming his wife got what she wanted, but I didn't stick around to find out. It was just my job to track him down, which I'd done. Of course, I ended up going to court as a witness. It was a big hassle."

"How long have you been a private investigator?"

"Twenty years. Almost twenty-one."

"Ever do anything else?"

Keoph shook his head. "Nothing else ever interested me. I'm not sure I could do something else if I had to."

They arrived at Davey's house and went inside.

"I'm a little too wound up to sleep," Keoph said. "I think I'll take one of those sleeping pills."

Davey got it for him and he drank it down with a

glass of water. He wished Davey a good night, and went to bed. He lay naked in bed, staring into the darkness, unable to think of anything other than what they were going to do tomorrow, and Karen. Keoph was not a hero. He typically was not the kind to walk into a dangerous situation. But neither was he the kind to walk away from one if someone's life was in danger. He hoped Karen was okay. He felt responsible for her abduction, for the whole investigation. He'd had a weird feeling about it from the beginning and he should have said no—maybe Karen would have declined then, too.

The pill kicked in half an hour later, and Keoph drifted off to sleep.

CHAPTER THIRTY-THREE

The next morning, Davey drove them to Mrs. Dupassie's. On the way, he kept yawning.

"You look tired," Keoph said.

"Like I said, this isn't the best time of day for us," Davey said. "I drank more coffee than usual, but I still feel tired, weak."

"Are you guys going to be up to this?" Keoph said.

"Don't worry, as long as we can shoot those guns, we'll be fine."

The plans of the Royal Arms Hotel were in the backseat. Davey took the rolled up sheet with him when they got out of the car.

Mrs. Dupassie had had a new screen door installed, and Davey knocked on it when they arrived.

The old woman came to the door slowly and looked heavy with fatigue.

"I just woke up," Mrs. Dupassie said as she let

them in, "so you'll have to forgive me if I'm a bit muddy. Coffee's on if you want some."

Once inside the apartment, Davey said, "Have you picked up anything more, Mrs. Dupassie?"

"I just gave it another try," Mrs. Dupassie said. "I'm afraid it's not good. Your friend feels filthy, defiled. It seems she's been raped multiple times, from what I can tell. She feels lost, abandoned. She assumes you have no idea where she is, and will never be able to come get her."

Keoph sighed. Once again, he wished they hadn't taken on the investigation.

Hearing that Karen Moffett had been repeatedly raped made Davey wonder what Casey had gone through before they killed her. He felt another hole rip open inside him when he thought about Casey. He tried to keep his mind on the task at hand.

"Tell me something," Mrs. Dupassie said. "Are you boys sure you know what the fuck you're doing?"

"We're going to be fine, Mrs. Dupassie," Davey said. "We'll be armed to the teeth, and we have surprise on our side."

Keoph said, "What can you tell us about Victor Barna, Mrs. Dupassie?"

She led them over to the dining table, where they sat down.

"You want coffee?" Mrs. Dupassie said. When they both said yes, she poured for them and took the mugs to the table. "Victor Barna. That rat-prick. You won't run into him at the hotel. He keeps his distance and has others running things for him there. He stays in his office and penthouse in the city. Of course, he doesn't want to be connected to the Royal Arms, and he's gone to great lengths to see that he isn't. He may show up there once in awhile for all I know, but it's probably fucking rare, and probably only in the middle of the night."

Norman, Darin, Steve, and Neil arrived about fifteen minutes after Davey and Keoph.

Norman sat at the dining table while the other three stood nearby. They yawned repeatedly. Mrs. Dupassie poured coffee for them.

"Out in the car," Davey said, "I've got your guns, ammo, and stun grenades in canvas satchels. That way, we won't have to carry the guns out in the open when going from the car to the manhole."

"How do we get in there, Davey?" Norman said.

Davey put the plans on the table and Keoph helped him unroll them. They put a coffee mug at each end.

Davey said, "We go down the manhole. We find our way to this sub-basement," he said, pointing to the sub-basement on the sheet.

"What if we can't get in?" Neil said.

Davey sighed. "That's a very good question. I'm afraid we haven't gone down there and planned this thing out that carefully. We'll figure that out when we get down there. We get into the sub-basement and climb up to the basement. From there, we take an elevator. Norman, I want you on the second floor, Steve and Darin the third, and Neil the fourth. Gavin and I will take the top floor. The woman we're looking for is on one of those floors. Mrs. Dupassie has determined that she's not on the first floor, so we won't even bother with it."

"How do we find her?" Darin asked.

Keoph said, "Davey and I have decided our only choice is to go down the hall calling her name. That'll draw attention. Since all the victims are most likely locked up, you're probably going to see nothing but vampires. When you do, shoot them. Keep shooting them until they go down and stop moving. You know as well as I do that just a few bullets won't cut it. We have to keep shooting so they don't have time to heal up, keep shooting until they're dead."

"Boys," said Mrs. Dupassie, "I want to make sure you understand how dangerous this is."

"Don't worry, Mrs. Dupassie," Norman said. "We do. We've talked about it. It's okay. We don't get a chance to take out brutals very often. We all want to do this."

Mrs. Dupassie looked at the other boys. "Is that true? You all want to do this?"

Darin said, "Yes, ma'am," and Neil said, "Yep," and Steve said, "Uh-huh," all at once.

"All right," she said with a tilt of her head. "I just wanna make sure you know what the fuck you're doing."

"Do you all feel confident you can handle the guns?" Davey said.

They all agreed that they did.

"Well, then," Davey said, "that's it. Let's go." He rolled up the plans. "Mind if I leave this here, Mrs. Dupassie?"

"Fine with me," she said. "Soon as you leave, I'm hittin' the fucking sack."

Darin scratched his head and said, "Mind if I go to the bathroom before we leave?"

Davey said, "All of you should. We won't have time for bathroom breaks once we get in there."

Norman, Darin, Steve, and Neil squeezed into the backseat of the Mercedes, and Davey drove away from the Hollywood Palms Apartments.

Keoph looked back at them and said, "Where did you guys meet?"

"At the gym," Norman said. "The 24/7 Gym in Sherman Oaks."

"A lot of vampires go there at night," Steve said.

"Is it owned and operated by vampires?" Keoph asked.

Neil nodded and said, "Yeah, but plenty of mortals go there, too. They don't know about us, of course, they just go there to work out."

Keoph faced front again. He wondered how many times he had come in contact with vampires without knowing it. He wondered if anyone he knew was a vampire. He knew a guy named Andy Cork in San Francisco who had a night job as a security guard—could Andy be a vampire?

Knowing vampires really existed made everything look a little different.

Davey parked the Mercedes at the curb on Halley, near the manhole, and took a flashlight from the glovebox and handed it to Keoph. They all got out of the car and, after getting the crowbar from behind his seat and handing it to Norman, Davey went to the rear of the car and opened the trunk. He handed the satchels out to them and they hitched the straps over their shoulders. He took out his shotgun, the strap, and the purse filled with cartridges, which he slung over his shoulder, and closed the trunk. He held the shotgun down, parallel with his right leg as he led them to the manhole.

Norman handed the crowbar to Steve, who lifted the manhole cover with it. Norman put a hand on each side of it and pulled it off the hole. It clunked heavily on the pavement when he let go of it.

"Okay, quick now," Davey said. "I'm going first, then Gavin, then you guys. Norman, I want you to go down last and pull the cover back in place, okay?"

Norman nodded.

After looking around to make sure no one was watching them, Davey climbed down the rungs first and Keoph followed. The sound of running water got louder as they went down the metal rungs.

When he reached the bottom, Davey waited for Keoph. Once he was down, Davey said, "Turn on the flashlight, then help me with this strap."

Keoph clicked on the flashlight, but looked up at the open hole and wondered if Norman was going to fit through it. He attached Davey's strap to the gun and put it over his head onto his left shoulder. Davey slipped his left hand through the loop and Keoph cinched the Velcro. The shotgun was already loaded, and he had plenty of cartridges on the strap and in the purse.

There was a sound somewhere in the dark—something skittered and splashed through water. Keoph turned to Davey.

They whispered when they spoke.

"You hear that?" Keoph said.

Frowning, Davey said, "Yeah."

A minute later, they heard the crunching clatter of the manhole cover being dragged back over the hole. When it fell into place, it became very dark.

There was another sound—like something being dragged through the water.

"What the hell is that?" Davey whispered.

"Which way do we go?" Norman said.

Keoph closed his eyes a moment and saw the plans in his head. "This way," he said, pointing to the left. "The door to the sub-basement should be close by."

Davey said, "I think it might be a good idea to get your guns out now. I don't like those sounds."

They opened their satchels and removed the submachine guns.

The air was damp and dank. Exposed pipes ran overhead and on the sides.

They trudged through the flowing water as Keoph's flashlight cut through the darkness in the narrow tunnel like a sword.

Something splashed behind them and Keoph swung around and pointed the flashlight toward the sound. The light fell on the flowing water, swept back and forth up the concrete walls, but revealed nothing.

Another sound, this time in the direction they'd been going. Keoph spun around again, but found nothing with his light.

"What the hell is that?" Darin whispered.

"Rats?" Steve said.

"Too big to be rats," Keoph said.

"Come on," Davey said. As they walked on, Keoph kept shining the light on the wall to their left, until it fell on a door. They stopped.

It was a heavy steel door, and it was open inward a few inches.

"I think this is it," Davey whispered. The hinges squealed when he pushed the door the rest of the way open.

Keoph went in first with the light, and Davey and the others were right behind him. They stood so close, they kept bumping into each other.

Keoph's shoes and feet were soaking wet, but he hardly noticed. He was tense and trembling a little. He held his gun down, like the others, but was ready to use it at a moment's notice.

Once they were all inside the sub-basement, they stopped as Keoph moved his flashlight around.

There were shuffling sounds in the room, the sound of breathing.

"Hello," a voice hissed from the dark. "Have you come to feeeed ussss?"

The light fell on a small figure hanging upside down from one of the pipes overhead. It was a child with a badly disfigured face—half his face appeared to be melting—an arm on the left side and a single wing folded up on the right. It smiled around a mouthful of fangs. It dropped from the pipe and landed on its feet, which were not feet at all, but large talons.

The sounds of movement came from all around the room.

"Oh, Jesus help us," Davey whispered. "It's the mutants."

CHAPTER THIRTY-FOUR

Oh, my God," Keoph said as he watched the darkness move.

"Everybody step back out of the room," Davey said. "Gavin, reach into your satchel and get a grenade."

Keoph eased his hand into his satchel, afraid to move too fast. He pulled out one of the grenades.

"Go ahead, pull the pin," Davey said, "and throw it in there. Everybody out."

Keoph waited until the others had left the sub-basement, then he pulled the pin and tossed the grenade underhanded into the room. He quickly went out the door and joined the others in the storm drain waiting for the explosion.

When it came, it made Keoph's ears ring.

They slowly made their way back to the sub-basement door. Keoph and Davey went in first.

The grenade left behind a sound—screaming. The creatures in the basement screamed high, shrill screams, throaty guttural screams, and some just whimpered loudly.

Rather than being stunned by the grenade, it seemed to do nothing more than piss them off.

Davey passed the flashlight over them slowly. Deformed faces, twisted claws, pink tails, bulbous eyes—they screamed and hissed and groaned.

Fear gripped Keoph and he found he could not move as his heart thundered in his throat. Gooseflesh rose on his arms and shoulders as he watched them move through the darkness.

A beautiful woman with useless legs pulled herself forward over the filthy concrete floor with webbed hands. Something small hopped up onto one of a few dark barrels, something with a hunched back and short limbs and eyes that bulged from their sockets. A thing with a bloated face and no arms rose up from behind a stack of wooden crates. Something that dragged a tail crawled crablike over the floor. A creature lowered itself from the web of pipes overhead and dropped to the floor—its face was covered with hair and it had a pronounced brow and a flat-nosed snout. Something with a gelatinous face, no eyes, and a yawning mouth crawled around one of the barrels. All the while, they whispered.

"Hungry . . . I'm sooo hungry . . ."

"Deee*lic*ious . . ."

"Company! I looove company."

Others made garbled, guttural sounds—their faces were so disfigured, they could not speak clearly, or their minds were no longer functioning.

The darkness was alive with them, and they all

moved forward, toward Keoph and Davey, Norman, Darin, Steve, and Neil.

Something short, with a large mouth full of fangs, flew out of the darkness on leathery wings and latched onto the front of Steve. He started to cry out, but before he could make a sound, the thing closed its jaws on his throat and ripped it out. Steve made a harsh gurgling sound as blood gushed down his grey shirt. He fell backward, and his gun skittered over the floor as the creature continued to slurp and chew at his throat. Steve kicked his legs and tried to push the creature off, but it held on and its wings spread over him.

Keoph surprised himself when he stepped forward and kicked the creature once, then a second time. With the third kick, the creature let go, slid over the floor, and slammed into one of the barrels. Norman aimed and fired his gun at the thing. The sound of the submachine gun was deafening in the small sub-basement. Shell casings jingled musically on the concrete floor as the creature jerked and jittered.

Norman stopped firing. The damp air carried the acrid odor of cordite. The creature was a torn-up, bloody mess and lay still on the floor, its wings destroyed by the bullets.

Keoph quickly went to Steve and turned the flashlight on him. The creature had nearly decapitated him. His trachea had been torn in half and the wound went all the way back to the base of his neck. Steve's eyes were open, but he did not move. His skin quickly turned a greyish-yellow and began to crack and peel.

"Shit," Darin said, distress in his voice. "He's . . . *dead*."

Keoph picked up Steve's gun and stuffed it into his

satchel. He didn't like the idea of one of *them* getting its hands on a machine gun.

Spinning around, Davey faced the group of creatures. "Anybody comes any closer, and you get the same," he said.

The things fell silent and stopped moving. Eyes stared from the dark. The glow of Keoph's flashlight glimmered on moist fangs.

The small, short-limbed thing on the barrel made a vomiting sound and dove from the barrel toward them. Neil and Keoph fired together, and the thing slapped to the floor in a splash of blood. They fired at it a moment longer.

"I'm not kidding," Davey said. "Move back or we start firing."

"What did we ever do to you?" one of them said in a gurgling whisper.

"Nothing," Davey said. "And let's keep it that way." He shone the flashlight all around the room until it fell on rungs that went up the wall to their left. "See it?" he said.

Keoph nodded. "I see it. But with these things down here, you know it's going to be locked."

"Shit, you're right," Davey said. "Norman."

"Yeah?"

"We've got to climb those rungs over there and get out through that door in the ceiling. But it's going to be locked. Think you can do something about that?"

"If not," Norman said, "I'll just shoot it till it's not locked anymore."

Darin said, "But Steve's dead."

"I'm sorry, Darin," Davey said, "but we'll just have to leave him here for now."

The things in the dark watched and waited, but they did not move.

Davey said, "Blow 'em away."

Keoph, Darin, and Norman sprayed the darkness with bullets. There was a great rush among the creatures to move backward and hide, while some of them fell to the floor. Shell casings rained down noisily onto the concrete.

"Come on," Davey said once the firing stopped. He moved fast as he led the way across the room to the rungs on the wall. "Get up there, Norman, and get us through that door."

"Here," Norman said as he handed his gun to Keoph. He climbed the rungs with his satchel over his left shoulder.

Something moved close behind them, and Davey spun around and fired his shotgun blindly. The creature made a horrible gagging sound and hit the floor. It tried to crawl away, but Neil fired his machine gun at it until it stopped moving.

At the top of the rungs, Norman pushed on the door. It opened about an inch, but was locked from above, perhaps by a padlock in a hasp on the front edge of the door. Norman lowered his head, put the back of his shoulders against the door, and pushed. But that was too awkward. He reached up with his right arm, put his hand flat against the door, and shoved as hard as he could. It did not work—he couldn't get any leverage on the rungs. Norman climbed down a few rungs and said, "Hand me the gun."

Keoph handed the submachine gun to him and he climbed carefully back up the rungs. He aimed the gun at the center of the front edge of the door, where the lock was, turned his head away, and fired, almost at point-blank range. Wood splintered and bits of it dropped down from the door. He stopped firing and pushed up on the door. It opened all the way up and flipped over, slammed against the floor.

"Okay, let's go, fast," Davey said. He pointed his gun downward and climbed up behind Norman. He climbed slowly and awkwardly because of the shotgun strapped to him, the purse slung over his right shoulder.

The others climbed the rungs awkwardly, too, with guns in hand, satchels hanging from their shoulders, Keoph behind Davey, and Neil and Darin behind them.

Keoph found himself in a small dark room with an enormous water heater to the right and a closed door directly in front of them. Light came through the window in the top half of the door.

A figure appeared in the window, someone on the other side of the door. Neil saw it first and opened fire on the window. The glass shattered and the figure dropped. Davey went to the door and opened it inward.

The figure on the floor was a man in a yellow T-shirt and blue sweatpants. He started to get up again, but both Norman and Neil fired their guns at him.

The man on the floor convulsed as the bullets entered his abdomen. The T-shirt was torn up and blood spattered in all directions.

Norman stopped firing first, then Neil. The man lay still on the floor, his abdomen torn open by the bullets.

"What about the sub-basement?" Keoph said. "Should we close that door?"

Standing in the doorway, Davey shook his head. "Leave it open. Let them out. It'll take attention off of us."

Seven feet to their left was a wall at the end of the corridor. To their right, it made a T-intersection with another corridor.

"Come on," Davey whispered. "Let's find the elevator." He led them to the intersection and carefully peered around the corner to his right, then to the left. "Okay." The others followed him to the left, down the corridor to the elevator, where Davey punched the button.

Twenty seconds later, the elevator opened, and the five of them got inside. Davey pushed buttons two, three, four, and five.

"Okay, things have changed," Davey said as the elevator door closed. "Norman, I want you on the second floor, Darin on the third, and Neil on the fourth. Gavin and I will take the fifth floor. Is that clear?"

They all answered in the affirmative.

The elevator stopped on the second floor.

"What's her name again?" Norman said.

"Karen Moffett," Keoph said.

Davey said, "If you don't find her once you've gone through the whole floor, go back down to the basement and go out the way we came in. Go back to the manhole. We'll all meet there afterward."

Norman muttered Karen's name a few times. The elevator door opened and he bent forward to look in both directions. He stepped out of the elevator, gun held at the ready.

Davey hit the button to close the door. The elevator began to ascend again.

* * *

"Karen Moffett!" Norman shouted. He kept calling the name as he went down the corridor. There were doors on each side, all numbered. He continued calling her name until a door opened on the left up ahead and a tall woman in a smart blue-and-white suit with short dark hair stepped out and faced him.

"Who the hell are—" she said.

Norman started firing before she finished her question. She stumbled backward as bullets entered her chest, bumped into the wall, and went down, smearing blood on it. Norman rushed to her side, aimed the gun at her face, and squeezed the trigger. The shell casings fell silently to the carpeted floor as the woman's face disappeared in a mass of blood and torn flesh.

"Karen Moffett!" Norman shouted again when he stopped firing. He turned around to look down the corridor and saw a man come out of the stairwell. He was tall, with dark hair, and wore a longsleeve white shirt, a red tie, and black slacks. He wore a shoulder holster and immediately drew his gun, and fired.

Norman grunted when he felt a bullet enter his belly. He opened fire as he walked toward the man, who went down fast and dropped his gun. Norman went to him and kept firing into his chest.

The man turned grey and started to decay almost immediately.

"Karen Moffett!" Norman shouted again and again as he went down the corridor.

The wound in his belly ejected the bullet, which fell out through the hole in his shirt, and the wound quickly healed over.

* * *

The elevator door opened on the third floor and Darin leaned out to look in both directions. He pulled back in immediately and said, "Shit, there's a whole crowd just a little ways to the right."

"How many?" Davey said.

He peered around the edge of the elevator door, then pulled back. "Four men, two women." He reached into his satchel with his left hand and removed a stun grenade. He pulled the pin with his teeth, stepped out of the elevator, and tossed the grenade toward the small group in the corridor, then went back into the elevator and winced as he waited for the explosion.

When it came, it was loud. Afterward, Darin said, "Okay, I'll see you at the manhole later." He hurried out of the elevator and ran down the hall to the six vampires, who were now lying on the floor in a stunned state.

He stood over them and filled them with bullets, one after another. They began to decay quickly. He had to change magazines midway through the task of killing all of them.

As he hurried down the corridor, Darin repeatedly called, "Karen Moffett! Karen Moffett!"

After Neil left the elevator on the fourth floor, Keoph and Davey went up to the fifth.

"You ready for this?" Davey said.

Keoph's hands trembled and he licked his dry lips. "As ready as I'll ever be," he said. "You've got an advantage over me. I die a lot easier than you do."

"Don't worry," Davey said. "They're not going to be ready for us."

The elevator stopped.

The door opened.

Davey peered out. "All clear." He pointed left and said, "You go that way." He pointed right. "I'll go this way."

They parted outside the elevator, and both began to shout, "Karen Moffett! Karen Moffett!"

Keoph stopped when a door opened in front of him. A short, dowdy, middle-aged woman with short brown hair and glasses stepped out into the corridor. She stood looking at him a moment, her mouth open in surprise.

She wore a green-and-yellow dress and squinted slightly as she looked at him. "Who're *you?*" she said.

She looked so . . . *normal,* that the idea of shooting her did not occur to Keoph right away. He said nothing and just stared at her.

She looked at his gun for a moment, then pulled her lips back and bared her fangs.

Keoph opened fire.

At the other end of the corridor, Davey heard the gunfire, but did not look back.

"Karen Moffett!" he shouted again and again, gun held ready to fire.

A door opened to his left and Davey turned to face it.

A tall woman with long dark hair stood in the doorway wearing a cream-colored nightgown. Davey was about to squeeze the trigger, but he suddenly recognized her.

It was Anya.

CHAPTER THIRTY-FIVE

Anya?" he said.

She smiled. "Davey Owen. With a shotgun. Why am I not surprised?"

Davey felt a clutching at his heart. A storm of feelings moved through him.

"This is all your fault," he said, barely above a whisper. "You made me what I am, you . . . you *started* all this."

"You wanted *me*, Davey. Remember? You wanted me, you had to have me."

"Yeah. Well. Suck on this, you cunt." He fired the gun.

Blood exploded from Anya's chest and she was knocked backward. She fell to the floor on her back, eyes and mouth open in shock. She immediately began to get up again, moving quickly but clumsily. She dropped back to the floor, mouth open, and grunted as she tried again.

Davey hurriedly moved forward. Using his left arm in the Velcro strap, he lowered the gun until the muzzle was just a couple inches from her face. He fired again.

Anya's skull opened up in an explosion of red, black, and grey. Teeth and bone scattered. Davey found himself smiling as he fired again and destroyed what was left of Anya's head. He stared down at her bloody body as she began to rapidly decay. A foul stench rose from her as her skin sloughed and peeled. She seemed to melt before his eyes. Every sinew rotted away, leaving behind clothed bones, some of which cracked and crumbled.

Davey watched her decay with wide eyes. He thought she had burned in Live Girls when it exploded and went up in flames. There was something unreal about the experience of watching her decay. He had not even *thought* about shooting her, he'd simply done it, as if he had been ready to kill her all along. He had been—he'd wanted to kill her for eighteen years, and had always regretted that she'd burned in the fire and robbed him of the chance.

Davey vaguely noticed a thumping sound coming from nearby, but he paid no attention to it. He wondered how long Anya had been in Los Angeles, how long she had been working for Victor Barna. He assumed she was there because she worked there. He knew how much Anya enjoyed her work.

The thumping continued, and something else—a muffled voice. But he heard them only peripherally. His mind was on Anya, and the fact that he had actually killed her after all these years.

He tore his eyes away from Anya's remains. He stood in the doorway of what appeared to be an office.

"Karen Moffett!" he shouted as he turned to continue down the corridor.

It got his attention, then—the pounding and the voice.

Davey frowned as he walked into the office. It was spacious, and not very feminine—he assumed it was Anya's office—with lots of dark wood paneling and antiques. There was a painted portrait of Anya on the wall behind the large antique desk.

The sounds came from his left. He turned and saw a door with a deadbolt lock.

"Karen?" he called.

"Yes!" the voice on the other side of the heavy wooden door shouted. "Yes!"

He turned the doorknob. It wasn't locked, but the deadbolt kept him from opening the door. He turned the deadbolt latch and pushed the door open.

Karen Moffett stumbled out of the room in a nightgown and slippers. Her face was pale and swollen and bruised, as were her bare arms.

"Oh, my God," she said, her voice trembling. "You found me."

"Yeah, but we haven't gotten out of here yet. Come on." He quickly led her through the office and to the door. Davey poked his head out the door and looked around. He saw no one but Keoph down the corridor a distance, calling Karen's name. He led her out into the corridor and hurried back to the elevator.

Keoph had emptied the submachine gun into the frumpy woman with glasses, and had to change magazines.

"Gavin!" Davey shouted from the other end of the corridor. "I've got her, let's go!"

Keoph jogged back down the corridor toward them. They hurried to the elevator.

Karen moved as fast as she could, but she limped along. She looked terrible. He flinched a little at the bruises on her face and arms. She had a black eye.

In the elevator, Keoph turned to her and said, "I'm sorry it took us so long, Karen. We did the best we could."

She nearly fell on him, and he put his arms around her as she fought back sobs.

The elevator went down to the fourth floor and opened up.

"You two stay here," Davey said. "I'm going to get Neil." He stepped out of the elevator and started to go left, but stopped, mouth open. He said, "Oh, my God."

Keoph stepped out of the elevator to see what Davey was seeing, and Karen grabbed his left arm and went with him.

Fifteen feet away, Neil was sprawled on the floor on his back. A white-haired figure in black clothes straddled Neil and sucked loudly on his neck, long fingers clutching at Neil's shirt. Neil's gun lay on the floor a few feet away.

Neil's skin had turned the telltale yellowish-grey of a decaying corpse.

The elevator door closed.

The figure sat up and looked at them. His skin was pale as death, his eyes pink. He stood as Keoph and Davey raised their guns, blood smeared around his mouth, vivid against his white skin. The albino became a blur, and was gone.

Karen cried out, and Keoph and Davey turned as the albino pulled her away from them from behind. He jerked her back with him, left arm across her waist. He raised his right hand, which held a closed knife. The silver stiletto blade appeared with a sharp click. He put the knife to Karen's throat. Then he smiled around his bloody fangs.

CHAPTER THIRTY-SIX

Martin Burgess sat beside his wife's bed in her hospital room. She had been given stitches and something for pain, and she was sleeping fitfully. There was another bed over by the window, but it was unoccupied.

The police had left him alone for awhile, but they would be back. Burgess expected them anytime and had to make sure Denise had something sane to tell them. He waited for her to wake up.

The vampire story wasn't going to fly. Officer Keaton hadn't bought it, even though Davey Owen had, if only for a moment, turned himself into something about which Burgess expected to have nightmares. It had happened right in front of the cop, and he'd managed to convince himself he hadn't seen it, that it was some kind of trick.

Denise stirred. She awoke with a gasp.

"Honey?" Burgess said as he stood and put his hands on the bed's rail.

"Muh-Martin?" she whispered.

"Oh, baby," he said as he lightly touched her hand. She had been so brutalized, he was afraid to touch her for fear of hurting her.

"Vam . . . vampires, Martin, they were vampires," she breathed.

"Yes, I know, honey, but listen to me, okay?" He bent down close to her. "Can you hear me?"

"Yes."

"You can't tell the police they were vampires. Do you understand me?"

"Whuh-what?"

He repeated himself slowly: "You can't tell the police they were vampires, Denise. Just tell them you don't remember much, okay? Tell them the last thing you remember is being in your car in the garage, and then they had you. Are you hearing me, Denise? This is very important."

"No . . . vampires?"

"No vampires."

"But . . . thuh-they *were* vampires."

"Yes, sweetheart, *I* know that. Remember? I tried to tell you about them."

"Yes, I re . . . member. I . . . I'm . . . sorry, Marty, I'm so sorry."

"No, no, you've got nothing to be sorry for. Just remember what I said, okay? Don't say anything to the police about vampires. Say you don't remember much. You were badly beaten, honey, so it's perfectly believable that you don't remember much."

"But . . . I do. I *do* remember. Marty, I was . . . I-I

was . . ." Tears welled up in her eyes as she silently mouthed the word *raped*.

"Oh, baby, please, just relax now, you're safe. Nobody's going to hurt you again. Nobody."

"We're *not* safe, Marty," she said, just above a whisper. "Nobody is. They're . . . thuh-they're horrible, Marty, they're awful. They enjoyed every second of it. They *enjoyed* it," she said aloud. She shifted her position under the covers and winced in pain. Her voice dropped again as she said, "They loved it. They *told* me they loved it. The bloodier, the better, they said. They beat me while they raped me. They beat me till I bled, then they sucked on my wounds." She sniffled as a couple tears fell. She talked gradually faster. "They were monsters, Marty. Not . . . not the kind of people we usually think of as monsters, like, like rapists or child molesters, but, but these things, they, they were . . . *real* . . . *monsters*. The kind we were afraid of as kids, Marty, the kind of monsters we used to have nightmares about after watching a horror movie." She tried to sit up and groaned in pain.

"Calm down, honey, please," Burgess said. "Don't try to sit up. I'll raise the bed, okay?"

"No, no. Not now."

"Okay, whatever you—"

"We're not safe anymore, Marty. Do you realize that?"

"That's not true, Denise. You're safe now. Please, relax."

"None of us," she breathed. "None of us is safe."

"Would you like me to ask the nurse to give you something to relax you?"

"No. No. I'll be fine." A laugh escaped her like a

cough. "What am I saying? I'll never be fine again. Never."

"Don't say that, sweetheart."

She took in a deep breath. "If you call me *sweetheart* . . . or *baby* . . . one more time . . . I'll pull this needle out of my arm and stick it in your eye."

Burgess's eyebrows popped up a moment, then leveled out. "I'm sorry," he said.

There was a long silence between them, then Denise said, "No. I'm sorry. I shouldn't've said that. I'm not thinking clearly, this medicine they're giving me . . . I feel all mixed up."

"Why don't you go back to sleep," he said.

She closed her good eye and whispered, "Yeah . . . yeah."

He watched her drift off again. He hoped she would remember what he'd told her.

About twenty minutes later, the door opened and Officer Keaton leaned into the room. "Can I see you?"

Burgess got up from the chair and went out into the corridor with Keaton.

"The nurse tells me she's talking," Keaton said.

"Now and then. The painkiller is pretty strong. She's not herself when she's awake."

"Have you talked to her about what happened?" Keaton said.

"She says she doesn't remember much. She remembers being beaten, and raped. But not much more."

"Does she remember being taken?"

"She said the last thing she remembers well is being in her car in the garage."

"She was taken from her car?"

"Yes."

"And you . . . what, didn't notice?"

"I told you, she was angry with me at the time."

"When did you tell me that?"

"Didn't I tell you that?"

Keaton shook his head once. "I don't remember you telling me that, no."

"Well, that's what happened. She was angry with me, and she left. I was in my office, on the other side of the house, listening to a CD on headphones."

"Were you working?"

"Yes, I was."

"You always listen to music on headphones while you work?"

"Often, yes."

"What music were you listening to?"

Burgess thought about his CD player and the last thing he'd listened to on it. "It was *Tusk*. Fleetwood Mac."

"When did you notice your wife was missing?"

"I went out to the kitchen for something to eat—"

"When? How long after you thought she'd left?"

"Oh, uh . . . I'm not sure. I didn't check the time."

"You don't know what time this was?"

"Like I said, I didn't check the time. The way I work—I don't pay much attention to time. I try to become immersed in whatever I'm writing. I can't be checking the clock all the time. I have no reason to."

"And what did you notice?"

"I heard her car running out in the garage. I looked out there and found the garage door open, her car parked, and the engine running. But she was gone."

"Where did you think she had gone?"

"I thought probably one of her friends had come by, and Denise had taken off with her. That happens a lot."

"Why would she leave the car running?"

Burgess's heart was pounding. He was good at coming up with lies, but he had no confidence in his ability to deliver them.

"No reason," Burgess said. "My thought was, she'd been in her car, a friend had driven up, and she'd gotten out of the car to talk to her. They probably talked a little while, then her friend invited her to come along with her and go shopping, or whatever, and Denise completely forgot about leaving the BMW running."

Keaton folded his arms slowly across his chest as he studied Burgess's face. "What did you do?"

"I turned the car off and closed the garage door."

"You didn't wonder where she was?"

"Like I said, it's very common, when her friends come by, for Denise to drop what she's doing and run off with them."

"Did you call anyone?"

"Yes, I called a couple of her friends, but neither of them answered." Burgess immediately doubted the wisdom of that remark.

Keaton uncrossed his arms and took a notepad from his shirt pocket. "Who did you call?"

Burgess took in a deep breath, let it out slowly. "Okay. I didn't call anybody."

"Listen to me, Mr. Burgess," Keaton said firmly, pointing a finger at Burgess's chest. "I will not stand for anymore bullshit from you, do you understand me? Yesterday, you were talking to me about vampires that worked for Victor Barna, for crying out loud. Now you're telling me you *didn't* call any of her friends?"

"Yes, that's right."

"Why did you say you did?"

"Because you seem to think I'm some kind of cold, uncaring husband, I can tell, and I didn't want you to continue thinking that of me. It's not true."

"Why *didn't* you call any of her friends?"

"I know my wife, Officer Keaton. She was pissed off at me, and the way she usually punishes me is by going out and spending a buttload of my money." That part was not a lie. "It never *occurred* to me that she'd been kidnapped. It's too common for her to just up and take off with someone, especially if it's to go spend a buttload of my money. I was pretty sure that was what had happened."

"What did you do?"

"I worked awhile longer, and then I went to bed."

"What time was that?"

"I don't know, two o'clock, two-thirty, two-forty-five."

"And she hadn't shown up?"

Burgess shrugged. "Like I said, we'd been fighting, and she was really pissed at me."

"Did it have anything to do with the fact that you reek of garlic?"

"Yes, as a matter of fact, it did."

"Why *do* you reek of garlic, Mr. Burgess?"

Burgess smiled. "I eat a great deal of garlic. For health reasons. The garlic pills really aren't enough, and they don't work as well as real garlic. I cook with it all the time."

Keaton narrowed his left eye as he looked intensely at Burgess for several seconds. "It wouldn't happen to have anything to do with *vampires*, would it?"

"I'm sorry about that. I, uh . . . I'd gotten too wrapped up in something I was writing, that's all."

"Do you do that often?"

"I'm in therapy for it." It was true, he had a therapist, but it had nothing to do with his writing. It was, instead, about some midlife doubts he'd been having about himself. Personal doubts, cosmic doubts. "I've been in therapy for almost three years."

"I see," Keaton said with a nod. "Well, I let the vampire story go. I could've arrested you for obstructing justice, but I let it pass, I want you to remember that. I won't be so generous if you start lying to me again."

"I'm not lying to you. I'm telling you what I should've told you in the first place."

"Do you have any idea—even a vague *guess*—as to who might've done this to her?"

Burgess shook his head. "I don't have a clue. Everybody loves Denise. People who can't stand me love Denise."

"No call demanding ransom?" Keaton said.

"No."

"How was she returned to you?"

Burgess told him how it had happened—no lie was necessary.

"And you took her to the hospital?"

"Immediately."

Keaton pointed at him again. "If I find out you're lying, I'm gonna charge you with everything I possibly can, you understand?"

"Yes, I understand. But I'm not lying."

"You're saying you didn't realize she'd been kidnapped until they brought her *back* and dumped her on the *porch?*"

"I swear to God, it never crossed my mind. I was

too busy getting drunk because I was afraid my marriage was over. I thought she'd left me."

Keaton nodded. "I'm going to monitor your wife's condition, and as soon as she's off that painkiller, I'm going to talk to her."

"I don't know how long that will be," Burgess said. "She has a broken arm, a broken leg, and a fractured collarbone."

"All very small fractures. Fortunately. I talked to her doctor. I'm very interested in what Mrs. Burgess has to say about what happened to her." He reached over and patted Burgess's shoulder once. "I'll be in touch." He smiled, turned around, and ambled off.

Burgess went back into Denise's room and stood beside her bed. He watched her sleep for a long time.

CHAPTER THIRTY-SEVEN

Karen Moffett!" Darin called.

There was no response, and he'd seen or heard no one since the six stunned vampires he'd killed in the center of the corridor. He reached the end of the corridor, calling Karen's name repeatedly. He passed the rotting corpses on the floor—he winced at the awful smell emenating from them—then went on past the elevator.

"Karen Moffett!"

He slowed his pace a little when he heard something—scratching on a door, and someone crying loudly on the other side—and ran his left hand back over his buzz-cut hair.

Darin felt bad that he had to ignore whoever it was who scratched at that door. He only had time for one rescue, and then they still had to get out of the building.

He reached the end of the main corridor, turned around, and stopped so suddenly, he almost tripped over his own feet. Standing a few feet behind him was a tall, beautiful woman with short dark-red hair and freckles on her cheeks. She wore a sleeveless black blouse and a dark green broomstick skirt. The top three buttons on the blouse were loose and displayed a scoop of cleavage. His eyes met hers, and he found he could not look away.

She smiled and said, "Where've *you* been all my life, honey?"

Darin wanted to raise his gun, but he found himself overcome with lust for the redhead. He felt a familiar tightness in his pants.

She unfastened the next button on her blouse, then the next, still smiling. "You're a vampire, sugar. You shouldn't be living the way you do. It goes against everything you are." With her blouse completely un-buttoned, it fell open in front and revealed pale, round breasts with rosy nipples. She unfastened the skirt and let it drop to the floor. She wore nothing underneath.

Darin felt everything but his desire for the beauti-ful woman in front of him drain out of him, as if he'd sprung a leak. He was losing his will—it was being sucked out of him.

She stepped toward him, reached out for him, and flashed her fangs.

Norman was very suspicious. Since he had shot down the man with the shoulder-holster, he had seen no one and heard nothing. The corridor had about it a creepy emptiness, even though he knew there were people beyond those doors. Mrs. Dupassie had told him about this place last night. He was disturbed by the fact that they were there to rescue only one person, when the hotel was fully occupied by people who desperately needed help. But he was very realistic about his situation—he knew the chances of them getting out of there with Karen Moffett were slim, as were their chances of getting out at all. But if he were to die that day, Norman was determined to take as many brutals with him as he possibly could.

He had traveled the length of the corridor and gone down the short side-corridors, calling Karen's name. Norman decided it was time to go back to the manhole. He went to the elevator and reached out to push the button, when the elevator's bell rang and the door opened up. Inside the car stood four men, two in front of two, wearing sunglasses and suits with slight bulges beneath the jackets on the sides.

Norman squeezed the trigger and moved the gun back and forth, spraying bullets into the four men. The two in front fell back on the two behind them, and all four of them slammed against the elevator's back wall. Norman followed them with the gun as they slid down to the floor. He stepped forward and shot at the heads, moving the gun from one to the next. Brains splashed against the faces of the two men in back, and against the wall.

Norman stopped shooting when the elevator door started to close. He held out a foot and nudged it, and the door opened up again. He stared at the four men, watched them begin to decay.

He quickly stuffed his gun in the satchel and grabbed the feet of one of the dead vampires. He pulled the corpse out into the corridor. He did the same with the other three. He kicked the elevator door every time it tried to close. When he was done, he got in the elevator and let the door close. He punched the button with a B on it, but the elevator started upward.

"Dammit," he muttered as he took the gun out of the satchel. He changed magazines as the elevator rose, then stood with the gun ready to fire.

As the elevator ascended, the smell of the blood on the floor and walls filled Norman's nostrils. He licked his dry lips as hunger clenched his stomach.

When he saw the fangs, Darin fired the gun. The bullets entered the redhead's guts at point blank range, and there was a spray of red behind her. Blood gushed from her mouth as she went down.

Darin stood over her and fired into her abdomen, until her tanktop was in tatters and her belly was mush.

The ringing in his ears from all the gunfire was worse when he stopped shooting.

The woman on the floor quickly began to stink.

Darin changed magazines, stepped around her, and headed for the elevator. He had no reason to believe Karen Moffett was on the third floor. It was time to go down to the basement and make his way back to the manhole.

"Shit," he said when he looked up at the floor lights above the elevator. It had already passed his floor and was on its way up. He pushed the down button.

Keoph and Davey stood frozen in place as the albino held his knife to Karen's throat.

"You're in over your head," the vampire said through his fanged smile.

Karen reached behind her and felt for the albino's genitals. She found them and squeezed his testicles with all her strength.

The vampire screamed and dropped the knife.

Karen dropped to the floor and shouted, "Shoot! Shoot! Shoot!"

Keoph and Davey fired. The tangy smell of cordite rose in the corridor. Davey fired only once and most of the vampire's head disappeared.

The albino vampire fell to the floor, but rolled over and started to get up again.

Keoph stepped over to him and fired bullets into his back as Davey destroyed what remained of his head. Karen crawled out of the way and got to her feet.

Keoph turned to her. "You okay?"

Karen said, "No, I'm not, but I'm ready to get the hell out of here."

"Let's go," Davey said as he stepped over to the elevator and pushed the button.

A moment later, the bell rang and the elevator door slid open.

Karen gasped when she saw all the blood.

Norman stood in the middle of the mess with his gun aimed at them, ready to fire. The instant he saw them, he lowered the gun.

"I don't know about you guys," Norman said, "but *I'm* ready to go."

They got in and the elevator started downward.

The smell of blood was heavy in the car. Davey closed his eyes a moment as a wave of hunger passed over him. The smell made something rise up in him, something he'd been fighting for eighteen years—a powerful lust, directed now at Karen Moffett, who stood beside him. He looked over at her neck and imagined he could hear the pulse of her blood through her veins and arteries.

The elevator stopped on the third floor and Davey

crushed the hunger inside of him, pushed it aside and focused on the situation at hand.

They raised their guns, ready for the worst.

The door opened on Darin, who stepped in without wasting a second.

"Let's get the hell out of here," Keoph said as he pushed the B button.

The elevator seemed to take an eternity to reach the basement. When it did, they heard the muffled sound of the bell outside, and the door slid open.

Something naked and bony with a gelatinous face and fangs bared bounded into the elevator.

CHAPTER THIRTY-EIGHT

Seated behind his vast desk in his massive Barna Tower office, Victor Barna opened a deep bottom drawer. It was filled with prepaid cell phones. He never used the same one twice—he did not trust them, and he believed it brought bad luck. He plucked a cell phone from the drawer and punched in a number. He waited for an answer. It was a long time in coming.

"Hello?"

"Who is this?" Barna said.

"Oh, Mr. Barna. It's Frank. Castlebeck."

"Castlebeck. What the hell is going on over there? I've called repeatedly, with no answer. Do you know how many cell phones I've gone through trying to reach someone over there?"

"There's something very strange going on here, Mr. Barna."

"What?"

"I'm . . . not exactly sure."

"Have you seen Anya?" Barna said, irritated. "I haven't gotten any answer from her office or her cell phone."

"I haven't seen her."

"Well, *find* her, and tell her to call me immediately. Got it?"

"Got it, Mr. Barna. But you should probably know what's going on here. There's been a lot of gunfire. Machine guns."

"*What?*" A chill passed through Barna. He quickly reminded himself that he had made sure there was nothing in or about the Royal Arms that could be connected to him. "Machine . . . guns. What the hell is happening there, Castlebeck?"

"I'm not sure."

"Well, for God's sake, don't you think somebody should find *out?*"

"Yes, probably."

"Well, Castlebeck, here's a thought—why don't *you* be that somebody." Then he raised his voice: "Call me back in ten minutes with some answers, Castlebeck, do you understand me?"

Barna pushed the phone's Off button and tossed it into the wastecan beneath his desk. The can already contained several cell phones.

His first instinct was to go over to the hotel and see for himself what was happening. But he did not dare go near the place, especially if something was happening that might draw attention from the outside. The fact that it was taking place in the middle of the day was not good—Barna had no friends on the police force who worked the day shift.

Barna had no choice but to wait.

* * *

Frank Castlebeck was afraid he would urinate into his pants before he could reach the employees' rest room down the hall. He sighed as he finally emptied his bladder into a urinal. He was in the back corridors of the Royal Arms, behind the front desk.

Barna wanted him to find out what was going on—it almost made him laugh. Castlebeck found it amusing that Barna actually thought he would run headlong into machine gunfire to find information for him.

Fat fucking chance, Castlebeck thought as he went to the sink and washed his hands.

He stepped out of the rest room and a completely hairless dwarf with flippers instead of arms, latched onto Castlebeck's left leg and sank its fangs into his thigh. Castlebeck cried out in pain and kicked at the dwarf with his right foot. He lost his balance and fell down. He crawled away from the thing, kicking his bitten leg, head turned back to look at the thing that was now making ugly sucking sounds.

When Castlebeck looked ahead, he stopped crawling.

A woman with dark, matted hair crawled over the floor toward him, digging the sharp claws of her webbed hands deep into the carpet to pull herself forward.

"Feeeed us," she whispered.

Castlebeck had been told by Anya and other vampires to stay out of the water-heater room down in the basement. He'd gone in there once, anyway. He'd seen the door in the floor. And he'd heard the sounds coming up from below. He'd visited a state mental hospital once to visit his half-sister, who was schizophrenic, and he remembered walking by the dayroom filled with people who babbled, groaned, or just made babylike noises as they wandered back and forth. The sounds he'd heard coming from under the basement floor were very reminiscent of the sounds he'd heard in the mental hospital. Babbling, groaning, or sloppy baby noises. It frightened and unnerved Castlebeck, and he hadn't been able to get out of there fast enough. He had never gone back down to the water-heater room.

He became sick to his stomach when he realized someone had opened that door in the floor down there. Someone had given the creatures that had made those sounds the freedom to roam the halls. And two of them meant to feed on him.

Castlebeck scrambled to his feet and kicked the dwarf hard against the wall once, then again, and a third time, when the dwarf's head struck the wall hard. He slid off Castlebeck's leg. Castlebeck quickly turned around and kicked the crawling, web-handed woman in the face once, then a few more times. Until something cracked and blood began to dribble everywhere, down her face in deep-red stripes.

The dwarf began to stir.

Castlebeck hurried over to the dwarf, lifted his right foot high, knee up, and stomped on the dwarf's head again and again. He kept stomping, even after feeling something collapse beneath his heel.

The woman started to crawl toward him again. He did the same thing to her.

It was Castlebeck's great hope that one day he would be turned by one of the vampires with whom he worked. He wanted it desperately. He wanted eternal life, but that wasn't even the best part of the deal—it was control over women for which Castlebeck lusted.

He was determined to keep from losing his life to the deformities on the floor, which would no doubt drain him of blood if given half a chance.

Castlebeck staggered down the corridor, his thigh bleeding, went out the door behind the front desk, and around the edge of the counter. He stumbled to a stop when he saw, through the glass doors at the front entrance, a police car doubled-parked outside—no doubt someone had called about the machine gunfire. Castlebeck limped backward a few feet, then turned around and headed for the elevator. The basement light was lit up overhead. The elevator seemed to be staying there.

He was parked behind the hotel. Castlebeck rushed back to the front desk, went around the counter. He swung the door open and headed down the narrow hallway that led to the breakroom, which had a door to the rear parking lot.

Something dropped down on him from the ceiling and wrapped its stubby wings around his face from behind. The creature sank its fangs into the back of Castlebeck's neck and started to gnaw.

Oh, this is bad, Castlebeck thought. *We're all done for.*

Castlebeck lost consciousness then and collapsed to the floor.

The creature remained on his back, sucking and chewing at his neck.

Castlebeck never woke up again. He would never have an eternal life filled with subservient women after all.

CHAPTER THIRTY-NINE

The naked creature with the gelatinous face also had talons instead of hands and feet, and it slapped onto the front of Norman. It's bony knees jutted upward as the talons at the end of its legs dug into Norman's beefy sides. Norman's gun fell to the floor of the elevator.

Crying out in pain, Norman nearly closed his hands all the way around the creature's waist, and pushed it away from his body. The talons tore at his back and sides as it opened its mouth and made gelatinous sounds.

"Somebody shoot him," Norman said as he held the thing at arms' length.

Keoph poked the barrel of his gun between a couple of the creature's ribs and squeezed the trigger. Norman let go of the creature and it flew backward out of the elevator. Keoph stepped forward and kept firing at the center of the creature. He quit just short of cutting the thing in half.

While he was outside the elevator, Keoph saw other things crawling around in the narrow corridors of the basement. He quickly stepped back in the elevator just as the door started to close.

"They're loose out there," he said.

"Then we shoot our way through them," Davey said. "We have to get down to that sub-basement and get the hell out of here. We've gotten off lucky so far, we caught them by surprise. That's not going to last for long." He looked around at them. "Everybody loaded?"

They nodded.

Davey led the way out of the elevator, turned to his left, and fired the shotgun.

Keoph shot down a bloated creature that looked like a large maggot with a human head and limbs that was crawling along the left wall. The bullets exploded its bulbous body, blood splashed in all directions, and it dropped to the floor. Keoph shot at it a bit longer to make sure.

When they got to the water-heater room, it was empty. They quickly climbed down into the sub-basement. Keoph took his flashlight from the satchel again and turned it on.

They were walking toward Steve's body when something wrapped around Keoph's left ankle and pulled his foot out from under him, knocking him onto his side. Keoph cried out as he dropped his gun and the flashlight. He lifted his head and saw, extending from the darkness to his right, a narrow, fleshy, baby-pink tentacle, the end of which was curled around his ankle.

As Neil stepped forward, he removed a long hunting knife from the sheath on his belt. He went to the tentacle and stood on it with both feet, legs apart. He bent down and attacked the tentacle with the knife until the blade went clear through to the concrete.

The tentacle bled red blood. It spurted from the end while it whipped back into the dark as something in there squealed like an injured pig.

Keoph scrambled to his feet and shook his leg to knock off the tentacle fragment, but without success. He had to unwrap it from his leg to get it off, then threw it into the dark from which it had come.

"Let's get the hell out of here," Keoph said as he retrieved his gun and flashlight.

They walked a little farther and came upon what remained of Steve. It was not much. Beneath his clothes, he was nothing more than a collection of crumbling bones.

"Damn," Norman whispered.

Darin whispered, "He was the oldest of us."

They left the sub-basement and walked to the rungs that led up to the manhole. They put their guns back into the satchels and zipped the satchels closed, and the vampires took their sunglasses from pockets and put them on.

Norman went up first to move the manhole cover. They heard it rumble over the pavement above with a crunching, clanking sound.

"Help me with this, Gavin," Davey said. Keoph helped him remove the strap. Davey dropped the gun to the ground and abandoned it.

Something behind them squealed as it splashed through the water toward them.

"Climb, climb!" Davey said as he pushed Keoph up, then Karen.

The thing was nothing more than a hunkering shape in the darkness. It continued to squeal as it sloshed closer.

Davey was the last one to climb out, and the second he'd cleared the hole, Norman moved the manhole cover and dropped it into place.

Davey and Keoph looked around carefully as they walked quickly to the Mercedes parked nearby. They could hear what sounded like a police radio—it seemed to be coming from the front of the hotel. Davey got into the car first and started the engine.

None of them said anything as Davey pulled away from the curb.

Adrenaline pumped through Keoph and he could hear his heartbeat in his ears. It was as if all his fear were catching up with him—his hands and legs shook as he sat hunched forward in the front seat.

"If that place weren't full of victims," Davey said after awhile, "it would be blowing up or in flames right now, I'd see to it."

In the backseat, Darin said quietly, "I can't believe Steve didn't make it."

"And Neil, too," Norman said. Half of his mouth turned up in a smile. "Wherever they are, they're probably pissed they didn't get to take out more brutals."

As he drove, Davey kept looking at Karen in the backseat. "Karen," he said, "I have to ask you this question. Did you and Anya exchange blood at any time? Did she ever make you drink her blood?"

"No, she didn't. But I think I would've preferred that to what she *did* do to me."

"What was that?" Keoph said.

"Please, I . . . I don't want to talk about it right now."

"Do you need to see a doctor?" Keoph said.

She shook her head. "No doctors. No police. I'll be fine."

"You're sure?"

"Keoph, I know you're concerned, and I appreciate it, but what exactly would I *tell* a doctor? I couldn't tell him the truth, and beyond the truth, I got nothing this time. I couldn't *make up* what happened to me. Right now, all I'm thinking about is one thing—I'm alive. I really thought I was going to die in that place. I can't thank you enough for coming in to get me."

Davey said, "You want to know the truth? I didn't think this many of us would get out alive. And that includes you, Karen. I'm sorry about Steve and Neil. But in spite of that, the truth is, we've been very lucky today."

CHAPTER FORTY

Keoph pulled a chair out for Karen at Mrs. Dupassie's dining table. Mrs. Dupassie sat across from her, reached out and took her right hand. A fat cigar protruded from Mrs. Dupassie's mouth. She took it out before she spoke.

"How are you, sweetheart?" Mrs. Dupassie said.

"Well, I'm not fine."

"Would you like to use my shower? Or, I have a tub, if you'd prefer. I think I have some clothes that might fit you, too, so you can get out of that nightgown."

"Oh, I would appreciate that so much."

Mrs. Dupassie stood and put the cigar back in her mouth. She led Karen down the hall to the bathroom. She opened a cupboard above the toilet and removed a white towel.

"There's the shower and tub," Mrs. Dupassie said, "and here's a towel. My robe is hanging on the back of this door. Put it on when you're done and go one door down to my bedroom. I'll set out some clothes for you on the bed."

At the table, Davey turned to Norman and Darin. "You guys are the best, I want you to know that. I can't tell you how sorry I am about Steve and Neil."

Norman nodded. "They died doing something they felt very strongly about. You know, Steve had a fascinating life. His parents brought him to this country from Germany when he was just a baby over a hundred and fifty years ago. When he was ten, his parents were killed by brutals, right in front of him."

"Vampires have been here that long?" Keoph said.

"Vampires helped settle this country," Norman said. "The good ones, anyway."

"What about the brutals?"

Norman said, "Well, the elements and poor medical treatment weren't the *only* things responsible for the high mortality rate among settlers."

Keoph nodded. It made sense.

"Steve was turned when he was in his late teens," Norman said. "He's been after the brutals ever since. He always knew it was going to get him killed one day, but he didn't care as long as he died taking brutals down with him. He fought in the Civil War, for the North. He fought in World War One and Two, but he killed more brutals than German soldiers in Europe, both times. The daylight almost killed him in World War Two, but he survived. That's what he was. Steve was a survivor. Until today."

"Neil was pretty shy," Darin said. "I don't know anything about his background. He never talked about himself, always about the people he was talking to. You know what I mean? He was always interested in people."

"He was a good listener," Norman said.

Davey said, "Nothing would make me happier than going in there and killing *all* of them, and getting those people locked up in the hotel the help they need."

"You'd need more people," Darin said.

"Oh, yeah, it would take more people, and a lot more bullets," Davey said.

"If you ever decide to try," Norman said, "give us a call, okay?"

"You'll be the first ones I call," Davey said with a smile. "I don't know how soon that'll be, though. I'm going to lay low, maybe do some traveling."

No one said Casey's name, but Keoph and Davey both thought about her at the same time. Keoph wondered to himself what such a horrible loss must be like, while Davey told himself he probably was going to have a long grieving period.

"I need some time alone," Davey said as he looked down at the tabletop. "Preferrably out of Los Angeles. I plan to pamper myself on a long trip to . . . somewhere."

Mrs. Dupassie came out of the hallway and passed the dining table to go into the living room. When she came back and seated herself at the table, she said, "It's on the news."

Keoph and Davey got up and went into the living room.

An attractive blond woman said, "—anymore gunfire for awhile now, that seems to have stopped. But police are getting no answer when they call the hotel on the phone. A SWAT team is on the way. We will keep you up to date as the story develops. We return you now to our regularly scheduled program, already in progress."

A rerun of *Everybody Loves Raymond* came on.

Keoph and Davey slowly returned to the table.

Mrs. Dupassie puffed on her cigar, took it out of her mouth. "That girl's in a lot of fucking pain," she said.

"Karen?" Keoph said.

Mrs. Dupassie nodded. "It's just dripping off of her. Her aura is not looking healthy. She needs help. I know a good therapist who sees victims of brutals. He's a vampire, but he's on our side. That way, she can tell her whole story and won't have to make up a bunch of lies to cover for what *really* happened."

"That's a very good idea, Mrs. Dupassie," Keoph said.

"I'll get his card for her next time I get up off my ass," Mrs. Dupassie said.

"I thought you were going to bed when we left earlier, Mrs. Dupassie," Keoph said.

"I couldn't sleep," she said. "I was too fucking worried about you guys. I didn't think you'd be coming back. That's what I thought. You had me real worried. I'm amazed, you wanna know the truth. Not only did most of you get outta that fucking place alive, you found who you were looking for."

Keoph let out a deep breath as he nodded. "You're right. And I want to thank all of you for your help. There's no way I could've done it without you."

Karen came in wearing a white T-shirt, a pair of grey sweatpants, and mocassins. Her hair was wet and combed straight back.

"How would you like some coffee, honey?" Mrs. Dupassie said.

"That would be wonderful," Karen said.

Mrs. Dupassie got up and went into the kitchen. She said, "Karen, why don't you come in here with me for a minute."

Keoph watched as Karen went into the kitchen and Mrs. Dupassie talked to her quietly. Mrs. Dupassie went to a drawer beneath the counter and rummaged around. She retrieved from the messy drawer a small business-sized card. She closed the drawer and gave the card to Karen, speaking to her quietly again. Karen responded and nodded, then took Mrs. Dupassie's hand and seemed to thank her.

When Karen returned to the table, Keoph said, "Is there anything I can do for you?"

She smiled. "Yes. Just stop treating me like a porcelain doll. I'm going to be fine, Keoph. Don't worry."

"Mrs. Dupassie told you about the therapist?"

"Yes, and I plan to see him. He's a psychiatrist, actually."

"Oh, good, I'm glad. I hope you get some good out of it."

"Thank you, Keoph."

"Are you in pain?"

"My whole body is killing me, but the shower helped a lot. You know, we should call Burgess."

Keoph nodded. "I'll do it. You just sit here and—"

Smiling again, she said, "I told you, Keoph. Stop it. You're going to drive me insane."

He returned her smile and said, "Okay."

CHAPTER FORTY-ONE

Martin Burgess sat in the chair beside Denise's bed, his head tipped forward, hands joined across his stomach. He snored quietly.

His cell phone went off and he sat up, rubbed the back of his neck, and yawned. He took the phone from his pocket and opened it.

"Burgess," he said.

"Mr. Burgess, it's Gavin Keoph."

"Oh, Mr. Keoph, it's good to hear from you. How are you?"

"We got Karen away from the brutals, and we—"

"Brutals?"

"Can I explain the details to you later?" Keoph said.

"Yeah, sure, if you'd rather."

"Karen's been beaten and raped."

"Oh, my God."

"How is your wife?"

"Heavily sedated. She's going to be in pain for awhile, but she'll be okay, thank God."

"Has she told you what happened to her?"

"She was raped and beaten as well."

"That seems to be their way."

Burgess said, "Who's way?"

"The brutals. They're vampires that prey on mortals. They also prey on other vampires."

"You'll write a full report for me?"

"Of course. But I want to *tell* you what happened first. Mind if we come by?"

"Sure, not a problem. But would you mind coming here to the hospital? We can go the cafeteria and get something to eat, maybe. I just . . . I don't want to leave the hospital."

"I understand. We'll see you in awhile."

Burgess slipped his phone into his pocket. He stood and went to Denise's bedside.

She was sleeping.

He wanted her to be well, to recover. He also wanted to hear her say that she forgave him for getting them involved with vampires. He wanted to tell her he'd spend less time writing, and more time with her. He'd just write his books a little slower. What was the rush, anyway? He already had more money than he could possibly use for the rest of his life.

Burgess reached down and took her right hand in both of his. He stroked the backs of her fingers with his thumbs.

"Please get better soon," he whispered. "And please forgive me."

Davey drove Keoph and Karen back to Karen's Lexus at his house in Topanga Canyon.

"Thanks again, Davey," Keoph said as they stood in Davey's driveway. "And again, I'm so sorry about Casey."

"I know," Davey said. "Thank you."

"I want to thank you, too, Davey," Karen said. "You have no idea what you saved me from."

"I have some idea," he said. "I'm . . . glad I could do it." There was an emotional thickness to Davey's voice, and he did not make eye contact with them.

They said their good-byes, then Keoph and Karen got into the Lexus, with Keoph at the wheel. He started the engine and headed back down the driveway to the gate.

"Can you take me to my place so I can put some clothes on?" Karen said.

"Sure."

They stopped at Karen's house, and she went upstairs and changed into a white-and-yellow blouse and blue jeans. She applied some makeup and the bruises on her face looked much less severe. She could not hide that black eye with makeup, though. She put on a pair of sunglasses.

"You don't mind driving again?" she said. "I'm hurting too much to drive."

"I don't mind at all."

In the car, Karen opened her cell phone and called Burgess. He was still at Cedars-Sinai hospital, and agreed to meet them in the cafeteria.

With Karen giving him directions, Keoph headed for the hospital.

"What are you going to do now that we're done, Keoph?" Karen said.

"I don't know. I'm not anxious to go back home, to be honest. I'd like to give my ex-wife a little more time to cool off. Or slash her wrists. It's up to her, really, either one would be fine with me."

Karen smiled. "You've still got your sense of humor, Keoph. That's a good sign."

Keoph said nothing for awhile, then, "I may stay here another two or three days. See the city. Go to some museums. Maybe see a movie at the Chinese Theater. How would you like to be my guide?"

Karen turned to him.

Keoph held up his right hand. "Not like a date, or anything like that."

Karen's eyebrows rose. "Why *not* like a date?"

"Because we may be working together again, and I've got rules about that."

"Working together again?"

"Don't you remember what Burgess said?" Keoph asked. "He said he was just *starting* with the vampires. He didn't come right out and say it, but I got the impression he plans to hire us for other investigations. Think you'd be up to it?"

"Well, it's pretty hard to turn down that much money."

"You got that right."

"I guess I'd be open to it. It would depend on the investigation. I'm sure as hell not going anywhere near vampires again, though. I won't do that."

"I don't blame you. Are you going to call that psychiatrist, make an appointment?"

"Yes, I am."

"Good. As long as I know you're getting some help, I'll keep my mouth shut about it."

Karen smiled wearily. "I appreciate your concern, Keoph. It's just that . . . well, I'm not exactly made of gossamer, you know?"

"I know. Anyone who's not ashamed to knock back a scotch in the middle of the day is probably able to take care of herself."

Karen chuckled. "Thank you for that vote of confidence."

They arrived at the hospital and Keoph parked. They followed the signs to the cafeteria, where Burgess was seated at a table eating a sandwich. He wore a black T-shirt—written on the front in dripping red letters was the caption, WANNA COME UP AND SEE MY CHAINSAW? He looked like he'd dropped a little weight. His face was drawn and weary.

Karen and Keoph went to the table and seated themselves across from him.

"Miss Moffett," Burgess said, "it's so good to see you. You had us all very worried."

"It's good to be seen, Mr. Burgess."

Burgess turned to his briefcase on the chair to his right, opened it, and removed two white business-size envelopes. He closed the briefcase and handed the envelopes over the table to Karen and Keoph. "Your final payment," he said.

They took their envelopes.

"We haven't put together any kind of report yet," Keoph said.

"I know you will. Somehow . . . I don't know, it just doesn't seem as important as it did before. Now, all that's important is that I got Denise back."

"Davey Owen wasn't as lucky," Karen said. "Casey was murdered."

Burgess lowered his head for a moment. Finally, he looked at Keoph and said, "You wanted to tell me about something?"

"I wanted to tell you about everything that happened," Keoph said. "We'll write it all up, but I want to tell you now."

For the next hour, Burgess listened as Keoph and Karen spoke. He slowly ate his sandwich and drank Diet Dr Pepper from the can next to his plate.

As they spoke, both Karen and Keoph—especially Keoph—realized they *needed* to talk about it. They had to tell someone, to hear themselves say it all, and to know that someone was listening, someone who would believe them. Burgess occasionally interrupted them to ask questions, but most of the time, he listened intensely with a deep frown on his forehead. They told him about Mrs. Dupassie, and about the night the brutals burst into her apartment to take Karen and Casey. Karen told them about the dark room she and Casey were kept in, about the horrible sound that went off at regular intervals. Keoph told him about the mutant vampires in the sub-basement of the Royal Arms Hotel, about the deaths of Steve and Neil, and about the search for Karen.

When they were done, none of them spoke for awhile.

There was a television suspended high in one corner of the cafeteria, and Keoph glanced at it. He did a double take when he saw the Royal Arms Hotel on the screen.

"Excuse me," Keoph said as he got up and went over to the television, turned his ear toward it.

"—shooters were not found," a male voice said over the shot of the hotel, "although police are mystified by the discovery of several corpses in various states of decay. The corpses were found in the corridors of the hotel by the SWAT team that entered the building. Some were little more than bones. According to a source close to the police, the hotel's residents appear to be more like prisoners. Some have been badly beaten, raped repeatedly, and even starved. A small film studio was discovered in the basement, as were many pornographic videos, along with what appear to be two torture chambers. According to a source close to the case, the police will probably be piecing it all together for some time. We will bring updates to you as they are released."

The newscaster appeared then, perfectly coiffed, and went on to the next story.

Keoph returned to the table. "Well, it's a big story in the news. It sounds like any remaining vampires fled the building right away. All they've found are the dead people, and all the people locked up in the rooms."

"What if it breaks?" Burgess said. "I mean, what if the vampires are found and exposed?"

Keoph shrugged. "I'll be back in San Francisco going about my business."

Karen said, "As long as we're not connected to it, they can do whatever they want with them. My opinion? They should kill every last one of them."

"They'd have to catch them first," Keoph said. "I bet there's a lot of scrambling going on in the vampire community tonight."

Burgess finished his soda, then said, "How do you two feel about ghosts?"

"Ghosts?" Keoph said.

"What kind of ghosts?" Karen said. "You mean, literal spirits?"

Burgess smiled briefly. "There's an allegedly haunted house I've been keeping up with over the years."

Keoph looked at Karen, and she looked at him.

"We're going to need time to recover from *this* investigation, Mr. Burgess," Keoph said.

"The pay will be the same," Burgess said.

Keoph and Karen looked at each other again.

"Not right away, Mr. Burgess," Karen said. "But please don't take that as a no."

Burgess smiled. "I can live with that."

"Sure you don't want to show me around the city, Moffett?" Keoph said. "I'd like to see all the museums, all the major points of interest. And Disneyland, of course."

"Nothing personal, Keoph, but I plan to spend the next couple days in a hot bath. But I'll be happy to do that the next time you're in town."

"Fair enough. Ah, I suppose I should go back, anyway. Things are screwed up at the office."

"Now you can pay off your ex-wife, and it won't hurt," Karen said.

"Believe me, it always hurts, no matter how much money I have." He sighed. "I guess I'll go to my hotel, where I haven't been staying. I'll get on the phone and arrange for a flight home. You going to be able to drive home from there?"

"Yes. It'll hurt, but I'll do it. Everything hurts, anyway. That two-day bath will make a big difference."

Keoph smiled. He drove to the Chateau Marmont on Sunset and double-parked.

"Moffett, it's been a pleasure working with you," he said.

"The pleasure was mine, Keoph."

They shook hands.

"Sounds like Burgess wants to hire us again," Keoph said.

"Yeah. Ghosts. Well, they don't sound as dangerous as vampires." She reached into her purse and removed a business card, which she handed to Keoph. "You want to write that report for Burgess, or shall I?"

"I'll write it. You take that two-day bath."

"My e-mail address is on the card," she said. "Send me a copy, okay?"

"Will do."

They both got out of the car and met in front of it.

"You'll let me know when you're ready to do another job with Burgess, won't you?" Keoph said.

She gave him a half-smile that was very appealing in spite of her bruises. "I will. We'll talk then."

As Keoph went into the hotel, Karen got behind the wheel and pulled away from the curb.

That night, Davey sat naked on a rock at the foot of the Y in the Hollywood sign. The red blanket was still there, as were the ice bucket and the overturned vase that held the dozen roses, all of which had died and shriveled. The ground was muddy from the summer rain. It was a dark night—there were still clouds in the sky obscuring the moon and stars.

He sat there for a long time without moving, thinking of Casey.

Before they got together, they had been friends and coworkers at Pendant Publishing. She had stood by while Davey had gone through one bad relationship after another. She had finally pointed out to him that he gravitated toward women who were bad for him, and all the while, she was there, in love with him. She had turned his life around. Looking back on the relationships he'd had, he realized he had never really been loved until Casey. She had taught him how to love and be loved.

Tears fell from his eyes, and were quickly followed by chest-cracking sobs. He wailed as he cried for his loss, wailed like a small injured child. The sound of his crying echoed over the mountain and sent birds flying from their perches.

He sat there for a long time, crying in the night.

RAY GARTON
LIVE GIRLS

The garish neon lights of New York City's Times Square can be very seductive. And so can the promises of dark pleasures on the seedier side streets. To Davey Owen, the lure of a glowing sign advertising LIVE GIRLS is too hard to resist. He was looking for a little entertainment. He finds instead a nightmare in the form of a beautiful but strangely pale woman. A woman who offers him passion, ecstasy—and eternal life—but takes in exchange his lifeblood and his very soul.

"*Live Girls* is gripping, original, and sly.
I finished it in one bite."
—Dean Koontz

RICHARD LAYMON

THE BEAST HOUSE

The Beast House has become a museum of the most macabre kind. On display inside are wax figures of its victims, their bodies mangled and chewed, mutilated beyond recognition. The tourists who come to Beast House can only wonder what sort of terrifying creature could be responsible for such atrocities.

But some people are convinced Beast House is a hoax. Nora and her friends are determined to learn the truth for themselves. They will dare to enter the house at night. When the tourists have gone. When the beast is rumored to come out. They will learn, all right.

THE
FREAKSHOW
BRYAN
SMITH

Once the Flaherty Brothers Traveling Carnivale and Freakshow rolls into Pleasant Hills, Tennessee, the quiet little town will never be the same. In fact, much of the town won't survive. At first glance the freakshow looks like so many others... lurid, run-down, decrepit. But this freakshow is definitely one of a kind....

The townspeople can't resist the lure of the tawdry spectacle. The main attractions are living nightmares, the acts center on torture and slaughter...and the stars of the show are the unsuspecting customers themselves.

Jessica